LORI WICK

Leave a Candle Burning

HARVEST HOUSE PUBLISHERS

EUGENE, OREGON

All Scripture quotations are taken from the King James Version of the Bible.

Cover by Terry Dugan Design, Minneapolis, Minnesota

Cover photo © Terry Dugan Design

Covered bridge interior drawing by Abby Wick

LEAVE A CANDLE BURNING
Copyright © 2006 by Lori Wick
Published by Harvest House Publishers
Eugene, Oregon 97402
www.harvesthousepublishers.com

Library of Congress Cataloging-in-Publication Data
Wick, Lori.
    Leave a candle burning / Lori Wick.
        p. cm. — (Tucker Mills trilogy ; bk. 3)
    ISBN-13: 978-0-7369-1373-7 (pbk.)
    ISBN-10: 0-7369-1373-4 (pbk.)
    Product # 6913734
    1. Physicians—Fiction. 2. Widowers—Fiction. 3. Massachusetts—Fiction.
    I. Title. II. Series.
    PS3573.I237L43 2006
    813'.54—dc22   2006007246

Printed in the United States of America

06 07 08 09 10 11 12 13 14 / BP-MS / 10 9 8 7 6 5 4 3 2 1

For Andrea—
*who colors my world with joy.
I'm so glad Tim found you.*

Acknowledgments

It's so fun to finish a series. It brings such a sense of accomplishment, but more than that, it's good to look back and see the changes that have occurred in that time. I want to use this page to give special thanks to special people who were a help, some of whom probably didn't even know it.

Thank you...

- Abby Wick—whose covered bridge will always make me smile. It was one of the highlights of this series, but then that should be no surprise. Having you for a daughter is a highlight beyond description.

- Corina Joy Kenney—for how very sweet you are and for allowing me to use your name. And also for having a tough time with those hard *c*'s.

- Todd Barsness—I needed that reminder about the battle we're in. I had been putting my feet up much too often and forgetting to fight. Thank you for leading the charge. It's so obvious in your life.

- Phil Caminiti—your example has brought salvation so many times. Your words of wisdom and fellowship are very dear. I do not take them for granted. And thanks too to your Denise, whose precious friendship and listening ear have been lifelines for me again and again.

- Darwin Parman—your teaching from 1 Timothy was fabulous. I can't tell you how much I learned. Your hard work was so evident. You made the book come alive.

- Bob Wick—you always surprise me. After 25 years, I'm supposed to be able to read your mind, and ofttimes I do, but the surprises just keep coming. Your willingness to keep growing and keep learning is why we have had 25 years. I don't leave a candle burning for you because you know I would burn down the house, but I hope you can always tell it's burning in my heart.

‭Characters‬

Maddie Randall — recently had a baby
Jace Randall — her husband
Valerie — their daughter
Clara — works for Jace and Maddie
Doyle Shephard — Maddie's uncle, owns the general store
Cathy Shephard — Maddie's aunt
Conner Kingsley — owns and operates the bank
Reese Kingsley — Conner's wife, expecting a baby in the fall
Troy Thaden — Conner's business partner
Eli Peterson — bedridden man, owns rental properties in Tucker Mills
Scottie Peterson — his wife
Iris Stafford — the Peterson's cook
Finn — Eli's man
Pastor Douglas Muldoon — pastor at one of the meetinghouses in town
Alison Muldoon — Douglas' wife
Hillary, Joshua, Peter, Martin, and Jeffrey — Douglas and Alison's children
Dannan MacKay — nephew to old Doc MacKay and new town doctor
Grant MacKay — Dannan's cousin
Annie MacKay — Grant's wife
Corina MacKay — Grant and Annie's daughter

Some of the townsfolk:
Mrs. Greenlowe — Reese Kingsley's former landlady
Mr. Leffler — the bank teller
The Webers — part of the church family
The Peternells—part of the church family
The Reverend Mr. Sullins — pastor at Commons Meetinghouse

Prologue

"I have your mother's things in order," the young woman reported to the bedridden man.

"Was it hard?" he asked kindly, his eyes not missing a detail about her. "Did it make you miss her more?"

"At times. And then at other times, I felt as though she were still here."

"What are your plans now?" he asked next.

"I'm not sure. I've found a house where I can board, but I don't know about income."

"May I make a suggestion?"

"Certainly."

"Would you consider marrying me?"

The woman's face betrayed all the astonishment she felt inside.

"How long have you worked here?" the man asked, changing topics.

"Since I was 12," she answered, her voice reflecting her confusion even as she wondered what the last six years had to do with his proposal.

"You know you've always done more than just assist my mother," the man began, stating his case. "She so depended on you in the latter years that she would say she couldn't have managed without you. Well, it's no different for me. Who will be here to take care of the small details and see to the shopping and the meals? Mother wasn't the only one to depend on you for those things."

The woman's heart crowded with sudden compassion.

"This is not what you really want," she told him gently. "You're upset about your mother."

To her surprise, the man smiled into her eyes.

"I am upset about losing my mother; I'll miss her more than I can say, but I can't lose you too. If you stay as my wife, then life can go on as it has, and I'll have the peace of mind knowing that when I'm gone, you'll be taken care of."

The woman looked confused by this as well.

"As my wife," the man explained, "this house and the properties will all be yours."

The woman began to object, but the man stopped her.

"Please just think about it. A marriage of convenience is in both our best interests. Take as much time as you need to decide and let me know."

Feeling a great deal of shock, the woman exited the room. She walked slowly down the open staircase, her eyes taking in the house that had been her home for a long time, a home she could only have dreamt about at one time in her life.

At the bottom, she looked back up, even though there was nothing new to see. She suddenly realized his suggestion held great merit. She didn't want to leave, and she did care for him, just as she had his mother.

"I'll marry you," the woman said when she arrived back by his side just minutes later. "If you're sure."

"I'm very sure," he told her, smiling again. "We'll do it soon."

Like the old friends they were, the two talked about the

details for a few minutes more before the woman exited, leaving the man alone.

During the day he was propped up against the headboard of his bed, slightly bent to the side because of his spine, but comfortable nonetheless. At the moment, he was more than comfortable. He was delighted.

It would be a marriage of convenience, but there was another truth involved, one that he would never let her know. For the time he had left, he would know that she would be by his side, but that wasn't what caused him to sigh with a deep contentment. That came from another fact: He was going to marry the woman he'd loved for years.

One

Tucker Mills, Massachusetts, 1840

Reese Kingsley stood in her bedroom and studied her shape in the tall mirror. Since she didn't carry extra weight, her protruding abdomen had been obvious in her second month. Now in her fourth month, she was beginning to look as though she might be carrying twins.

She wasn't. She was sure of that. But the fact that her spouse was the size of a small mountain could explain the additional inches around her middle. As though thinking of him might make him appear, Conner Kingsley came to the door, looking for her.

"Back in front of the mirror?" he teased quietly, which was his way.

"What do you mean *back?*" Reese turned her back on her reflection, working to look innocent.

"I saw you in this same spot a few mornings ago," Conner answered, slipping his arms around her.

"I'm sure you mistook me for someone else," she said.

"I can see how that might happen," Conner went along as soon as he'd kissed her nose. "There are so many expectant women moving around this house."

Reese smiled into his eyes, her own voice whispering that she loved him just before she slipped her arms around his neck. For a time the two were in a world of their own, up to the moment when Conner's stomach rumbled.

"Oh, my," Reese laughed. "I think I'd better get to the kitchen."

"Troy started the coffee," Conner volunteered, referring to his business partner, who also lived with them.

"If I wait long enough, will he start breakfast too?"

With a soft laugh and an arm around his wife, Conner moved them to the door. It was time to head downstairs to start the day.

Maddie Randall held her small daughter lengthwise in her lap, bending slightly to speak into her small face. Three-month-old Valerie Randall smiled into her mother's eyes, not even remembering she was hungry.

"You slept almost all night," Maddie congratulated her. "Didn't that feel nice? So much better than waking up before morning."

Valerie smiled as though she'd helped out on purpose, and Maddie laughed in delight, scooping her close to kiss her tiny cheek. This was the way Jace Randall, proud husband and father, found them.

"Well, good morning," he greeted, having just come downstairs. "You two are up early."

"Yes, but not in the night, so we feel very rested."

Jace bent and kissed Maddie, and then spoke to his daughter.

"Val, tell your mother that you sleep through every night," he teased. "I never hear you, so you must not be waking up."

Valerie gave another smile that assured her parents she was brilliantly taking in every word, and Jace, unable to keep his distance, took her in his arms.

"Very soon now she'll figure out she's hungry," Maddie said, moving toward the stairs. "But I'm going to get dressed anyway."

"We'll be just fine," Jace assured her, eyes still on the small bundle in his arms.

Valerie was beginning to be quite distressed by the time Maddie came back down, but Jace only spoke softly into his daughter's crumpled face before handing her off when his wife made her appearance.

Pastor Douglas Muldoon was sitting at the desk in his study, head bent over his Bible, when he heard the door. He looked up to see what looked like his wife's hand, but she didn't enter. Instead it opened just enough to admit 15-month-old Jeffrey, who giggled and ran when he spotted his father and found himself scooped up into Douglas' arms.

"How's my Jeff?" Douglas asked, pressing a kiss to his soft, round cheek.

The little boy hunched his shoulders with delight, smiling into his father's face. Douglas turned with the little boy to speak to Alison, his wife.

"He was missing you," she informed him.

"How could you tell?"

"He goes to your chair at the dining table and tries to talk to you."

Douglas laughed, and Jeffrey put his head on his father's shoulder. Douglas knew he wouldn't get any work done this way, but at the moment it didn't matter.

"How's your day going?" he asked of Alison.

"I keep getting distracted."

"By Jeff?"

"Yes, and the garden. I think I put too much on my list."

"Where's Hillary?" he asked about their daughter.

"She's at Opal Berglund's, helping clean up after their kitchen fire."

"It was kind of her to go."

"Yes, it was, but I admit that I had big plans for the day."

Douglas caught it then. His wife's oh-so-subtle attempt to get him to watch Jeffrey for a time. Douglas tried not to smile, but it wasn't going very well. Alison saw the smile that crept into his eyes and had to fight her own grin.

"I have a sermon to prepare," he tried.

"It's only Wednesday, and you've been working so hard on this subject you know it backward and forward."

"Nothing much gets by you, does it?"

"Not when I'm trying to get into the garden," she answered with a coaxing smile.

Douglas shook his head in mock exasperation and agreed. When Alison kissed him and left, he settled himself on the floor to play with his youngest son. It was no end of fun, but it also made him long for a swift return of his three middle children, who were visiting their grandmother in Boston.

"Good morning, Dannan MacKay," Troy Thaden, who with

Conner was one of Tucker Mills' bank managers, welcomed the new doctor. "Come, have a seat by the desk."

The men had spoken to each other many times at the meeting-house and over meals but never talked about Dannan's personal business interests. Today would be different.

"How are you, Troy?" Dannan asked.

"Doing well. Yourself?"

"Fine. Still adjusting to a new town and letting folks adjust to a new doctor, but coming along."

"How many months have you been here?"

"Let's see." Dannan's head went back. "I've been here about four months, maybe a little more."

"Is there anyone to visit back in Willows Crossing?"

"Just a cousin and his family. I might go see them this winter if they don't visit here first."

"How is it coming with your patients?"

"Most of the time, it's fine," Dannan informed him, even as he began to smile. "I had a woman yesterday who came to the office. I could tell she wanted something, but it took a while for her to tell me what it was. I guessed for the better part of ten minutes about what might be bothering her, and she finally blurted it out."

"Well, that's progress," Troy said, smiling in return.

"Yes, but she also told me exactly how she felt about *old* Doc MacKay leaving, and that he had no business doing such a thing."

"He heard plenty of that before he left too."

"Yes, I'm sure. Now," Dannan began, "I won't take up more of your time on this. I'm wondering if the bank owns any small houses that it's trying to sell right now."

"Looking to move?"

"It's just a thought I had, and I don't believe my landlord wants to sell."

"Have you asked Eli?" Troy asked. He knew Eli Peterson, Dannan's landlord, owned several properties in town. "He just might want to discuss it."

"As a matter of fact, I haven't met him. My uncle paid my rent for months down the road, so we never got around to my meeting him."

"Well, it was just a thought. I have two houses, one that's available now, and one that will be going on the market very soon. I can tell you about them right now or show them to you some other time."

Dannan was on the verge of saying that he'd like to hear about them, but a man had rushed into the bank, and Dannan knew he was needed.

"Is the Doc here?" the man asked of the teller, even as Dannan and Troy both stood and were noticed in the office alcove.

"There you are," the stranger said to Dannan. "Can you come? It looks like Cathy Shephard has broken her arm."

"I'm on my way," Dannan replied with a calm that was genuine. "Thank you, Troy," he turned long enough to add. "I'll check back with you."

"Certainly, Dannan. Maybe I'll see you at noon."

Dannan agreed and slipped out the door. Troy and the bank teller, Mr. Leffler, walked to the front windows. They didn't speak, but their eyes were directed down the green toward the Shephard home and store, their hearts wondering how the accident had happened.

"Hold still, Cathy," Doyle Shephard cautioned his wife, having made her as comfortable as possible on the floor of the store office.

"It throbs," she gasped a little, holding her right arm close to her body, still unable to believe she had fallen down the stairs at the store.

Doyle and Cathy owned Shephard Store, Tucker Mills' general store. Cathy had come over to the store—their house was right next door—and found Doyle with three customers. He'd asked her to go upstairs to the storeroom and find an item. She'd lost her footing about halfway down and tumbled to the bottom. Now they waited for Dannan MacKay.

"It could have been my neck," Cathy suddenly said, bringing Doyle's eyes to hers.

"Considering how stiff your neck can be," Doyle teased her, "that would've been bad."

Cathy tried to glare at him, but a smile peeked through.

"Through the office," they heard someone out front say. Their customers had given them space but were not willing to leave. Dannan appeared a moment later.

"Well, Mrs. Shephard," Dannan teased gently, "lying down on the job."

"It's my arm," she said a bit breathlessly. "Do you set bones, Dannan?"

"I've done my share." He knelt beside the couple. "Let's have a look."

"It hurt every time I tried to help her up, so we stayed here," Doyle put in.

"I think you were wise," Dannan encouraged as he began to probe gently on the arm and wrist. Cathy's breathing quickened. Dannan murmured words of comfort, but both knew there was a break, and the following minutes were not going to be very much fun.

❦

Reese loved old Doc MacKay. More than old enough to be her father, they had been fast friends for many years. And it was with a great many tears that he had departed their community, but not all was lost. He had left Dr. Dannan MacKay, a fine doctor and his brother's son, in his place. Reese and Conner had taken to him in a hurry, and whenever he could make it, he joined them for dinner, enjoying the meals Reese prepared and the leftovers and baked goods she sent his way.

Today was no different. It had taken some doing to make Cathy Shephard comfortable, but by the time the clock climbed toward noon, Dannan was at the Kingsley home, known around town as the big house, readying to eat with Conner, Reese, and Troy. Troy prayed and the meal began.

"How bad was the break?" Conner was the first to ask.

"Not as bad as it could have been. The bones in Mrs. Shephard's arm are not broken, but the break in the wrist is bad enough that the pain is going to radiate up the entire arm. She'll have to keep still and be patient while it heals."

"Will it heal properly?" Reese asked.

Dannan nodded. "It should. I'll check on the splint tomorrow, to make sure it's still holding well."

"Will she be in town or out at Jace and Maddie's?" Reese asked practically.

"I hadn't thought of it," Dannan admitted.

"If I know Doyle," Conner put in, "she'll be at the farm by the end of the day."

No one commented further on Cathy Shephard's condition, but both Reese and Troy silently agreed with Conner. Doyle would see to it that his wife was taken care of, even if that meant moving her out of town to the farm.

"I can't move out of my own home," Cathy was still saying when the wagon pulled into the yard at Jace and Maddie's after teatime that evening. Her husband ignored her, and seeing Maddie come out the kitchen door, Cathy stopped talking.

"Hello," Maddie spoke with surprise and confusion in seeing her aunt and uncle after tea. Her eyes also took in Cathy's cross face. Nevertheless, Maddie was ready to welcome them both when she noticed her aunt's arm. "What's happened?"

"She fell down the store stairs and broke her wrist," Doyle said simply. "Dannan set it but says she needs to rest it."

"He won't even listen to me," Cathy cut him off. "How am I going to look after things from out here?"

"It sounds like looking is all you can do, Cathy," Maddie said reasonably, watching Cathy climb from the wagon and wince in pain. "Come in and see the baby," she invited warmly, not wanting to get into a dispute with her. It helped that Jace was coming from the house, Valerie in his arms.

Cathy's face lit with a smile as soon as she saw the baby, and Maddie knew at least one thing: Cathy might grouse about being there, but Doyle's decision to bring her was the very best medicine.

"How are you?" Reese asked of Mrs. Greenlowe, her former landlady, as soon as she was seated at her kitchen table on Friday afternoon.

"I'm not the one!" Mrs. Greenlowe answered in her indomitable way. "You increase every time I see you. I need to be the one asking!"

Reese couldn't stop her smile and assured her, "I'm fine."

"Not sick?"

"Not sick."

"Well, that's good! It's miserable when you're sick."

"I'm more tired," Reese admitted.

"How does one get *more* tired when she's never been tired in the first place?"

Reese had to laugh. It was an old saw between them. Mrs. Greenlowe was convinced that Reese could go forever without sleep or rest. And in fact, her energy level was high, but not as high as the older woman liked to proclaim.

"What's that banker husband of yours doing today?"

"I think he's at the bank. A property in town has recently come back to the bank, and he and Troy are having to deal with readying the house for the market."

"Was it Corgiat? Did he owe the bank?"

"It is his house, but the bank might only be handling it for the family because they don't live in Tucker Mills."

"Doesn't Conner tell you these things?"

"No, and I don't want to know."

Mrs. Greenlowe sat back. She'd been leaning toward her guest in anticipation but now relaxed. Reese smiled at her, able to guess her thoughts after all this time. Mrs. Greenlowe was the next to speak, confirming Reese's suspicions.

"What's the point of being married to a banker if you can't learn simple things like that?"

"Even if I learned them, I couldn't share," Reese reasoned, fighting laughter over how close she'd come to reading this woman's mind. "Would you want me to leave here and tell others your business?" Reese asked gently.

Mrs. Greenlowe sat up as though she'd been stung. "You wouldn't do that!" the woman defended her as though there was a need. "How's Cathy Shephard?" she asked next, jumping topics at lightning speed.

"I haven't checked on her, but I suspect she's at the Randall farm."

"Maddie will take good care of her," Mrs. Greenlowe stated confidently. "Who will see after Doyle?"

"Well, I imagine he'll head to the farm each evening. I don't know about breakfast and dinner." This said, Reese leaned in her chair to see the clock on the parlor wall.

"I've got to go."

"Already?"

"Yes, but I'll be back."

"And I might visit you."

"Yes, you might. Why don't you come to dinner next week?"

"Will Dannan be there?"

"Probably."

Mrs. Greenlowe sniffed. "I don't know if I can have dinner with two bankers and a doctor."

Knowing this lady's views on several professions, including bankers and doctors, Reese only smiled and said, "Well, if you change your mind, I've plenty."

"Thank you," Mrs. Greenlowe returned, tempering her voice and speaking sincerely. She saw Reese to the door, hugging her in return when Reese bent to embrace her.

Mrs. Greenlowe watched Reese walk away, not aware that Reese's mind was on her as well. Reese was asking herself if she should have invited Mrs. Greenlowe to the meetinghouse on Sunday, and then realized from her many invitations of the past that the offer was always on the table. If Mrs. Greenlowe wanted to come, she knew she was welcome.

Dannan settled by the fire that evening, wondering when

he'd ever been so lonely. It hadn't been like this when he first arrived in town. His uncle was still here, and the newness of Tucker Mills had given him little time for reflection. But now Jonas MacKay was gone, moved to warmer climes with Dannan's own parents. Dannan was settled in the house, unpacked, and completely moved in, which meant if he wasn't enjoying tea with a family in the village, he was very much on his own come evening.

His closest friend and cousin, Grant MacKay, with his wife and small daughter, still lived in Willows Crossing. They had exchanged letters since he'd arrived, but Dannan had just recently written and had not yet heard back.

Dannan knew that sitting and feeling sorry for himself was not the answer. He owed a letter to his mother, and he knew if he could tell anyone how he was feeling, it would be her.

Dannan took time to pray for his family and then for the patients he'd treated that day. Of all the valuable things he had learned from his uncle, praying for his patients was his favorite. Not until he covered each one did Dannan start his letter home.

Two

Dannan was at Shephard Store first thing Saturday morning, but Conner had been right: Cathy was no longer in town.

"She wasn't happy about it," Doyle admitted, his eyes sparkling a little. "But you said she needed to keep still for proper healing, and that wasn't going to happen here in town."

"No, I imagine not." Dannan laughed softly, having seen from the start that Cathy Shephard was a woman who liked to get things done.

"You headed out there?"

"Yes. Probably in the next hour."

"Can you take a basket of things she forgot?"

"Certainly."

"Oh, and you got a letter."

"Thank you," Dannan looked down at the missive he'd been handed. It was from his father. Dannan might have started the letter on the spot, but Doyle was suddenly handing him a basket.

"Tell Cathy I'll see her as soon as I close up and that I'm not starving."

Dannan laughed again and headed toward the door. Interested to know how life was going for his parents with his uncle living with them, Dannan went back to trying to read when he exited, never seeing the rake handle that was headed his way. Dannan felt something hard poke him sharply in the head. It was not a soft blow, and it stopped him dead in his tracks.

"I'm sorry!" a female voice gasped. "Are you all right?"

The fingers Dannan put to his forehead had blood on them. His ears rang a bit, so it took a moment to look at the woman addressing him.

"Are you all right?" she repeated.

"I think so," Dannan answered, realizing he'd seen this young woman at the meetinghouse. She was hard to forget.

"Can I do something for you? I don't have a handkerchief." She looked down at her basket, and the rake handle, whose end was very jagged and the evident object of his attack, swung near him again. Dannan reached out and took it. The woman never noticed.

"I must have something to put on your head," she spoke into the basket as she was searching. "You're bleeding, and I'm so sorry."

"It's all right," Dannan assured her, shifting the objects in his hand to reach for his own handkerchief. "I've got something here."

The green-eyed woman stared up at him, her face filled with concern. Dannan handed the rake back to her and then mopped his head.

"I'm sorry," she said again.

"Please don't be. I'm fine."

"Fine people don't bleed," she reasoned, and Dannan had to smile. When she saw that smile, the woman relaxed a bit. Dannan was glad to notice her apparent calm. He was all right, or he would be very soon; it was not a serious injury. Indeed, for looking at those green eyes and the light red curls peeking out of her dark yellow bonnet, Dannan had forgotten all about his head.

"Why don't I ask Doyle if he has an ointment handy?" the woman suggested.

"I do thank you for your concern, but I'm headed home and have all that I need there."

"All right," she agreed, still looking troubled. "But if you do need something, I live at the Peterson house. I hope you'll let me know."

Seeing that she was not going to go inside until he took his leave, Dannan thanked her with a slight bow of the head and wished her a good day. He then made himself walk away. What he wanted to do was stand and talk to her some more, or maybe he just wanted to look into those green eyes and hear the soft sound of her voice. At any rate, Dannan turned and made his way down the green, all the while seeing the small redhead in his mind's eye.

"She's been fed and changed, and she's ready for you to hold her," Maddie told Cathy after breakfast. "Are you comfortable?"

"I'm fine. You just give me that girl and go on your way."

Maddie surrendered her daughter into Cathy's good arm and then slipped into the kitchen. She shut the door so she wouldn't spend all her time peeking in at them and then got to work.

Saturdays were usually busy because she was preparing meals for Sunday as well. She had been planning to invite Conner, Reese, and Troy for dinner after services, but since Cathy had become a guest and wasn't always very comfortable, she would leave them for another week.

Maddie got to work on dinner for that day, but she could tell she was distracted. When Doyle had brought Cathy, Maddie had been sorry for her but was glad for the opportunity to take care of her. And always it lingered in her mind that her aunt might wish to speak of spiritual matters. Maddie's life had changed dramatically while she'd been carrying Valerie, and she was eager to share. Cathy had occasional questions, but Maddie was never sure how far the door was open.

Realizing that she was standing still with her thoughts, Maddie forced herself to get back to work. She had a new recipe to try and needed to concentrate, but when her mind had time, she kept asking God to save her aunt. She also asked that her own patience level—no matter how long it took for Cathy to see the truth—would remain strong.

"Did you get that handle?" Iris Stafford asked Scottie Peterson when she arrived home.

"I did. Doyle put the rake together."

Scottie showed the tool to Iris, who nodded her approval. Anyone watching them would never guess that Scottie was the mistress of the house and Iris her cook. Iris was well old enough to be Scottie's mother and had been looking after her long enough to take such liberties.

"Eli's been asking after you," Iris informed her.

"I'll go right up."

Scottie moved from the kitchen to the open stairway that led out of the spacious parlor. She moved along the upstairs hallway and slipped into the first door on the left.

"Hello," she greeted the two men inside, Eli in the bed, and his man, Finn, standing by the window.

"How did it go in town?" Eli asked as Finn, always willing to fade into the background, quietly made his way from the room, closing the door behind him.

"Fine. I got that new rake handle."

"And dress material?" Eli questioned. "You picked out something for your new dresses?"

By now Scottie had taken a seat on the edge of the bed. Her brow creased before she answered.

"I don't think I need new dresses, Eli."

Just watching her, Eli began to smile. He knew she would have a proper argument for her side, and he looked forward to hearing it.

"When did you realize this?"

"As I walked into town," Scottie informed him. "I had several new dresses made when we were married."

"Scottie," her husband said patiently, "that was five years ago."

"No, it wasn't," she argued without heat, her brow creasing again.

"It was," he insisted, still patient. "Five years next month."

"How could it be that long?"

Eli didn't comment, but his smile grew.

"I'm being laughed at."

"Just a little," he admitted as he reached for her hand. "How many years did you think it had been?"

"I hadn't thought about it," she confessed, her eyes on nothing, wondering where the time had gone.

Eli reached up and gently stroked the creases on her forehead until she relaxed. He did that whenever he thought she might be worrying. This time it reminded Scottie of the man and the rake handle. She suddenly sat up straight and told her husband about the incident.

"He bled?" Eli clarified when she was finished.

"Yes. I wanted to do something, but he said he was all right."

Eli's eyes had rounded a bit, but Scottie knew she was not in trouble. Eli was rarely upset with anyone, and never with her. Nevertheless, the man's injury lingered in her mind.

"Who was it?"

"I don't know," Scottie admitted. "I think I've seen him at the meetinghouse, but I don't know him."

"You didn't think to ask Doyle?"

"No."

The couple was silent for a moment.

"But you think he was all right?" Eli questioned.

"He said he was, but it might have been all politeness."

Eli nodded thoughtfully, knowing his wife had that effect on some men. "I can tell Finn, and he can keep an ear out. I'm not sure we can do anything else."

"Maybe I'll see him on Sunday," Scottie added as the realization struck her.

Eli agreed that she might, but just moments later his mind was on something else. He asked Scottie to bring the account books. He had some numbers he wanted to go over with her.

Dannan slipped into the workroom at his house—the one where he mixed medications and worked on experiments—long enough to check the cut on his head. It wasn't overly deep, but the skin was tender. He cleaned it up, making sure the bleeding had stopped, before heading out to ready his rig. He wanted to check on Cathy Shephard's arm before another thing interrupted him.

In the kitchen at the Peterson house, Finn sat at the worktable sipping the tea Iris had made him. A newspaper was open in front of him, but it wasn't long before Iris needed the space to roll out crust, and Finn was forced to shift to one corner.

"Anything new?" Iris asked after a few minutes of quiet.

"I think the Corgiat house is for sale."

"By the bank?"

"It would seem. Did he have debt?"

"I doubt it," Iris answered but then gave a small grunt. "But then no one thought old man Zantow had debt either, and none of us will soon forget that debacle."

Finn huffed a little himself at the point. It was an incident from the past that had long been resolved, but memories in Tucker Mills could be longer.

Both stopped talking when they heard Scottie on the stairs. They didn't fear reprimand, but if she was coming downstairs already, she probably needed one of them.

"Finn," Scottie wasted no time in saying, "Eli can't get into position to take a deep breath. Can you shift him around?"

"I'll go right up," the man offered and left the table immediately.

"Is he hurting?" Iris wished to know. "Does tea or broth sound good?"

"He's not hurting, but tea sounds nice. Thank you, Iris."

Scottie left her to it and returned to her husband's side. She told herself it was wrong to worry or fear, but she was doing a lousy job listening.

"Come in, Dannan," Maddie invited the town's doctor, not surprised to see him.

"Thank you, Maddie. This basket is from Doyle," Dannan said, offering the handle to his hostess. "Some things for Cathy," he added.

Maddie took the basket with a word of thanks and led Dannan

to the parlor, where Cathy was sitting in the rocking chair. Valerie had fallen asleep and was in the cradle in the corner.

"Dannan's here," Maddie announced quietly, seeing the thundercloud on her aunt's face.

"How are you, Mrs. Shephard?"

"Tired of sitting!" Cathy all but snapped, but she softened when she saw Dannan's smile. "It aches, but I'm keeping still."

"You'll be glad of that," Dannan gave his approval. "I saw Doyle this morning," he continued conversationally, checking the splint and rewrapping it with a careful touch. "He seems to be faring well."

"Probably living off the cookie jar," Cathy grumbled.

"I think he said he had cake and pie for breakfast," Dannan replied, catching Cathy by surprise. She laughed when she saw the glint in his eye.

"Oh, go on with you," she said, swatting at him with her good arm.

Beyond telling her that all looked well and she was doing a good job, Dannan didn't comment further.

"Job?" Cathy was outraged over the word. "I've not done a thing!"

"Right now, that's your job," Dannan continued calmly. As he was in the process of putting his hat back on, Maddie invited him for a cup of tea. Dannan accepted, and a short time later, the three sat around the table in the parlor, tea and freshly baked scones before them.

"Do you cook for yourself, Dannan?" Cathy asked.

"When Conner and Reese Kingsley aren't taking me in, I do."

"Reese is a good cook," Maddie complimented. "I have more than one recipe from her."

"She is a good cook, but then I would say that about most of the women whose homes I've visited in town."

"Spoken like a hungry man," Cathy commented, and Dannan laughed.

A small sound from the corner just then brought Maddie to her feet. Dannan hid a smile. It wouldn't be too many more months before Maddie would allow Valerie to wake on her own, but like most new mothers, she was waiting for any excuse to hold her baby.

Dannan decided not to linger. He didn't have anything pressing, but a doctor on the outskirts of town—when he didn't need to be—was no help to the townsfolk. Finishing his tea with a genuine compliment, Dannan took his leave.

∞

Conner sat at the desk chair at the bank, his eyes gazing out the window but not really seeing anything. Troy watched him and waited. Eventually Conner looked at his partner.

"What's going on?" Troy asked.

"Just thinking," Conner said, his voice as quiet as ever.

"About?"

Conner hesitated. Troy waited.

"Reese."

"What about her?"

"Do you think a woman can be that hale and hardy and still die in childbirth?"

Troy sighed. It was an easy question to ask at this point, but the answers were tougher.

"I think any woman can die in childbirth," Troy said honestly. "But I can't but wonder whether being as healthy as Reese would help. You might want to ask Dannan what he thinks."

"I might do that."

"This is where trust comes in, Conner."

"You're certainly right about that," the younger man agreed before putting his mind back on banking.

"I can't believe you're still here!" Cathy exclaimed when she rolled over in bed Sunday morning and found Doyle beside her. He had obviously been awake and was lying on his side facing her.

"Where would I be?"

"I thought you'd be gone with Jace and Maddie to the meeting-house this morning."

"And leave you on your own?" Doyle asked quietly.

Cathy was not quiet at all. "Well, it's not as if I'm an invalid, Doyle Shephard! What are you thinking?"

"I'm thinking about my wife having needs, and me being all the way in town when I don't have to be!" he answered a bit hotly himself. "Why would that surprise you?"

Cathy didn't answer but stared at him.

"Cathy," he started over, calm again. "I can miss a Sunday gathering for you and still believe in who God is and what He expects from me."

Cathy looked almost startled and then humbled.

"I shouldn't have flown at you. I was just surprised."

"And I shouldn't choose so many things over you that it would surprise you."

"You don't do that," Cathy argued.

"I must to some degree, or we wouldn't be having words over it. I've even been rethinking the hours I keep at the store."

Cathy looked thoughtful but didn't speak.

"How's your arm?" Doyle asked.

"It aches," she said simply, and Doyle, just as simply, slipped an arm around her and brought her head to his shoulder. They lay together in the quiet house for a long time. Not until Doyle's stomach rumbled did either one feel a need to move.

"Do you realize we're in a battle?" Douglas asked. It was the same opening question he had asked of his flock the last four Sundays. He watched some of them smile.

"Are you weary of this topic?" he asked next. "I know I can get tired of it, but then that reminds me of what a weak soldier I'm prone to be, and I can't afford weakness. Because as soon as I let my guard down, sin—which we read about last week—is already crouching at the door waiting for me. It then has an opportunity to come in. I've got to keep fighting because I'm too vulnerable to attack.

"Let's turn to some more passages," Douglas said as he opened his Bible. "I want us to start in Romans 7:23. I've asked Nate Peternell to read that verse this morning."

Nate stood and read, "'But I see another law in my members, warring against the law of my mind, and bringing me into captivity to the law of sin which is in my members.'"

"Thank you, Nate," Douglas said when that man sat down. "Please do not let your mind pass swiftly over the word *warring*. This is important. This is urgent. It needs our attention. We also need to pay attention to the use of the word *captivity*. I like that word in this verse. It reminds me of the war we're fighting. Let's move on."

Troy was the next man to read. His verses were from 2 Corinthians 10. He also stood to read: "'For though we walk in the flesh, we do not war after the flesh: For the weapons of our warfare are not carnal, but mighty through God to the pulling down of strongholds; casting down imaginations, and every high thing that exalteth itself against the knowledge of God, and bringing into captivity every thought to the obedience of Christ.'"

"Thank you, Troy," Douglas commented and then wasted no time getting to his point. "Did you hear the war that is being described here? It has nothing to do with our physical bodies. It can't be fought with knives or rifles. It's spiritual warfare. And did you catch the use of the word *captivity* again? We are at war for the daily salvation of our souls. I'm not talking about that once-and-for-all step we take when we trust in Christ's blood for eternal salvation, but I am referring to that salvation we need each and every day if we're going to serve God with all our hearts; that salvation we need if we're going to keep our thoughts on obedience and not let our hearts be distracted by things that go against the knowledge of God.

"But even as I say these things, I want you also to know that the battle is already won. We're still here fighting, but Satan has been defeated. We still have battles because our natural man is fleshly and wants his way and will until the day God calls us home, but in reality, God has triumphed over Satan, and we need to trust Him in that.

"When temptation makes an appearance, we can resist because God promises us that strength. We can believe Him when He says that sin won't overpower us because He does not give Satan that kind of control.

"Let's look at one last verse that tells us that very thing. Turn to John 17:15 and listen while I read the words of Christ, 'I pray not that thou shouldest take them out of the world, but that thou shouldest keep them from the evil.' The evil at the end of that verse is Satan—the evil one or the son of perdition as he is called back in verse 12. We are at war with a foe whom God has already beaten. And we don't have to yield when Satan tempts us."

Douglas stopped for a moment and looked at them, knowing he'd given out a lot of information in one morning. He loved each person in the room and ached to have them all walk well with their heavenly Father.

"Please come see me if you've not understood something," Douglas felt he had to say, "or if I've overwhelmed you. It's my heart's desire that you understand and believe this, and I hope you won't hesitate to come if there's a need."

Wondering all the time if he had been clear, Douglas closed with a song. He didn't pray at the front of the room, but his heart begged God to use him in a way that would aid each person.

The service ended, and little by little the congregation dispersed. Dannan had not been looking for the small, redheaded woman, but she suddenly walked past him toward the door. He wanted to have eye contact with her but didn't know her name, and he knew it would be awkward if he followed her. She was moving along, bidding folks goodbye but not stopping to talk. Dannan watched her all the way out the door, going so far as to study the window until she went by.

It was a relief to have Conner appear and invite him to dinner. Otherwise he might have stood for way too long thinking about that woman and wondering who she was.

Dannan was not the only guest invited to the Kingsley house for Sunday dinner. The four Muldoons still in town were there, as were the Weber family and Judson Best.

"So tell us, Dannan," Conner invited during the meal, "what do you hear from Doc MacKay?"

"I just had a letter from my father, and Uncle Jonas is enjoying the area immensely. The house is roomy enough for each to have his own bit of space, and I guess they're rubbing along together quite nicely."

"Will your folks visit you here, Dannan?" Alison wished to know.

"My mother's health doesn't allow her to travel, and my father hates to leave her, so probably not."

"Will you go for a visit later in the year?"

"I don't know when I'll be going that far south. I'll probably visit my cousin in Willows Crossing before the summer's over."

"Has your mother been ill long?" Douglas asked.

"About five years. She fell while hiking with my father and injured her back. Sitting for long periods is excruciating."

Most of the heads at the table nodded with understanding, but no one commented. It was certainly easy to see why his mother could not travel. She would have been miserable.

"She's an amazing woman," Dannan felt a need to add, looking at the compassion on Hillary Muldoon's face. "She doesn't spend a moment pitying herself, and because we write to each other almost weekly, I never feel out of touch."

Conversation drifted to Judson, a young man, fairly new in town, who was working part-time with Jace on the farm and part-time for Will Barland, who grew a broomcorn crop. That business was expanding to the point that Judson was helping Will ship brooms across New England.

Judson's charming way of describing his job had everyone laughing in very short order. Indeed, they were still enjoying his humorous anecdotes when Troy rose from the group to answer the knock on the front door.

Three

"Do not tell me you've put dinner on," Maddie said to her aunt when they arrived back at the farm and caught the aromas wafting from the parlor as soon as they stepped into the kitchen.

Doyle suddenly appeared in the parlor doorway, a large smile on his face.

"She didn't lift a finger, but she certainly enjoyed telling *me* what to do."

Maddie laughed when Cathy looked as pleased as Doyle.

"Come on," Cathy urged. "Wash up and we'll eat."

Maddie and Jace were not going to argue with that order. Valerie was settled in the corner, and the four adults sat down to the meal. Maddie noticed in a hurry that Doyle was swift to cut meat and butter rolls for Cathy. For a moment the younger woman couldn't remember if he had been that solicitous the night before and then wondered if something might have happened between them that morning.

"How was the sermon?" Doyle asked when all plates were served.

"Excellent," Jace was swift to say. "Douglas is still talking about the war with sin."

"Is that normal?" Cathy asked, and the other three diners looked at her.

"Is what normal?" her husband asked.

"Staying with a subject for so many weeks. At the Commons Meetinghouse, the Reverend Mr. Sullins didn't keep to a topic for more than one week. Does the Bible say pastors should do that?"

"In a way it does," Jace said as he fielded this one. "When Scripture stresses something, we've got to pay attention to that."

"How do you know when something is stressed?" Doyle asked.

"Sometimes by how often the topic is addressed. Sin's warring against us is one example of a subject Scripture covers very thoroughly."

"But it's been several weeks," Cathy said. "Did he have *more* verses today?"

"Yes," Maddie answered, "and Jace talked to Douglas afterward. It seems he has more sermons planned on the topic."

Cathy looked surprised but not put off. Indeed, she looked intrigued, as if she might be interested to see how far Douglas Muldoon could take this.

Doyle asked more specific questions as the meal went on, and Jace and Maddie told him all they could remember. At one point, Jace brought his Bible to the table and read some of the verses to them.

It was the beginning of a great afternoon.

Scottie was downstairs after lunch. She had eaten with Eli, as she always did, but he wanted to nap soon after the meal ended, and she had moved downstairs and picked up her sewing. Iris had Sundays off, but Finn was always in attendance. He found her in the parlor not long after she'd settled in.

"He's having trouble breathing," Finn informed her quietly, his face serious.

"Is it his position? Can he get comfortable?"

"I've shifted him many times, and it's not working."

"Find the doctor," Scottie ordered, wasting no time. "Find Doc MacKay's nephew—I can't remember his name."

"I'll find him," Finn promised and exited out the front door.

Scottie went directly to her husband's room. He didn't look very distressed, and Scottie stared at him, a bit confused.

"Are you all right?"

"Yes," he said in soft surprise because it was true. "I wasn't, but things seemed to have suddenly cleared." Eli cleared his throat and shifted his shoulders a bit.

"I sent Finn for the doctor," Scottie admitted, her voice apologetic.

"Well, it's too bad to disturb him on a Sunday, but it will be nice to meet him." Eli's voice told of his calm.

Scottie smiled at him. It was just his way to comfort and take care of her, even making light of the way he felt. She could tell he was not completely comfortable when he continued to clear his throat.

"Are you sure you're all right?"

"I was struggling for a bit, but it really is better. I was serious about that."

Reaching for his hand, Scottie sat on the edge of the bed and studied his eyes. Sometimes he said things to make her feel better—she was sure he did—but a moment's study of his dark brown eyes told her that his claim to feeling better was every bit the truth.

Finding Dannan took some doing. Finn began his search at the doctor's house, and when his knocking produced no response, he started down the green—the town center—remembering that it was Sunday. The Muldoons' house was the next stop, but again, he found that home empty. Finn knew it would not be wise to run around without a plan—Tucker Mills was too large for that—but for a moment he was at a loss. Not until he spotted an extra carriage at the big house did he think the banker might have a suggestion for him.

He was at the large front door a few minutes later and was relieved to see Troy answer the door. He knew him from the bank.

"Well, Finn," Troy greeted him. "Come on in."

"Thank you, Mr. Thaden." Finn stepped just inside and saw Conner come into the hall. He nodded in that direction but wasted no time. "I need to find the doctor. Would you have any idea where he might be?"

"He's here, Finn," Troy assured him, a hand to his arm. "I'll get him right now."

It wasn't two minutes before Dannan was leaving with Eli's man. They stopped briefly at Dannan's house so he could get his bag. The two walked swiftly back down the green and then west to the Peterson house. Beyond a brief explanation of what was needed, Finn had not spoken. His legs were not long, but his stride was swift, his heart hoping things had not grown worse in his absence.

"He's better," Scottie was waiting to tell Finn the moment

he arrived. She glanced at the doctor, but her eyes were mainly on Finn. "He began to feel better just after you left, but thank you for going."

"Of course," Finn assured her.

"Maybe I'll just take a look anyway," Dannan put in, not sure he was comfortable with what Finn had told him.

"Come this way," Finn said, starting toward the stairs. Dannan followed. Scottie held her place in the parlor. She had never been a part of her husband's medical exams, always waiting for Finn to summon her when Eli's clothing and bed covers were back in place.

She took a seat, her eyes going up the open staircase to the upstairs hall and resting on her husband's closed bedroom door. She wasn't anxious, but neither did she want to be out of sight when Finn came looking for her.

"Your pulse is good," Dannan announced, still bent over Eli. Having checked his eyes and listened to his heart, he put the stethoscope away, having also summed up the fact that the man in the bed knew more about his condition than any doctor ever would.

"It came on suddenly," Eli supplied as he buttoned his shirt and Finn adjusted the covers, "and went away just as suddenly."

"Is that normal?" Dannan asked. "You've had that happen before?"

"Not quite so sudden, but shortness of breath is sometimes a problem."

Dannan was vaguely aware of Finn exiting the room, but he was mostly concentrating on the man in the bed. It was obvious that he had not been up and around for many years, if ever, but that he was also at peace with his situation. Dannan also didn't miss the fact that this man possessed a keen mind. Dannan found him fascinating.

However, almost all thoughts of the man flew out of his head when the small, redheaded woman from downstairs came in the open door. Dannan had forced himself to concentrate on the task at hand, but now that he could see that Eli Peterson was breathing well, his mind made an immediate shift to the redhead, especially when she stopped short and looked at him in surprise.

"I stabbed you in the head!" Scottie exclaimed, her eyes looking at Dannan and then at her husband.

"This is the man you hit with the rake handle?" Eli confirmed.

Scottie's eyes were very round as she nodded in the affirmative.

"Our new doctor?" Eli added, not having pictured anyone like this when his wife told her story.

"Well," Scottie reasoned quietly, "at least he's a doctor."

Eli's slim fingers came to his mouth, but they would not hide the smile.

"I didn't mean that the way it sounded," Scottie said as she tried to recover, looking between the men and then back at her husband.

"Dr. MacKay," Eli began, a full-blown smile now covering his mouth.

"Everyone calls me Dannan," that man said, offering a smile of his own.

"Dannan," Eli said, starting over. "Please meet my wife, Scottie, and trust me when I tell you she is not a violent person."

Dannan's smile froze a little, but he still managed to offer his hand to Scottie, who shook it and apologized.

"Please don't give it another thought," Dannan told her, the oddest mix of emotions running through him.

"Did it hurt or bleed very much?"

"No," Dannan answered.

Scottie looked unconvinced. She felt terrible about what she had done, and even the things she'd said today.

"I'm fine," Dannan assured her again, not wanting her to trouble over the point and also wanting to exit as soon as possible.

Eli sensed this and rescued him.

"Thank you for coming. I'm sorry to interrupt your Sunday."

"It's no bother. I'm just glad you're doing well. May I stop back tomorrow for one more check?"

"If you think that's wise, certainly."

Dannan nodded, put his hat back in place, and said, "Until tomorrow, Mr. and Mrs. Peterson."

After both Eli and Scottie bid him goodbye, Finn saw Dannan to the front door, not aware of the way the doctor walked just out of sight of the house, leaned against a large tree, and laid his head back, his eyes on the leaves above him.

He had done such a good job of keeping his mind on Eli Peterson, telling himself he could later enjoy the fact that he'd learned where the redhead lived. Not any scenario in his mind had included marriage. And to Eli Peterson, a man who looked to be 20 years her senior! It was none of his business how this marriage had come about, but he wished desperately that he knew.

What does it matter, Dannan? he asked himself. *She's not available, and that's the end of it.*

Dannan pushed away from the tree, knowing he was going to have to keep his mind busy whenever he saw her. He didn't know why he was so drawn to her, but it had happened on that first meeting, and he'd done nothing to deal with it. Well, now he had no choice.

Walking back down the green, Dannan remembered his uncle's advice to pray fervently for all of his patients, and Eli Peterson now fit that bill. Dannan covered the distance to his house, praying all the while, completely unaware that his patient's wife was thinking about him at that very moment.

"I'm feeling terrible," Scottie told Eli from where she was sitting on the bed beside him. "Just awful."

"I don't think you need to," Eli said honestly. "You don't smile like Dannan did when you're upset."

Scottie's brow furrowed. "So you think he's all right?"

"Yes," Eli answered her kindly. But he also thought, *A bit taken with you, but physically all right.*

Scottie studied her husband, wondering if something more might be on his mind, but before she could ask, he reached up to rub her forehead in an attempt to erase her troubled expression. It worked, as it usually did, and Scottie relaxed.

"I'm glad you didn't really need him."

"I am too. It's not much fun when I get sick."

"You haven't been for a while, have you?" Scottie suddenly realized.

"Not for at least two years."

A contented silence fell over both of them. Scottie was the one to break it.

"How about an early tea tonight?"

"How early?" Eli asked.

"Now?" Scottie suggested—the visit from the doctor and Eli's trouble breathing had made her hungry.

"Can we wait an hour?"

"Yes," Scottie agreed, but she didn't linger long in the bedroom, needing to find something to do. She went to the kitchen and spent more time than she needed preparing the tray. But it did the trick: The hour seemed to pass at a rapid pace.

"Well, Hillary," her mother said after tea that evening, finding her daughter sitting on the back porch stoop. "I didn't know you were out here."

"I was hot in the kitchen and looking for air," the younger woman explained.

"It's a nice evening," her mother agreed, sitting beside her.

"Is Jeff sleeping?" Hillary wished to know.

"Yes. He cried when your father left to see the Petersons and didn't take him, and because he didn't get a nap, he fell asleep on my shoulder. I changed him and put him to bed."

The women fell quiet then, both deep in their own thoughts. Hillary was thinking about dinner that afternoon and the fascinating mix of people around the dining room table. Alison's mind was on her three absent sons and hoping they were having a wonderful time with her mother.

Hillary glanced at her mother, whose face was a bit wistful, and guessed her thoughts. "Thinking about the boys?"

"I am," Alison admitted. "Part of me wonders if they might not be a little homesick."

"I suspect Grandma will keep them very busy."

Alison heard a note in her daughter's voice. "Do you wish you could have gone, Hillary?"

Hillary's smile was just a bit wicked before she answered. "No. Next time it will be my turn, and I'll get Grandma all to myself."

Alison loved this and continued to chuckle about it until they went back inside.

"Well, Douglas," Eli spoke with pleasure when his pastor was shown into the room. "I didn't expect you until tomorrow."

"And I didn't expect you to need the doctor."

Eli smiled. "Heard about that, did you?"

Douglas smiled back. "I hear everything. Eventually."

Eli laughed, and Douglas pulled up the chair he used each Monday to give Eli an abbreviated version of the sermon.

"So how are you?"

"I'm well. A bit of breathing trouble earlier, but it seems to have mended itself."

"What do you say to yourself during those times, Eli? What does peace look like?"

Eli thought about this for a moment. He'd not thought about it in those terms.

"I try to remember, long before my breath shortens, that each breath is from God. That way I can trust Him for the next one, or even if there isn't a next one."

"Do you fear at times?"

"It's not fear, but this time the problem came on swiftly, and I was startled. I was suddenly gasping, and I had no idea why. It took a moment to figure out that I hadn't done anything to cause it, and I was going to have to work through it."

"So you weren't eating? You hadn't started to choke?"

"No, nothing like that. That's why it came as such a surprise. I just suddenly couldn't draw a deep breath."

"What if you had died? Any concerns or regrets there?"

"Only for Scottie. She'll do fine, but she's never been

completely in charge here, and I hurt when I think about her trying to adjust."

"Not to mention the way she would miss you," Douglas added with quiet sincerity.

"Yes," Eli agreed, knowing how true it was.

With plans to return on his regular afternoon, Douglas didn't stay overly long, but the men had a good visit. When Douglas took his leave, glad to know his friend was faring well, Eli and Scottie had their nightly ritual, the one where Scottie read to her husband from one of the many books on his shelves.

On Monday morning, Eli talked Scottie into going back to Doyle's store to look at dress fabric. She still wasn't sure she should agree, but she did as he asked, thinking at the very least she would bring home a swatch or two. Something in green or yellow. He liked those colors.

Iris had given her a short list of pantry needs, and Scottie exited the house just minutes before Dannan left his own abode, the Peterson house his destination.

Dannan felt his footsteps slow as he neared the Peterson home. At some point after he'd left the day before, he remembered this man was his landlord, but that wasn't what made him dread this return trip.

He did not want to have thoughts of interest toward another man's wife; it was all wrong. But since seeing Scottie Peterson outside the mercantile that first time, she had lingered at the back of his mind.

Dannan shook his head a little and had a little talk with himself as the house came into view. *You live in the same town,* you attend services at the same meetinghouse, and now her husband is a patient. You're going to have to make this work.

Even having said this, Dannan knocked on the front door, not sure he was ready.

"How is Cathy doing?" Scottie asked of Doyle before she headed toward the bolts of fabric.

"Coming along," he answered. "She'd like to be doing more, but that'll have to wait."

"It must help to have the baby to play with."

"I suspect," Doyle's eyes twinkled, "that Val might be the only reason Maddie is not losing her mind."

Scottie laughed at his mischievous face more than his words. She was still chuckling when Doyle asked what she needed. Scottie stalled and started with Iris' list but before too long had no choice but to ask about the fabric.

"I just got some new pieces in. I think you'll like what you see."

Scottie didn't comment about her reluctance to do this but followed Doyle to the wall with fabrics and watched as he took down some lovely prints and calicos. Unable to help herself, she was taken with several, her hand going out to finger them.

Doyle watched her face and smiled a little, knowing that she would be pleased with the colors and subtle prints.

"I might need to get some swatches, Doyle," Scottie finally said.

"I'll get a pair of scissors."

"This is an amazing collection," Dannan said to Eli, surprised at the turn of the conversation in the last several minutes.

"My mother indulged me," Eli admitted, "or I should say spoiled. And Finn took up where she left off."

Dannan had seen in an instant that his landlord was feeling just fine, and almost at the same moment noticed the bookshelves he'd missed the day before. There were four of them, tall and filled from side to side with volumes that could not have been easy to come by. Some authors Dannan did not recognize, but others were like old friends. James Fenimore Cooper and Sir Walter Scott jumped out, as did Johann Wyss, author of the *Swiss Family Robinson*.

"You're welcome to borrow whatever you like," Eli offered. Not many folks had access to these shelves, but he liked Dannan MacKay and felt confident that a book loaned to him would be returned in good shape.

Without moving his body, Dannan swung his head around and looked at his host.

"Have you been in that bed long?"

"Since I was ten," Eli had no trouble admitting.

"What happened?"

"I was born with a crooked spine. Walking was always an effort, it took me years to learn, and when it became too awkward and painful, I was forced to stop."

"And your mother took care of you," Dannan put the pieces together.

"Until puberty, and then she found Finn."

"Your father?"

"Died before I was born."

"That must have been hard on your mother."

"If it was, she never let me see it."

Dannan nodded, thinking what a strong person she must have been. Eli didn't say anything else just then, so Dannan's eyes went back to the shelves. He spotted several textbooks and realized that this man had quite literally lived his life in this room. Dannan looked to the bed again and found himself under Eli's scrutiny.

"Pick a book," Eli said, not wanting to give his thoughts away just then.

"Thank you, I will," Dannan accepted.

"Now it comes with a condition," Eli warned before Dannan had even made a choice. "When it's read, you must come back and discuss it with me."

"Something tells me I'll be in over my head."

"What makes you say that?" Eli asked, unable to mask the laughter in his voice.

"You've been through each of these volumes a thousand times. I'm a novice."

Eli let a smile break through but wasn't given a chance to reply. Both men heard Scottie's voice in the hall. Eli turned toward the door with a welcoming smile, but Dannan did everything he could to brace his heart for her appearance.

Four

"You'll be so proud of me" were the words that escaped Scottie before she realized her husband had a visitor. "I'm sorry, Dr. MacKay," she said as she pulled up short and stopped.

"Please call me Dannan," that man requested. "My uncle was the doctor in this town for so long, that title makes me feel old."

Scottie smiled at him before turning to her husband.

"Are you all right?"

"Yes. If you recall, Dannan said he wanted to check back with me today. We've been talking about my books."

Scottie turned again to the doctor and found a volume in his hand. She couldn't stop another smile.

"Did he tell you they come with conditions?"

"He did, and I'm looking forward to our first discussion."

The eyes she turned on her husband were full of laughter and fondness. Eli smiled at being caught out, and Dannan felt something catch inside. The things he'd been imagining about this couple were fading away. Clearly there was love and caring and not just an unaffectionate or convenient arrangement.

"I'll be going," Dannan announced when it seemed the time was right. "I'm glad to see you so improved."

"Thank you for stopping," Eli said sincerely. "Do let me know what you think of the book."

"I'll do that," Dannan promised. "And if you like my evaluation enough, maybe I'll be trusted with another."

Eli's eyes twinkled as he agreed to this, and Dannan noticed absently the way it took years off his face. A moment later, Dannan was gone, and husband and wife were alone.

"That was kind of him," Scottie said, sitting on the edge of the bed.

"Yes, it was. I think kindness comes easily to him."

"You must be impressed if you trusted him with a book after such a short acquaintance."

"I am impressed," Eli agreed, keeping most of his thoughts concerning Dannan MacKay to himself. "Now, to you. You said I would be proud."

Scottie smiled and reached for the shopping basket she'd placed on the floor. Spreading her swatches carefully, she put samples from six different fabrics on the bed. The first had a green background with a yellow pattern running over it; next was a small yellow and blue check; then a yellow on yellow print; and then a green fabric with small white flowers. The last two were vertical stripes, one in green and the other in rust.

"You've been busy," Eli said, picking up each one and examining it closely.

"Do you like any of them?"

"I like all of them."

"But which one should I choose?"

"One?" Eli teased her, knowing he would want her to have more than she did.

"Yes, one. I'm sure I don't need more."

Eli reached for her wrist. The fabric on her dress was frayed at the cuff, a tear threatening during any daily activity.

"And all your dresses are doing this," Eli said as though

Scottie had argued. "I want you to choose three of these. I don't care which."

Scottie opened her mouth to argue and then realized how unthankful that would seem.

"I'll do that," she said, having trusted this man for a long time and seeing no reason to stop now.

Eli nodded and smiled at her, already looking forward to seeing which fabrics she chose. Not many minutes later, Scottie said she had work to get done. Eli didn't try to detain her.

Reese frowned down at the recipe for veal soup, wondering why it didn't taste the way she expected. She was getting ready to add more pepper when she wondered if it might be her. Many foods tasted differently right now, and she thought it might be wise to wait and hear what Conner thought. The only problem with that idea was that by the time he arrived home for dinner, the soup needed to be on the table.

Reese suddenly sat down. Why did such small things make her feel like crying? Conner never complained about the food. He and Troy were always thankful for meals, and their praise never sounded hollow. So why did she feel almost sad? She was not a melancholy person to begin with, and since coming to Christ and understanding the way He died for her, she had learned on a regular basis how much she had to be thankful for.

Reese pushed to her feet, telling herself she had better things to do than sit around and cry. She left the soup as it was and went to work on a dessert.

"How is dinner coming?" Scottie asked of Iris, who was in the kitchen bent over the worktable.

"I don't have the biscuits cut yet. Do you have time?"

"Indeed I do." Scottie didn't hesitate, uncovering the bowl on the table corner and going to work.

"What did the doc say about Eli?"

"He was just checking back in," Scottie explained. "Eli was fine before he even got here yesterday."

"I didn't meet him," Iris noted, referring to the physician, "but Finn says he's a decent sort."

"He certainly seems to be," Scottie had to agree. "Eli liked him. He left here with a book."

Iris turned surprised eyes to her employer's wife. Eli Peterson was a kind and giving man—extremely generous but ever so careful about his beloved book collection.

"What book was it?" Iris asked out of curiosity.

"I don't think I noticed, but he said he's looking forward to giving a report."

Iris smiled. She liked it when Eli had company. She went up every day to visit with him for at least a few minutes and had done so every day she'd worked for the family, moving onto 18 years now.

"All set," Scottie announced. Having cut the dough, she wiped her hands and laid out the biscuits in neat rows on the pan. "I'm headed into the garden for a bit. Call if I'm needed."

"Don't you be filling that water bucket until it's too heavy," Iris warned, giving her standard caution as Scottie slipped outside. Scottie agreed, knowing that no matter what she said, it wouldn't be long before Iris sent Finn to check on her.

∞

A corked jug dangling from one hand, Maddie walked across the field to where her husband worked. He wasn't in the sawmill at this time of the year, but the fields and spring planting had a habit of eating up every available hour.

She had left Valerie in Cathy's care, wondering how Jace was feeling. Clara, a woman who worked for Jace and Maddie a few days a week, suggested apple water when she learned that Jace's stomach had been acting up the night before. It was a relief to get close enough to call to him and see the way he smiled at the sight of her.

"Apple water," Maddie explained when he tipped the jug and took a huge drink. "How is it?"

"It's good."

"Clara suggested it when I mentioned your stomach."

"Leave it to Clara to know such things."

Maddie had no choice but to agree. She had learned plenty at the knee of her Aunt Cathy, but Clara sometimes knew things of which no one else seemed to be aware.

"How do you feel?" Maddie asked when Jace drained the jug and used his handkerchief to wipe the sweat from his face.

"Not bad. I won't mind coming in for dinner, so I take that to be a good sign."

"Do you want to eat a little early?" Maddie asked, knowing how little he'd eaten the evening before.

"That might not be a bad idea."

Jace handed the jug back and smiled down on her.

"How's it going with Cathy?"

"I can tell she wants to be home. She's over the moon about having Val to play with all day, but she misses her home."

"What does Dannan say about her healing?"

"Nothing new that I know of. I think he might be out today. Cathy's hoping he will be."

"And what of you?" Jace reached up and fingered the ties on her bonnet. "Are you weary of company?"

"Not until evening," Maddie admitted, "when I'd rather have you all to myself."

Jace's hand closed around the bonnet ties. He bent his own head even as he pulled until Maddie's face was close to his own. Making himself hold back, he kissed her once gently when all he wanted was to put his arms around her and keep right on kissing.

"I was thinking," Maddie whispered while their faces were still close. "I haven't had a swimming lesson in a while. And it's a warm day."

Jace's eyes lit with little flames before he kissed her again.

"Tonight," he promised, watching his wife smile.

Maddie was still smiling when she turned and started back for the farmhouse.

"How is the soup?" Reese asked, and both men assured her it was delicious. Reese still thought it tasted off but kept her opinion to herself.

"I've heard from my daughter," Troy said, his soup bowl half empty.

"Which one?" Conner asked.

"Eliza. She wants to know if they can all come to visit."

"Of course," Conner said with no hesitation.

Troy looked to Reese and then back to Conner. "You agreed rather swiftly. Are you sure Reese is up to it? It's three adults and two small children."

"I'm up to it," Reese put in. "I've wanted them to visit for a long time."

"I'll write back and tell them. It will probably be for a weekend, Reese. I don't know if Harris," Troy spoke of his son-in-law, "can be away during the week."

"Anytime is fine."

Not until she said this did Conner catch something in her face and voice. She sounded almost tired or discouraged. He watched her during the rest of the meal and didn't hear it again, but when dinner was over, he told Troy he would catch up with him.

"Are you all right?" Conner wasted no time asking.

Reese had already started to work in the kitchen. She stopped and looked at her husband.

"I'm fine, why?"

"Is it the family's coming?" Conner asked, ignoring her declaration of *fine*. "Troy would understand if you don't want a houseful right now."

"I want them to come. I was quite sincere about that."

Conner studied her. Something was wrong, but he could not put his finger on it. Reese was not one to evade questions, so he knew better than to accuse her of keeping something from him, but he could hear in her voice and see in her face that all was not well.

"Conner, what is it?" his wife asked.

"I'm not sure. You just seem a bit low, as though you're upset about something."

"I have been feeling like I could cry," Reese admitted, thinking she was the only one to know this. "But when I can't figure out what's bothering me, I just go back to work."

Conner had to smile. It was such a *Reese* thing to say. She had such amazing energy and drive that it was hard to imagine her being brought low over anything.

"But something is bothering you?"

Reese thought about this. Earlier when she had wanted to cry, she would have said yes, but right now she didn't know.

"I'm not going to press you," Conner said when she stayed quiet, but he moved until he could touch her. "I'll finish early at the bank."

"I don't know if I'll understand my feelings later, Conner. I just can't tell."

"Well, either way, I'll be home early to check on you."

Reese nodded as Conner put his arms around her. He held her for a moment before bending to kiss her. Not until he was ready to leave did he realize Dannan had never made an appearance for dinner.

"No word from Dannan?" Conner asked from the doorway.

"Not today."

Conner only nodded and left. Reese went back to work.

"You have something on your mind," Finn said to Eli as soon as dinner was over and the two were alone.

"What makes you think that?" Eli asked but didn't deny the statement.

Finn's brows rose. They both knew that the only person who knew Eli better than himself was Finn.

"Is it something Pastor Muldoon said today, something from his sermon?" Finn asked, not willing to be put off quite yet.

"No," Eli said but didn't elaborate.

Finn debated pressing him. He knew he would find out in time, but sometimes his curious nature got the better of him. Eli enjoyed stringing him along, but at the moment Finn realized his employer's eyes were too serious to tease.

"Let me know when you want to talk about it" were Finn's parting words, having settled Eli for the night and ready to seek the privacy of his own room.

"Thank you, Finn," Eli said, his gratitude sincere. He did want to talk about what was on his mind, but not tonight. It had been a full day, and at the moment he was simply too weary.

Sitting on the edge of his bed that night, Dannan thought back on the day. His last stop had been the Randall farm, where he found Cathy Shephard in good shape. He told her to give her wrist a few more days and to ease back into her duties, favoring her wrist until it was completely comfortable. He had seen that she was delighted with this news and also witnessed the same pleasure on Maddie's face. He knew she got along well with her aunt and wondered what might have been going through her mind.

Before the visit to the farm, Dannan had been at a house on the outskirts of town, a location that kept him from joining the folks at the big house for dinner, seeing to the needs of a young girl. She had a rash on the backs of her legs that made walking very painful. Her mother had tried several poultices with no relief. Dannan suspected poison sumac, but when he questioned the mother, she said the little girl had not been out.

Dannan had stood still for a moment, his mind at work. He was almost certain of the diagnosis, but he couldn't very well argue with the mother when she said the child had been indoors. In Dannan's favor, the family dog had chosen that moment to come into the room. Dannan had looked down at the big animal as he came to stand by the bed. In obvious affection, the dog had laid his head on the mattress, and the little girl had reached to touch him.

An explanation of where the exposure might have come from was easy to make. The mother hadn't looked delighted with the idea but took Dannan at his word, and she listened carefully to his suggestions to make her daughter more comfortable.

While Dannan was still sitting on the edge of the bed, his mind finally wandered backward to the beginning of the day. He could easily see Eli Peterson sitting against the headboard of his bed, slightly bent to the side, his face too thin but redeemed by the short, neatly combed beard he wore. Remembering Eli's eyes as being dark in color and keen with intelligence, Dannan doubted they missed a thing.

He had felt instant warmth from Eli, not just that morning but the day before as well. Dannan didn't know how much company he had, but he clearly knew how to make visitors feel welcome. And Dannan had been serious in his compliments about the full bookshelves. He'd not seen such a fine collection in many years.

For a moment, Dannan thought about some of the other titles, but without warning, he saw Scottie entering the room. Dannan's heart did the strangest things when that woman was in view. Dannan had thought he'd prepared his mind to see her, but then there she was, smiling in delight. Her beautiful face had been completely distracting with those light red curls peeking out from the brim of her bonnet.

For several minutes Dannan let his mind slip away. He thought about what his new life in Tucker Mills might have been like if she hadn't been married. He pictured her smiling up at him and not Eli and felt his pulse quicken.

Dannan shook his head and stood up, knowing that thinking about her was the worst thing he could do; it was also wrong in the eyes of his Savior. He couldn't remember if he'd left the book he'd borrowed from Eli in the parlor or the kitchen, but it was time to find it. And he did just that, right after he confessed to the Lord yet again that he'd been dreaming about another man's wife.

⚮

"When do your boys come home, Alison?" Reese asked on Tuesday afternoon.

"This Friday."

"Have you missed them?"

"I can't tell you how much," Alison confessed, and every woman in the room smiled at her in understanding.

It happened once a month, sometimes more often. The women of the church family gathered in Alison's parlor at the time of Jeffrey Muldoon's nap to visit and share for whatever time their schedules would allow.

Today Maddie was there, the baby in tow. Reese had come, as had Beth Peternell and Ora Weber. Maddie and Beth were regulars, but the other ladies came only when they could. They had been doing this for the past few months, and each time the women grew a little closer.

"How is Cathy doing?" Ora asked of Maddie.

"Physically, very well. I think when Doyle comes tonight for tea, he'll be taking her home. Dannan gave her leave to return to her life, albeit carefully."

"Why did you specify physically?" Reese asked, having caught this.

"Because I can't tell how she's doing spiritually," Maddie admitted. "She does a lot of listening, and she does ask the occasional question, but I can't tell what she's thinking."

"She attends services nearly every week," Beth pointed out.

"And she enjoys them," Maddie added. "I can tell by the

things she says and the way she interacts with everyone, but that's the way she was at Commons Meetinghouse, so I'm not sure there's much to hang my hope on."

"You mean outside of Christ?" Alison asked, smiling graciously.

Maddie's own mouth stretched into a smile before saying, "I do now."

The women all laughed together before the next topic of conversation came up. Ora wanted to talk about a verse she'd been learning, and Alison was encouraged to learn that all of these women had been memorizing Scripture. She had been struggling with that herself, admitted as much to the women, and was challenged to get back to work.

The time raced by, and almost at the same time all the women departed, everyone save Reese. That woman hung back a bit and asked Alison if she had any extra time.

"Certainly, Reese," she invited. "I just need to run up and check on Jeff."

Reese stayed in the parlor, wondering how she would explain. As she sat still, her last conversation with Conner came rushing back.

"How did the rest of your day go?"

"It was fine."

"You feel okay?"

"I think so," she had said, a bit helplessly, and then, *"Conner, what exactly do you see in me right now?"*

He had picked up her hand. *"The Reese I know is a ball of energy. She radiates strength and stamina."*

"And now?"

"You're just a little bit on the quiet side, almost sad."

She had nodded, wondering what to think.

"Do you know how much I love you?" Conner had pressed.

"Yes, and how much God loves me. I spent all day thinking about

*the blessings and promises I have in Him, and yet I still feel a bit off,
and you see that too."*

Even at that, her eyes had filled. Conner had reached up and
put his large hand against her cheek. His thumb had stroked over her
cheekbone, his touch light.

"It must be the changes in your body due to your pregnancy.
Things might be a little thrown off during this time."

She had only nodded in agreement.

"Why don't you talk to Alison? She's had enough children to
know how to advise you."

"That's a good idea."

"You go there tomorrow, don't you?"

"Yes, but there will be other women there."

"Then go early or stay late. You know that you're always welcome."

She was still remembering what Conner had said when
Alison arrived back. When she did, the older woman found
Reese looking very thoughtful.

"You have something on your mind," Alison began, her
voice kind. "I can see it in your eyes."

"I'm just trying to figure out where to begin. Conner suggested I talk to you, and it seemed easy at the time, but now
I'm not sure."

"What does he want you to talk to me about?"

"About how you felt when you were expecting. We talked
about it for a while last night, and when Conner realized I was
going to see you today, he said to ask you about it."

"How I felt emotionally or physically?"

"Emotionally. I want to cry all the time."

Alison had to laugh.

"What did I miss?" Reese asked, smiling at the other woman's
reaction.

"I'm laughing at myself," Alison admitted. "I cried for three months with Hillary and probably six months with Marty."

Reese laughed and sighed with relief all at the same time. Alison, still chuckling a little, had a question for her.

"Have you ever heard emotions compared to a train, Reese?"

"I don't think I have."

"I've heard it said that feelings make a wonderful caboose but a terrible engine."

Reese smiled.

"You get it, don't you?"

"I do get it. Even if I'm teary, I can't let my feelings pull me around."

"At the same time, Reese, tears are not all bad. Maybe your body just needs to cry right now. You might be experiencing some emotional changes because of the baby, but if you're still remembering God's truth about Himself and who you are because of Him, you'll do fine. If you're controlling your mind enough to praise God even when you want to sob, I call that a victory in Christ."

"Thanks, Alison," Reese said as she moved to stand.

"May I check on you again?" Alison asked in genuine concern.

"I hope you do."

Thanking Alison and hugging her goodbye, Reese headed home, wondering at the fact that she felt better for having talked. She walked down the green, fairly certain she'd stumbled onto the answer: telling Conner how she felt and listening to women who had walked ahead of her in the path.

Five

Cathy woke earlier than usual Wednesday morning. It had not been the best of nights, but she still smiled. She was in her own bed, in her own house, and the familiar sounds and smells were the most comforting thing she'd known in a long time. She would miss her time with Maddie and especially the baby, but even with the short time she'd been away, it was completely wonderful to be home.

She knew she was going to have to move slowly, and that included the extra cleaning she wanted to do since Doyle had been living on his own. He hadn't spent a lot of time washing dishes or picking up behind himself, but he'd threatened to cart her back to the farm if she overdid.

"You awake over there?" Doyle suddenly asked, his back to her.

"Um hm," she answered, doing nothing to disguise the smile in her voice.

"I don't smell my breakfast on the stove," Doyle teased. "You'd better get up and get to work."

"And find myself back at the farm? No, sir. I'm going to become a lady of leisure."

Doyle rolled over and looked at her.

"Is that right?"

"Yes, it is."

"Well, one of us has to make a living around here, so I cannot join you."

"Your loss," Cathy said with a cheeky smile before Doyle leaned to kiss her.

And she almost pulled it off. Doyle had to help her dress, and she only assisted him with breakfast, not able to do much with her arm still in a splint. In fact, she managed to keep rather still until she spotted the dust that had gathered on the furniture in the parlor. Not until she felt a sharp pain radiate up her arm as she reached to dust the clock that hung over the mantle, did she remember she could not carry on in her usual method. She did very little, and only with her good arm, until Doyle came for dinner, a meal that Maddie had sent with them the day before. Cathy's arm had stopped throbbing by the end of the meal. She didn't think she'd done any real damage, but even at that, she didn't mention her foolishness to her husband.

Dannan picked up his mail Friday in the late afternoon. He'd just been to see a woman with a toothache and was on his way back through town. He recognized his father's handwriting immediately, but it took some time for him to realize that something was wrong. The letter had come from Willows Crossing. Seated in the buggy, his horse half asleep, Dannan opened the letter and read. Later he would be thankful that his father had not beat about the bush, but at the moment shock filled him.

Dear Dannan,

Grant and Annie are dead. A flu epidemic swept through Willows Crossing, along with Carson Gap and

Headley. Corina was taken to the outskirts of town and is
still there. She is fine. Jonas and I are here and will wait
your arrival. Come as soon as you can. We may not be
able to hold the burial, but there is much to be decided.

> Love,
> Father

Reading the words over again didn't help. It was still there.
His father was still telling him that his cousin was dead. Their
family was already so small. Grant was more like a brother than
a cousin, and Annie had been the sister he'd never had. And
Corina.

Dannan's mind stopped. His heart couldn't take it in. The
horse shifted against the reins, and the buggy moved. Dannan
looked at the animal just before someone walked past and greeted
him. Dannan responded automatically, his hand going in the
air.

Not until this happened was Dannan able to focus on anything. His eyes caught sight of the bank, and without any more
thought, he climbed from the buggy and started that way. He
had no idea what he was going to say. He just wanted to see
Conner and Troy.

Only Conner was present. Walking past the teller's counter,
Dannan headed toward the desk that sat in the alcove of the
bank, Conner coming to his feet as he approached.

"Sit down, Dannan," Conner ordered without preamble,
reading something terrible in the other man's ashen face.

Dannan felt Conner's hand on his arm and the chair beneath
him, but nothing else.

"Tell me what's happened," Conner said.

Dannan held the letter out, wishing he could find words.
He didn't even look at Conner as he read. His mind could only
manage the fact that his cousin would never see this place. He

had planned to invite them. He had pictured them visiting and touring all around the town he'd claimed for his own.

"What plans have you made?" was Conner's next question.

Dannan looked at him.

"Dannan?" Conner tried again. "How will you get to Willows Crossing?"

"I think on the train."

"It's been and gone. There won't be another until Monday."

Dannan only stared incomprehensibly at him, and Conner saw that this was not going to work, at least not in the bank building. He went to the counter to have a brief word with Mr. Leffler. When he came back to Dannan's side, it was to take that man from the bank and lead him to the big house. Dannan went without complaint or question.

Conner had asked Mr. Leffler to send Troy to him as soon as he arrived back. Conner hoped it would be soon.

"Trains run more often from Worcester. We'll put him in a coach for there and get him on the next train for Willows Crossing."

"Who will you have drive the coach?" Reese asked, having sneaked a quick peek at Dannan, who sat motionless in the front parlor.

"I'll ask Eli if he can spare Ollie Heber for a few days," Conner said, referring to the man who performed odd jobs for the Peterson household. "I've already sent word to him."

This was no more out of Conner's mouth than someone knocked on the front door. It was Scottie.

"Is Dannan here?" she asked.

"Yes, Scottie. Come in," Reese invited. "In the parlor."

"Scottie," Conner's voice stopped her before she could go very far. "Is this about Ollie?"

"Yes."

"Then tell me. I've had to make plans. Dannan's not thinking very clearly right now. He won't even know what you're talking about."

Scottie nodded. "Eli's just spoken to Ollie, and he says he can leave at any time."

"All right."

"Eli asked me to tell Dannan we'll see to the house."

When Conner nodded, Scottie entered the parlor. Dannan sat so he could see out the window, but Scottie wasn't sure he noticed much.

"Dannan," she called and was surprised to see him startle. He stood but didn't speak.

"I didn't mean to disturb you. We got word about your cousin. I'm sorry. Eli wanted you to know that we'll take care of the house while you're away. Don't give it a thought."

"Thank you."

"And this is for your trip," Scottie added, holding out the basket she'd been tightly clutching in one hand. "A few baked goods from Iris."

"Thank you," Dannan said again, his heart so apathetic that all of this felt like an illusion.

"We've made plans for you, Dannan," Conner put in, seeing a tiny bit of life in the young doctor's eyes. "We have a coach and a man who will take you to Worcester. You can catch a train to Willows Crossing from there. If something should go wrong, the coachman will take you all the way to Willows Crossing."

Dannan's thanks was automatic and uttered without a trace of expression. Wanting to sit down, Dannan glanced at the sofa and noticed Scottie heading that way. He took the other end and looked at her. The Kingsleys were surprised as well and took chairs in order to watch.

"Was your cousin an older man?" Scottie asked, her voice and face kind but also matter-of-fact.

"No, he wasn't. Just a year older than me."

"With a family?"

"A wife and a little girl."

"I'm so sorry, Dannan. How awful for you."

Dannan nodded.

"Had you seen him lately?"

"Not since moving here."

"What will happen to his wife and child? Is there family nearby?"

"His wife died with him. I don't know right now what will happen to their daughter."

"How old is she?"

"She just turned three."

Scottie's hand went to her mouth, and tears filled her eyes.

"Did they share your faith, Dannan?" she whispered. "Did they know the Way?"

"Yes," he answered, his voice catching a little.

Scottie's glance went out the window, and Dannan watched a tear slide down her cheek.

"I'm glad," she said when she could speak. "I'm glad you have that to give you comfort, and one day their little girl will be old enough to be comforted by that as well."

Reese had all she could do to keep her mouth from swinging open. When Dannan had been so stunned, she had left him to himself, but Scottie's combination of compassion and boldness seemed to give Dannan just the outlet he needed.

"By her second birthday she was reciting dozens of Bible verses."

"Dozens?" Scottie repeated. "That's wonderful."

"She's very bright, and Annie worked with her on some passage every day."

Scottie didn't ask who Annie was. She knew it was the child's mother. She stayed quiet, and Dannan added a bit more.

"I can't think about her being so little and not understanding where they are." After putting words to some of his grief, Dannan's shoulders seemed weighted. "I should have been there. I'm sure I could have done something."

"Don't forget how much you learned from Dr. Collier," Conner reminded Dannan. "He must have done all he could."

At the moment Dannan didn't remember telling Conner about learning alongside Dr. Collier, but he was right. That older doctor knew more than he ever would. Dannan was on the verge of saying this when someone else knocked at the door. Conner went to answer it and returned with Ollie, Troy in his wake.

"I'm ready to leave anytime," Ollie said.

Dannan looked at this man and realized he'd seen him around town. He was not very old, early forties maybe, but he had a weather-beaten look about him that spoke of wisdom and keenness. Dannan had the impression that if needed, he could put his life in the man's hands.

"I left my horse and buggy at the store," Dannan suddenly recalled.

"Doyle took care of them for you," Scottie filled in.

Dannan stood. "I need to gather some things from home."

"I'll meet you there with the coach," Ollie said, slipping away.

Dannan didn't linger. He thanked Conner and Reese and then Troy. He nearly left before remembering Scottie. He turned to find her standing. She smiled when their eyes met.

"I'll pray for you, Dannan."

Dannan nodded and went on his way. He knew the numbness was complete. He hadn't felt a thing when Scottie Peterson smiled at him.

By the time Dannan sat aboard the train, his ride to Willows Crossing was little more than a few hours up the tracks. He hadn't been able to get the train at Worcester, and Ollie had been forced to take him on to Cherry Corners.

He hadn't let himself think while riding with Ollie, and that man had had enough to say to keep his mind occupied, but now he was alone with his thoughts. He knew he was tired enough to sleep, but fear that he would drop off hard and miss his stop kept his eyes open, no easy task since it was dark and the train moved slower than usual. He kept his head up, even when it bobbed with fatigue, and tried to pray.

Thoughts of Grant MacKay filled him. Grant's father had died when Grant was a young teen. He had lived with his mother but also spent untold hours with Dannan and his parents. And when Dannan's parents had made the decision to move south, the two young men stayed in Willows Crossing, even finding a place of their own to live. It had been the right decision. The church family had kept a close watch on them, and they'd both done a lot of growing up in those years. And to top it off, Annie had come into Grant's life.

A rumble on the tracks momentarily diverted Dannan's thoughts. He glanced around the dark, semifull train car. He could make out the shapes of the other passengers but not their faces. One minute he was looking around, and the next he was jolted awake as the train pulled into the station. Dannan's heart thundered over the fact that he could have overslept his stop.

It thundered again when he realized he was back in Willows Crossing.

Tucker Mills

"You're up early," Alison said to Douglas when she came downstairs Sunday morning and found him in the kitchen.

"I woke up and couldn't get back to sleep."

Alison put coffee on before joining him at the table. "Are you thinking about Dannan?"

"Almost constantly."

"Will you talk about it with the congregation?"

"I think we'll take some time for prayer, and if that goes long, I can adjust my sermon." He paused before adding, "I can't get that three-year-old off my mind."

Alison's heart was just as heavy, and both sat wondering whether Dannan would do more than return to Tucker Mills, gather his belongings, and head back to Willows Crossing, where he might be needed more.

Willows Crossing

Dannan was in the kitchen, a mug of hot coffee in front of him, when his uncle found him. Doc MacKay poured his own coffee before taking the chair by the fireplace.

"Did you sleep?" Doc asked.

"A little, I think. You?"

"Fairly well."

Both men were silent for a time. The funeral had been the day before. Dannan had arrived late to the house, after midnight, and Saturday had been full of the viewing, burial, and meal the women of the church family had prepared and served at the parsonage.

Dannan still couldn't believe he was in Grant and Annie's house. Even with Corina sound asleep upstairs, their absence was conspicuous. Annie's housekeeping had been excellent, but since they'd been so ill before they died, it looked as though nothing had been put to rights for weeks.

"I thought I heard you," Jathan MacKay, Dannan's father, spoke as he entered the room. He passed by the coffee and sat opposite Dannan at the kitchen worktable.

"I've been thinking since yesterday morning," his father wasted no time in saying. "I can't get over Corina's reaction to you. I was all ready to take her, Dannan. She's like a granddaughter to me, and I figured your mother and I could make it work.

"I mean, I knew, Dannan," Jathan rushed on, "I knew you were very close to Grant and Annie, but I didn't know how close. Corina got out of bed yesterday morning, found you at this table, and clung to you. She clung to you for an hour. Her little world had been turned upside down, and you'd made it right again."

"Get to the point, Jathan," Doc MacKay finally put in.

"You've got to take her, Dannan," his father said with tears in his eyes. "I know it won't be easy being single and balancing your work, but whatever savings Grant and Annie had will go to Corina, and that includes her care. You take her. Make her your own. Make her forget how hurt she is now."

Dannan shook his head a little. The thought was not abhorrent to him at all, but the words had come tumbling out of his father's mouth so swiftly, and he was low on sleep. He looked to his uncle to find that man in calm agreement. It was written all over him.

"You talked about this before I came?" Dannan asked.

"Actually not," Doc MacKay answered. "But it's like Jath said—we hadn't seen her with you. Young as she is, she would adjust to living with the three of us in North Carolina, but why add more trauma than she's already experienced?"

"Now, Dannan," his father continued. "We hate the thought of trying to talk you into this. We want to hear what you have to say. If you don't like the idea, you must say so."

"I don't like the idea of Grant and Annie being gone. About the only thing that makes that bearable is having Corina, but that doesn't change the immensity of the undertaking. As you mentioned, I am single."

Jathan had thought there would be more resistance. He'd half-expected to have to talk his son into the idea. When that didn't happen, some of the wind went out of his sails. He glanced at his brother and saw that he had expected the same thing.

"What can we do for you?" Doc MacKay asked. "Maybe I should return to Tucker Mills for a time. Help you settle in."

"No," Dannan said quietly. "I mean, I'd love to have you, but then it's goodbye all over again for Corina."

When it stayed quiet for a bit longer, Dannan realized he missed his mother. He would love to hear her calm logic on all of this but didn't think such a trip was a very good idea right now.

"How's Mom?" Dannan asked, not having had time to even think of her before.

"Crushed not to be here but praying constantly."

The words made Dannan want to cry.

"Corina and I will come when we can. Just as soon as it seems right, we'll come down for a nice long stay."

It was time for the older men to grow emotional. Neither one was overly surprised that Dannan was thinking so clearly—he often did. But watching him step up and take charge, even speaking of a time down the road when Corina was settled, caused fresh emotion to surface, emotions that only heightened when, a short time later, a certain little girl stumbled sleepily into the kitchen and immediately sought the comfort of Dannan's lap.

Tucker Mills

"We've heard from Dannan," Troy wasted no time telling Conner. After getting the mail, he went right to the bank with plans to tell the Muldoons and Petersons next.

Conner took the letter Troy handed him and read. It was brief but said much. He was coming just as soon as affairs were put in order, and he was bringing his cousin's little girl. The letter said her name was Corina Joy MacKay, and she was three years old.

In the letter Dannan also thanked everyone for their prayers and admitted he would certainly need them in the days to come. There was an estimated time of arrival more than a week down the road, but no firm promises of when he could return.

Conner handed the letter back to his business partner with one request—that he tell Reese the news just as soon as he could.

"How is Cathy?" Maddie asked when Jace returned from town.

"Doing well. Taking it easy but getting things done."

"I'm really quite proud of her, Jace. I never expected her to stay so quiet and be so patient."

"She's done well," Jace agreed. Then he put in, "There's news from Dannan."

"A letter?"

"Yes. He's not sure what day he'll be back, but he's bringing that little girl with him."

"Oh, Jace." Maddie's heart was broken and pleased all at the same time. It was wonderful to know Corina would have a home with Dannan but awful to think of her little heart trying to take it all in.

"What can we do?"

"I don't know of anything right now, but we'll stay in touch with Conner and Reese. I assume they'll know what's going on."

When Jace said he had work to do and left, Maddie put away the things he'd brought her from town. But she did so with a distracted heart. Until Valerie needed attention, all she could think about was Dannan and his new little girl.

"I know we need to respect the man's privacy," Eli said to his wife and Iris as soon as Troy left. "But I want something done at the house. I'm not sure Doc MacKay even had furniture in that extra bedroom upstairs."

"I don't know how we're going to go into the man's home, clean it, and possibly provide furniture, and not invade his privacy," Iris stated in plain terms, although she was not against the idea.

Eli looked thoughtful. "We'll send Finn. He can gain an assessment of the situation for us and report back the needs."

"Where is Finn?" Iris asked.

"He's checking with Ollie in case we need furniture moved."

Scottie had been quiet during all of this, but Eli didn't question her until Iris exited.

"Is something bothering you?"

"Just the situation. I hurt for them, and I don't want to complicate the situation by doing things to Dannan's house without first talking to him."

Eli patted the side of the bed, and Scottie sat down.

"If in fact there is no furniture in that small upstairs bedroom, we'll be doing Dannan a favor. We'll also make it clear that he may change or return to us anything he doesn't want or need."

"I just wish there was a way to know."

Eli watched her and was ready to continue his argument when she spoke up.

"Don't do anything yet; don't even send Finn."

"Okay," Eli agreed carefully.

"I'm going to see Reese. If she likes the idea, we'll proceed. If not, we'll ask Dannan what he needs when he returns."

"Does Reese know Dannan that well?"

"He takes almost every noon meal with them, and sometimes evening tea."

"I didn't know that."

"Reese was so close to Doc MacKay," Scottie explained, "that they've just taken him in. I believe Conner and Dannan are alike in age and get on very well."

"Yours is the best idea, Scottie. We'll wait and see what Reese says."

Scottie was relieved by this adjustment and told Iris on her way out not to send Finn just yet. But relief soon gave way to excitement. Scottie didn't even walk, eager to get to the big house and talk to Reese. She hitched the cart horse to the buggy and wasted not a moment of time.

Six

Dannan was on the Friday train back to Tucker Mills two weeks after he'd left for Willows Crossing. He had a very weary little girl in tow, and more trunks and baggage than he could manage. Corina had not cried on the train or even been fussy, but her sober countenance as she took in each new sight and sound was hard to watch.

"Mama here, Danna?" Corina asked, once they stood in front of the station, using her own pronunciation of his name.

"No, Corina," Dannan told her, taking her hand as the stationmaster headed their way. Dannan had a few words with him and then moved aside to wait for the unloading of his baggage. Once on the bench outside the station, the warm June sun across his lower legs, Dannan took Corina in his lap and tried to explain yet again.

"Mama is dead, Corina."

"Jesus died."

"Yes, He did."

"He's alive."

Dannan looked into her eyes and asked God, as he'd been asking for days, how he was going to do this. How was he going to make her understand that her mother was not coming back?

"Why did Jesus die?" Dannan asked, hoping he would not regret the way he changed the subject with her so many times.

"Sin."

"That's right. For our sins. That's very good news, isn't it?"

Corina smiled at him, and Dannan knew another question was coming, but a very large presence had joined them. Dannan looked up to see Conner sitting down on the bench to his right.

"Dannan," the big man whispered, all his throat would allow. "I heard the whistle and hoped you'd be on this train."

Dannan put his hand out to shake Conner's larger one and felt suddenly choked up. Although Tucker Mills hadn't been home for all that long, it felt amazingly good to be back.

"I need to tell you a few things, but first, is there anything I can get for you right now?"

"We're waiting for the baggage to come off, and then I'll tell the stationmaster which ones are mine."

"I'll send a wagon for those things," Conner offered, taking charge. "I'll stay and see to it, but before you head home, I need to tell you that folks have been busy in your absence, especially Eli Peterson."

Dannan's brows rose in question, and Conner smiled a bit.

"He sent for me earlier this week, and I'm to tell you what he's had done."

"At the house?"

"Yes. They asked Reese if she thought you would object, and she told them no. I hope she did the right thing."

"I'm sure it's fine," Dannan said, trying to picture what Conner could be talking about.

"I'm not sure you'll know the place," Conner continued. "Iris, Scottie, and two others cleaned like women on fire, and Eli had Scottie furnish and decorate a nearly empty bedroom upstairs. I've been told it was done with a small girl in mind." Conner glanced toward Corina but found he couldn't keep his emotions level if he looked into her eyes.

"Eli did not wish to overstep, and he offers sincere apologies if you feel he has. Everything is reversible if it's not what you had in mind."

Dannan could not speak. When Corina had napped on the train, his mind had been busy with the practical side of all of this, such as where she would sleep. Jonas MacKay had taken some furniture with him when he left Tucker Mills with Dannan's assurance that he would not need it. Now he found himself a father with one small charge. Grant and Annie had been renters. Most of their furniture belonged to the landlord.

"Dannan, are you all right?"

That man cleared his throat. "I'll go see Eli myself, but please rest assured that I don't feel he's overstepped."

Conner put a hand to the smaller man's shoulder and forced himself to do what had to be done. He looked at the child on Dannan's lap, taking in the dark hair and large hazel eyes, and said, "I should meet this person you have with you."

Dannan smiled at him in compassion before turning to Corina.

"This is Mr. Kingsley. Can you tell him your name?"

"Porina Joy," the little girl obediently answered.

Dannan smiled and then turned back to Conner. "Those hard *c*'s are proving a little tricky."

It was just what Conner needed. His smile was huge, not hinting of the tears he held inside as he formally addressed the little girl.

"It's nice to meet you, Corina. My wife is going to want you to call her Reese, and I think you'll be at my house enough to call me Conner. Do you think Dannan will agree to that?"

Corina looked up at Dannan.

"Can you say Conner?" Dannan prompted.

"Ponner."

"Close enough," Conner laughingly remarked, thinking that in a matter of moments, this little girl had walked straight into his heart.

The train began to move, and Dannan realized he'd missed the unloading. He headed back into the small, cramped station, Corina at his side and Conner bringing up the rear. He showed his bags to Conner, who took over and sent him on his way.

It wasn't far, but Dannan was suddenly tired. He felt too weary even to pick up Corina, but not too weary to notice the trusting way she kept her hand in his. Dannan made himself ignore the way he felt, and tightening his grip ever so slightly on Corina's small hand, they continued the walk home.

Reese had not been expecting Conner but somehow knew why he was home. She stopped in the wide hallway, 15 feet from the front door, and watched his face. "Was that the train? Have you seen them?"

Conner didn't speak until he was right in front of her. "They were there."

"You met Corina?"

Conner nodded. "She's so little and sweet. I can't stop thinking about her."

"How did Dannan seem?"

"Tired. I've never seen him so tired."

"And Corina? Was she tired too?"

"I don't think so," Conner guessed, smiling a little. "She must have been warm on the train because her hair was curled around her neck and forehead."

"What color?"

"Dark brown. It looked soft when she walked in front of me, and when I saw the back of her little neck, I—" Conner couldn't finish. He didn't have the words to describe what went through him at that point.

Reese put her arms around him. Conner laid his cheek on the top of his wife's head.

"She can't say hard *c*'s," Conner added. "She calls herself Porina and I was Ponner."

Reese's shoulders shook with mirth even before her mouth opened to laugh in sheer delight.

"I can't wait to meet her."

"I invited them for tea tonight, but Dannan said he wasn't sure."

Reese nodded, trying not to get her hopes up but also knowing she was going to have to force herself all afternoon not to march over there and meet that little girl.

It was a good thing Corina was occupied because Dannan couldn't speak when he saw the extra bedroom upstairs. A small bed sat low to the ground in one corner, a low dresser to the side. The ceiling had been painted, and the walls were covered in wallpaper, the print a bright, fun blue. It was a paper he wouldn't mind having in his own room.

The quilt on the bed, however, was as feminine as it could be. Every pastel of the rainbow was displayed, and it fit the bed as if it had been made especially for it. There was even a small rag doll against the pillow, and Corina had taken exactly five seconds to get her hands on it.

"Sit, Danna," she invited, having perched herself on the

edge of the mattress, whose frame was not many inches from the floor. Clearly she knew it was all for her.

"Thank you," Dannan said, lowering himself as carefully as his long legs would allow. He thought about reading her stories once she was tucked up for the night and wondered if he could find a rocking chair for the job.

"How do you like your room?" Dannan asked her, wondering how long it would hurt to see the mixture of Grant and Annie in her face.

"My room," she repeated.

Dannan slipped an arm around her, and she nestled against him for a moment, but it wasn't long before she spotted a basket in the corner and went to investigate. Dannan watched her from his place on the bed, his stomach starting to rumble. Had he been on his own, he might have slipped over to the tavern to see if they had anything left over from dinner, but he wasn't taking Corina there.

It was a good time to remember Conner's invitation. He pulled out his pocket watch and saw that if he could hold off, Reese would be feeding him in little more than an hour.

A messenger brought a note to Eli. Scottie, who answered the door, thanked the boy, who refused the coin she offered, saying that Mr. Kingsley had paid him. Eli had planned to nap, but Scottie still slipped upstairs to check on him. She entered with a smile when she found him awake.

"From Conner," she explained, passing the paper to him.

Eli read these words out loud to his wife, "'I talked with Dannan at the train station. He plans to see you himself but did not think changes to the house would be a problem. Thank you for all your work. Conner.'"

"So they arrived," Scottie confirmed, sighing a little. "I hope she likes the room."

"How could she not?" Eli teased. "I wanted that quilt myself."

Scottie laughed with him, but it wasn't long before they fell quiet. They sat together, both thinking on the changes ahead for Dannan and the little girl.

Eli's eyes had been directed out the window, but when they finally swung to his wife, he found her looking at him.

"It's a helpless feeling, isn't it?" Eli said, guessing her thoughts.

"Yes. I have to keep reminding myself that there is nothing helpless about our God."

Eli took her hand.

"Thank you for the reminder," he said softly, and Scottie could hear the fatigue in his voice. Leaving him alone to nap, Scottie exited the room, knowing that she was going to have to remind herself all afternoon about her own words.

"This is Reese," Dannan said, wasting no time with formal names. He nearly lived here and knew Corina would as well. "And this is Troy. Can you tell them your name?"

"Porina Joy," the little girl obediently replied, helping the adults to smile in her presence when the temptation to cry was so strong.

"Come in," Troy invited Corina and then led them toward the dining room. Corina looked into his face, the face of a young-looking grandpa, and followed without a glance at Dannan.

"How are you?" Reese asked after she'd given Dannan a hug.

"I'm not sure. I think there's still a good deal of shock."

Reese nodded in compassion and preceded Dannan into the dining room, only to find Troy making Corina right at home.

"I have two little granddaughters just about your size," he said as he helped her into a chair. "They were just here to visit me."

"Two?" Corina asked him, catching only that word.

"Yes."

Dannan had taken a seat next to his small charge, and once Troy prayed and the plates were passed, Dannan gave her small amounts. She had been a good eater so far, and he was glad of that. He buttered a slice of bread for her, made sure she could reach her water, and checked that her meat and vegetables were cut into small bites.

"I have pie too," Reese said, watching them and trying not to stare.

"We'll save room," Dannan promised, not sure Corina even heard.

"How is the house?" Conner asked when things grew quiet enough for him to be heard.

Dannan shook his head in wonder. "Have you seen it?"

No one else had.

"Corina's room is perfect for her. The bed is so low that she can sit on the edge of the mattress and have her toes on the floor. We were able to put some of her things away in the little dresser before we came over, and she giggled with excitement to reach and open the drawers herself."

"And the rest of the house?"

"As clean as I've ever seen it. Not a thing out of place, and any clothing I'd left out was all washed, pressed, and hung away."

"You don't feel intruded upon?" Reese checked.

"No. I don't think anyone went into my workroom, and my only concern there would be a bottle bumped over and broken."

"Danna," Corina whispered beside him. Dannan looked down to find a look of distress on her face. "I need a visit."

"Okay." Dannan was swiftly learning her phrases, so he excused them both and took her from the room. The other three adults were almost relieved. They had a chance to look at each other in wonder. None of them were lulled into the false belief that the days ahead would be carefree, but Corina was doing so well. She was bright and attentive to things around her when Conner, Reese, and Troy all thought she would be constantly asking for her mother.

They didn't talk about it before Dannan came back from seeing to Corina's needs, but everyone thought it. They had all prayed, not even knowing exactly what to say to God but asking Him to work in His way and to bless and keep both Dannan and Corina. It was so clear to all three of them that God was doing just that.

Weary as he was, Dannan had seen his chance after tea. Troy and Conner were playing a game with Corina, who was laughing in delight at the faces they made and the little ball that kept rolling from the parlor table.

Telling Corina he would return shortly, he slipped outside and walked past his own house toward a house he'd never actually seen. Sticking to the path that navigated a small group of trees, Dannan came upon a cottage not 60 yards from his back door. If he'd understood his uncle, it was the home of Iris

Stafford. She was the woman he'd suggested Dannan talk to about Corina's care.

With every step his heart prayed and worked at trusting. He felt almost desperate to have this plan work so life could settle in as soon as possible. He had patients to see to and a living to make. He could not do that without distraction until he'd secured a place for Corina while he worked.

"Mrs. Stafford?" Dannan asked politely, hat in hand, when the door opened to his knock.

"It's Miss. You must be Dannan."

"Yes. You must have received my uncle's letter."

"I certainly did," she answered in her matter-of-fact way. "Come in and sit down."

Dannan entered a small but neatly kept house with low ceilings and doors. He hadn't ducked to enter, but nearly so. The front door put him directly into a small parlor that held too much furniture but was clean in every direction.

"I heard about your loss even before the letter came. I'm sorry," Iris said as soon as they'd taken seats, Dannan in a chair and Iris on the sofa.

"Thank you," Dannan said.

"How old is the little girl, and what's her name?" Iris asked.

"Corina. And she's three, not four until December."

"Talkative or quiet?"

"A little of both. Some of her pronunciations can be a challenge, and she can be quiet around strangers."

"We'll get along fine," Iris assured him, having decided the moment the letter arrived that she would take care of this little girl. She added, "I work for the Petersons."

Dannan hesitated. This woman had just agreed to look after Corina during the day but now told him she would not be there.

"Will that be a problem?" Dannan asked, hoping he hadn't missed something and be forced to look for someone who had not been recommended by his uncle.

"Not at all." She dismissed his question with a slight wave of her hand. "Mr. Peterson will love it, and so will the missus."

"So will I bring Corina here or there?"

"I go each day around seven o'clock, so that depends on when you want to leave her. If she's not here by seven, I'll assume you're dropping her there."

"And the end of the day?"

"I'll probably still be at the Petersons' when you're done working, but you mustn't wait all day to see her," Iris told him kindly but plainly. "Come and visit, have dinner, or whatever works for your schedule. There's no reason you shouldn't stop in."

"And if there's an emergency in the night?"

"You just bring her here to my kitchen door. My bedroom is right above, and I'm a light sleeper. I'll just come down and take her back to bed with me."

They talked about several more details, the fact that she had Sundays off and preferred it that way, and the way she wanted to handle payment. They agreed that weekly was best, and Dannan knew the amount she charged was fair.

These details out of the way, Dannan's relief was indescribable. He knew this was not the ideal situation for Corina, but he would not let her or his cousin down. He found that his heart couldn't take thinking about his cousin right now, so he thanked Iris, making the mistake of calling her Miss Stafford.

"Iris," she corrected. "I go by Iris." A bit of a gleam lit her eye. "No woman at my age wants to be reminded that she never married."

"Iris it is," Dannan agreed, putting his hand out to shake hers.

He was on his way back to the big house in the next few seconds, his heart unbelievably light with relief and thanks. He suspected that Corina might have fallen asleep, and that would diminish some of the joy of putting her in her new bed this first night, but Dannan was swift to remember they had a lifetime ahead of them to experience that small act.

Her little nightgown was in place, her shoes and stockings off, and the covers were pulled back ready to take her. Dannan had not readied her for bed in her sleep before, but the job was almost done. He couldn't help but laugh when she woke up the moment her head hit the pillow.

"Danna?" she called.

"I'm right here. Go back to sleep."

She reached for him, and Dannan took her into his arms. He sat on the little bed, thinking she would be gone again in a moment, but the eyes looking up at him were wide open.

"What verse are we going to say tonight?" Dannan gave up and asked.

Corina's small brow furrowed before her eyes opened wide, and she said, "'In the beginning God created heaven and earth.'"

"Beginning" had come out *big-a-ning,* and "created" sounded more like *grated,* but Dannan still praised her in complete sincerity. It had been their nightly ritual since he arrived in Willows Crossing. Dannan would request a verse, and Corina would have one. Her pronunciations never failed to make him smile, but in the two weeks they'd been together, she had yet to repeat a verse.

"Can you sleep now?"

The small head that bobbed against him felt weighted. Dannan tucked her in and stayed close until her eyes slid shut.

When the little hand that held his went limp, Dannan reached for the candle and sought his own bed.

Not until he was settled in for the night, both bedroom doors open so he could hear Corina, did his emotions take over. For the second time since finding out that Grant and Annie were gone, he cried, wondering when anything had ever hurt so much.

∞

"We're having a girl," Conner announced when he and Reese had settled into bed.

"Is that right?"

"Yes."

"How do you know?"

"I'm sure it's God's will."

Reese laughed in the dark, not about to let this pass. "This wouldn't have anything to do with meeting Miss Corina MacKay, would it?"

"Not at all," Conner lied, still smiling over how precious she was.

Reese also smiled. She had been so sweet and cute.

"Well, we'd better get started," Conner spoke out of the dark.

"On what?"

"Names. We've got to have lots of girls' names to choose from."

"You work on names." Reese rolled to get comfortable. "I'm going to sleep."

"I like Valentina."

"No, Conner," Reese said, knowing she was being teased about her middle name; it had never been her favorite.

"Valentima?" he teased again, putting an emphasis on the changed letter.

Reese told herself not to encourage him, but that was difficult. She was sure that Conner felt the bed moving with her suppressed laughter, but he still took pity on her and let her go to sleep.

"I had a visitor last night," Iris told Eli as soon as she arrived.

"Dannan?"

"Yes."

"Did he like the house?"

"I wasn't sure if he knew who was involved, so I didn't ask."

"And the little girl? Did you meet her?"

"No, but that's what he came about. I'm glad Doc wrote to me, so I could say yes right away."

"And did Dannan understand how welcome they both are?"

"I told him. We'll have to see if he believes it."

"Will she come today?" Eli wished to know.

"Not until Monday."

"Well, if he doesn't come for dinner at least once next week, I want to know about it."

"What will you do?"

"Invite him up here and repeat what you said to make sure he understands. Maybe he doesn't think you have the right to make such an offer."

Iris knew it would work. Eli was charming and could usually talk his way around anyone in his acquaintance.

"I heard you loaned him a book," Iris teased a little before announcing she had work to do and heading to the kitchen.

Eli only smiled, having been caught out, but not minding in the least. He did like Dannan MacKay; he liked him very much. On the heels of this thought came thoughts of his wife, and Eli began to wonder how she was. Even though she had not felt well in the night, her husband couldn't wait to tell her Iris' news.

Seven

Dannan woke to the sound of tears. He had been sleeping hard and couldn't at first figure out what was going on. Wanting to move fast but feeling sluggish and disoriented, he scrambled from the bed as best he could.

Corina was standing by her bed, crying into her hands and calling for her mother. Dannan went down on his knees to take her in his arms, whispering soft words of comfort.

"Papa, Papa!"

The sound of a male voice changed her cry to one for Grant, and then Corina said several words Dannan couldn't make out. Feeling helpless, Dannan only held her until the cries turned to long, shuddery breaths and then to chest-jarring hiccups.

"What happened, Corina? Did you have a bad dream?"

"I want Papa," she stuttered out, and Dannan sat on the floor so he would have a lap for her. She climbed up and lay her head against his chest. Dannan stroked her soft hair, running his fingers through the short waves until her eyes began to droop. When she fell back to sleep, he put her back into bed and then went to look at the clock. It wasn't even 5:30, at least an hour before she normally woke.

Dannan was tired, but he knew he wouldn't fall back to

sleep. He picked up his Bible from the dresser and settled back into bed, not willing to go downstairs until she woke. His plans lasted only about ten minutes. He fell back to sleep, and when he woke again, Corina was standing by his bed calling his name with not so much as a hint of tears.

∞

"I've gathered everything I can find," Scottie reported to Iris. "I've stacked it in the parlor."

"You mean Eli's toys? I was going to take care of that."

"You just said you were behind on your baking," Scottie stated reasonably. "And Eli has been talking about it all morning."

"Well, behind on the baking or not, I've got to have a look at those."

Scottie followed Iris into the parlor, knowing exactly what her reaction would be. Scottie was right. The older woman laughed as soon as she saw the toys lined up on the table in the parlor.

"I haven't seen these for years," Iris said as she picked up the wooden meetinghouse from the Tucker Mills town set. "Mrs. Peterson had these made special for Eli's one-year birthday."

Finn chose that moment to come from Eli's room, and he joined Iris in her perusal of the toys.

"Why don't you gather a few of these, Finn," Scottie suggested. "I think Eli would love to see them."

"I'll do that. This town set especially."

Scottie watched him pick up the small painted block of his own house, a house he didn't use right now. The detail was amazing. Each little window and door was painted on with painstaking precision, and the slanted roof even looked as though it were covered with shingles. Even the bushes that sat outside the front door had been painted into place. And to top it off, a small chimney piece was adhered to the side.

And they were all like that. Scottie remembered seeing these somewhere along the line but didn't remember the bright colors and splendid detail. To pick each one up was like taking a walk down the green.

Finn gathered almost all of them into his arms and started back upstairs. Scottie trailed him, gaining her husband's bedroom in time to see his face light up with pleasure.

"The town set! I haven't seen these in years."

Finn had dumped the blocks on the side of the bed and gone on his way. Scottie pushed them aside just enough to make room for herself and watched her husband's inspection of each piece

"Finn's house." Eli's voice was fond. "And Iris'. What memories."

"Did it hurt to look at them and be stuck in bed, or did it help?" Scottie asked.

"It helped, because Mother always told me exactly where she was going or where she'd been, and I felt like I'd gone along. I wasn't anxious about her, but I would put them in a circle that began and ended with our own house." Eli picked that block up and smiled with contentment as he studied.

"Who made these?" Scottie asked, Doyle's store in her hand.

"I can't remember, but I suspect they're outdated, or at least incomplete."

Scottie continued to examine the block in her hand, and for a moment, Eli studied her. His mind had swept back in time to when she'd come to them. Scottie Davis had been her name then. She'd come on a trial basis to work for his mother and ended up staying on. She'd been too thin, too quiet, and too serious. They had all taken to her in a heartbeat, but it was some time before Scottie realized she could stay as long as she wanted; it was to be her home.

"What are you thinking about?"

"You," Eli admitted.

Scottie's head tipped as she looked at him. After a moment she smiled.

"I don't think I want to know any more."

Eli smiled back. "Why is that?"

"You have a mischievous look about you right now, and I'm not sure you can be trusted."

Eli laughed his soft laugh, still watching her. He didn't comment further, and neither did she. Finn joined them a short time later, and the subject did not come up again.

"I'm headed out," Conner told Reese Saturday morning. He'd been working at home for a time, and she now came from the kitchen to kiss him goodbye. "Valentrina," he called out before she reached him.

Reese stopped and tried to look severe. She had thought he was done with this topic.

"No, Conner. And if you really think it's a girl, how about suggesting some real names?"

"What fun is that?" Conner asked as he started toward her.

Reese was having none of it. She backed away and watched his brows rise.

"Is this how it's to be?" he asked, moving relentlessly closer.

"Yes," Reese answered, backing away all the while. "I'm not going to be hugged and kissed by such an insensitive man."

The smile he gave her was positively wicked, but Reese was up for the challenge. She scooted into the dining room, putting the table between them and waiting for his next move.

"Now this is tricky," Conner said, never taking his eyes from his prey. "If I chase you, you might fall. But I can't have you running away from me, now can I?"

"Oh, I don't know," Reese countered, keeping the table between them. "I think running from you is a lot of fun."

"Now or when I catch you?"

The smile she gave her husband quickened his pace. He was pursuing her in earnest when they both heard Troy at the door.

Reese was on the door side of the table and calmly walked to the hallway to meet him.

"Hi, Troy," she greeted lightly. "You're a little early."

"Yes, is Conner still here?" Troy asked absently, heading toward the study.

"He's coming right now," Reese said, her voice not giving a thing away.

The soft pinch Conner gave her as he passed and the meaningful look he shot her way told Reese that he was not done yet. She was still able to smile at him, however, knowing she had won this round.

It was slow for a Saturday, but Doyle didn't mind. There was always dusting and straightening to do, but besides that, he was thinking about his wife. Tomorrow was Sunday. They would attend services at the meetinghouse. It wouldn't occur to Cathy Shephard to do anything else, but Doyle desperately wanted to ask her why. Why did she attend in the first place? Why did she keep attending?

He might be able to do this. The simple question might make for good discussion or conversation between them, but it also might make her defensive. Doyle never knew.

This is when You want me to trust You, Lord. This is when You want me to believe that You are in charge and have a plan for all things. I do believe, Lord, but sometimes I'm weak. Help me trust You with all of myself, and help Cathy to that same end, Lord. Help her to find You. Let me be the husband she needs and never a hindrance in her path to You.

Doyle thought he might have stood there all day and asked for God to increase his faith and save his wife, but a customer came in. Doyle turned with a ready smile, but his mind was not entirely on his job.

Corina had been doing very well during the service. Dannan had seen to her needs prior to taking a seat, and so far the wiggles had been few. What Dannan hadn't planned on was the bee that had joined them in the meetinghouse. It hadn't come very close to him, so he hadn't noticed it, but it was a different matter for Corina. She saw it from a distance and wanted in his lap. Dannan didn't object, wanting her to stay quiet, but when the bee came close, nothing worked.

"Bee!" she cried out, and Dannan put some fingers on her mouth.

"It's all right," he whispered. "He's gone."

And it was gone for a few seconds. Corina was quiet and watchful until the bee landed on the pew in front of them.

"A bee, Mama! A bee! Help, Mama, help!"

Corina was attempting to scale Dannan when he stood and took her from the room. She sobbed and called for her mother the entire time, cries that could be heard until Dannan strode away from all the open windows.

No one older than 15 turned to watch Dannan. All had eyes for Douglas, who suddenly found himself without a voice. He stared at the door and then his wife, whose eyes had flooded. Douglas' head dropped for a moment as he worked to compose himself. When he spoke again, his flock could barely hear him.

"I feel brokenhearted for that little girl," Douglas admitted. "Dannan too."

The congregation—those who could see through swimming eyes—still stared in frozen silence at their pastor, not having seen him like this very often.

"I'm hoping that Dannan and Corina can join our family for dinner today so we can learn how he's doing. And I tell you that so you won't think me completely insensitive when I say that no matter how my heart feels right now, it knows nothing compared to the pain God feels when I choose my way over His."

Douglas swallowed and tried to clear his throat.

"I'm going to be done with the sermon now. I want you to come to me if you think I could have handled this better, but I'm nearly finished with my points, so I'll just wait and share those that remain with you next week. Right now, I want us to pray together for Dannan and Corina."

It was a relief for everyone to close their eyes. Douglas prayed, not a lengthy prayer, but his voice was still measured, as it had been since Corina began to cry for her mother. When Douglas was finished, he opened his eyes to find Dannan and Corina back inside.

"Again," he said, not dismissing them just yet, "I don't wish to seem heartless, but I don't want us to forget the good words we heard this morning from Scripture. We want to work hard this week or until we meet again. Know that I'll be praying for all of you this week. God bless you."

No one moved very swiftly. Their minds had been working their way through verses on the war with sin, and that had been going well. No one banked on such an emotional ending to the service—certainly not Dannan. He felt completely drained, and if Alison hadn't suddenly arrived at his side and asked him to dinner, he was quite certain he would have invited himself to the big house.

It was a quiet couple that pulled into the Randall farmyard after leaving the meetinghouse. Jace had said little on the ride home; Maddie was just as quiet. They entered the house in the same way, Jace to see his wife and child inside, and Maddie to stand and stare thoughtfully around the kitchen.

"We have to trust," Jace emphasized as though they'd already been discussing it.

Maddie looked at him, knowing he'd been struggling with the same thoughts. What if the two of them died and left Valerie? That question had been in their minds since hearing of the death of Dannan's cousin, but now that they'd seen Corina and heard her cries, it put new meaning on the whole situation. It also placed new meaning on their faith in the character of God. Was He a God who could be trusted with the life of their daughter? Their Bibles said yes, but their hearts were taking a little time to follow.

Jace suddenly put his arms around Maddie and spoke with his lips close to her ear.

"Everyone else is asking themselves the same questions. We're not alone in this. We're going to keep trusting and talking to others who are working to trust just as we are."

Maddie nodded against his chest, almost relieved that Valerie began to fuss. She thanked Jace after he kissed her and turned to take care of her daughter. Jace exited to stable the team and keep praying that he and Maddie would believe what they'd read and heard.

"Are you all right?" Reese asked Conner the moment they stepped inside their front door.

"What made you ask that?" Conner responded.

"You're quieter than usual."

Conner didn't immediately answer. He'd been very affected by Corina's cries and was still thinking about her but also about Dannan. That man had lost a close friend and a cousin, and yet he had to carry on. And without a wife, no one was there to share his tears and remind him that in God's care, all was going to be well.

"Conner?" his wife tried again.

"I am all right, but I can't get Dannan and Corina off my mind."

"I'm glad he'll be with Douglas and Alison today."

Conner agreed, but a part of his heart wished Dannan was with them. He wasn't sure why, but the desire to take care of Dannan was amazingly strong.

"Tomorrow," Reese said, and Conner looked at her. "He'll be here tomorrow for lunch. We'll have him then."

Conner wasn't sure how he felt about her reading his thoughts so clearly, but he still put his arms around her and held her until

Troy showed up. He had walked home, his heart just as heavy over Dannan.

"It was the most heartbreaking sound I've ever heard," Scottie whispered to Eli, still working to control her emotions. "She was so frightened of that bee. And then to call for her mother—" Scottie stopped, not sure she could think about it anymore but wanting her husband to know.

Eli took her hand. "You don't have to tell me."

"But she'll be here tomorrow, and I want you to know how precious she is, and what a good job Dannan is doing."

"But your telling me can wait until you feel better talking about it."

Scottie stared across the room for a moment. She didn't cry, but she wanted to. She usually never lingered long after services, but today she'd left without speaking to anyone. She wanted only to get home and talk to Eli, and now she couldn't find the words.

"I guess there's really nothing else to say," Scottie sighed. "Douglas handled it well, but he was shaken too. And Dannan came back in during the closing prayer. Corina was calm by then."

Eli gave her hand a little squeeze. "Tomorrow starts a great opportunity for us."

Scottie looked at him.

"Even though Corina is Iris' responsibility, you and I can both show her kindness and caring, in turn, making this time easier for her small heart."

Scottie nodded in agreement, suddenly so weary that she felt she was drooping on the side of the bed.

"Why don't you rest for a while?"

"Do you mind having dinner alone?"

"Not at all. I'll eat now and when you're ready, have Finn bring your tray up here."

"Thank you," Scottie said.

Eli smiled at her and watched her leave the room. He heard her door shut down the hall a few seconds later and knew she'd be asleep as soon as her head found the pillow.

"Cathy?" Doyle called for his wife when she wasn't in the kitchen or parlor. He looked up the stairs but didn't call again. Something told him she was up in their room, and he debated whether or not to disturb her. He vacillated for some minutes before climbing up to make sure.

"Cathy?" Doyle called softly from the doorframe, finding her on the edge of the bed. "Are you all right?"

"Her parents died so fast, Doyle," she said with her back to him and the doorway. "No warning at all. Just like Maddie's when she was a baby."

Doyle joined her on the side of the bed before saying, "And God gave Maddie to us, and Corina has Dannan."

Cathy looked at him, her face surprised. "It was all God's doing, wasn't it?"

"It certainly was," Doyle agreed. "I wouldn't have seen it that way six months ago, but it's clear to me now."

"But what about the bad part, Doyle?" Cathy's mind searched to understand. "If we get to thank God for the good—having Maddie as our own—are we not allowed to blame Him for the loss of your brother and his wife?"

"That's an interesting question," Doyle pondered. His face was thoughtful, and his brow furrowed. "I need you to do something with me," Doyle said next.

"What?" Cathy replied, her voice cautious.

"I want you to go see Douglas with me."

Cathy looked as horrified as she felt, but Doyle's face was determined. She frowned at him a moment but knew there was no fighting it.

"All right," she agreed quietly, and when he read how reluctant she was, he put a comforting arm around her. He did not, however, tell her they didn't have to go.

"How are you doing?" Douglas asked as soon as the children wandered off to play. Alison and Hillary were still in attendance, but Corina played at the far end of the kitchen with 6-year-old Martin Muldoon and 15-month-old Jeffrey.

"I can't always tell," Dannan admitted. "I don't think the reality of all this has actually hit me."

"You're so busy right now," Douglas said. "I don't know if your mind has had time to take it in."

Dannan looked thoughtful.

"What will you do with Corina while you're working?" Alison asked.

"She'll be with Iris Stafford."

"Iris does a great job with children," Hillary put in. "My friend, Mercy, stayed with her after her mother died. They're still close."

Dannan nodded. "My uncle said the same thing. He was so confident that he didn't even have a second suggestion for me if she said no."

A small *no* was heard from the kitchen, and Dannan excused himself. Douglas followed him.

"Is there a problem, Corina?"

"My doll," she fussed.

"But you can share it," Dannan said reasonably. "Even if Marty or Jeff touch it, it's still yours."

The little girl looked as though she didn't understand.

"Can you share?" Dannan pressed her.

"Come here a minute, boys," Douglas called to his sons. He spoke when they were near the worktable. "At least for today, let's let Corina keep her doll, okay? Jeff, Marty will remind you if you forget, and you listen to him. Just play with something else."

Martin nodded, and when Jeffrey saw it, he nodded too. Douglas smiled tenderly into their faces and thanked them. By that time, Dannan had spoken to Corina. The men met together in the doorway of the parlor, and Douglas was shaking his head a little.

"I think I need to apologize. I've just told my boys to let her have her doll today, and you just told her to share."

"It's all right," Dannan said with a laugh. "I'm not sure she was taking it in. I think we might need to head home pretty soon and give her a nap."

"Or she could lie down here," Douglas suggested.

Liking the idea, Dannan's brows rose and not many minutes later, Hillary had offered to take Corina to the corner of the kitchen, coaxing her into her lap with a storybook. The older girl read and rocked the three-year-old to sleep. Dannan was able to talk with Douglas and Alison for two more hours, and Alison sent food home for their tea. Dannan walked home slowly, carrying a groggy little girl in his arms and asking God to sustain them each day as He had today.

∞

Cathy was asleep in record time that night, but not so Doyle. He lay praying, talking to God about the day and wondering at the marvel of forgiveness. He let the truth of the cross roll over him. He thought about the blood that was shed—not just any blood, but the blood of God, and his heart sobered in an instant.

He then thanked God for Jace Randall. Jace had been studying the cross and Christ's sacrifice in detail and had been sharing all he'd learned with Doyle. Doyle had not given thought to much of this prior to now, but this knowledge had sustained him lately. He was tempted to discouragement that Cathy was still so undecided. Remembering the blood sacrifice caused him to think better about who God was, as well as His perfect plan.

Cathy chose that moment to shift in the bed, and Doyle began to pray for her.

Lord, she is so reticent to admit she sins. Please help her to see how forgiving You are. Help her know that You would not reject her humble plea. Help her to know the peace that can only come with repentance and confession to You alone.

Doyle was suddenly drained. His mind still full of his wife and his saving God, he drifted off into dreamless sleep.

∞

"I'm headed into the garden," Scottie informed Iris just after breakfast Monday morning.

Iris turned away from the fireplace to look at her. "Now why would you be doing that?"

Scottie was ready for this. "I don't think there's any need

to overwhelm this little girl with a houseful of adults. I'll just occupy myself outside until she's had a few hours to adjust."

"What if they don't come for a few hours?"

Scottie shrugged but was not put off.

"All right," Iris agreed, not sure what she was expecting or why she felt a little disappointed. These thoughts flew out of her head some 30 minutes later when Dannan, a very small girl at his side, knocked at the front door. Iris hid her feelings, but she had not been expecting someone so small or adorable.

"Come in," she greeted warmly, her voice softening a bit even as she wondered if she had forgotten how little a three-year-old could be.

"This is Iris," Dannan said to his little girl. "Can you tell her your name?"

"Porina Joy,"

"And what a pretty name it is," Iris was swift to compliment. "Is this your doll?"

The little head bobbed.

"I share," Corina informed her, remembering the conversation she and Dannan had just had over breakfast.

Dannan smiled down at her, wondering how he was going to leave her. He also wanted to talk to Eli but felt he should exit as soon as possible. He said as much to Iris, who understood completely. Forcing himself before he would lose all resolve, he kissed Corina goodbye and left.

For a moment he stood on the front porch and took some huge breaths. He then made a beeline for the bank. He had to speak with Conner.

Eight

The fence around the kitchen garden was a high one, but there was a large gap between two boards that allowed Scottie to look up and see Dannan on the front step. He was alone, so she knew he was leaving. She might have called a greeting, but the way he stopped on the front porch, his eyes closed for a moment, kept her silent. Scottie watched him walk away, knowing she hadn't been fully honest with Iris.

It was true that she didn't want Corina to be overwhelmed, but it was also true that her own heart was still aching over what had happened the morning before at the meetinghouse. She knew it would all come back as soon as she saw Corina. She wasn't sure if she was ready for that.

Scottie stood for a long time and stared at the inside of the fence, not really seeing it. It took some time, but with a new resolve, she eventually went back to work. Taking extra time, she was determined to have a basket of fresh goods for Dannan when he arrived back to take Corina home.

"This is the kitchen," Iris said as she showed Corina the

next room. "I work in here most of the day, and right here," she directed, "is a little table and chair where you can sit and play."

Corina looked at the small collection of toys and tiny table and chair and back up at Iris. Iris smiled at her and Corina smiled shyly back. Iris' smile grew when Corina went toward the table and carefully picked up a small cup from the miniature tea set displayed there. She watched her for a moment, giving an approving nod when Corina looked at her.

A moment later, Corina set her doll down and picked up the teapot, removing the tiny top and peeking inside. Iris then felt confident to turn back to her work. They were going to get along just fine.

"Can I speak with you?"

Dannan found Conner behind the counter and asked the moment he was close enough to keep his voice low.

"Of course. I'll let Troy know and be right with you."

Dannan waited outside, and as soon as Conner joined him, they began to walk. They didn't remain on the green but cut across yards until they were in an open field a few blocks away.

"Are you all right?" Conner asked, his eyes intent on the other man.

"It was hard to leave her," Dannan admitted. "I can't have her with me, but it was hard to walk away."

"Did you have second thoughts about Iris?"

"No, that wasn't it. I'm torn inside. The changes that have happened in my life in the last weeks have been over-whelming. Part of me needs a break and wants to have some time without Corina. At the same time, I know that I'm the one who understands her and knows what certain looks mean. It feels like I've abandoned her."

"But you haven't. You've provided for her. It would be ideal, Dannan, if she could be with you when she needs you, and at the same time, give you time on your own. But you'd need a perfect world for that, and we don't have one. These first few days will be hard on both of you, but you are still the best person to raise that little girl. Don't ever forget that."

Dannan nodded, working to take comfort in the words. He knew he had a job to do. It was more important than ever to make a living and support Corina, but even as he thanked Conner for his time and headed out on his rounds, he wondered whether keeping his mind on his work was even possible when his heart was so torn.

Scottie did not leave the garden until midmorning. She slipped quietly inside the kitchen door and smiled when she found Corina at the table. Iris grinned at her mistress and kept working on dinner. Scottie watched Corina a moment more, but when the little girl did not look up, Scottie slipped up the stairs—grubby hands and all—to see her husband.

"Have you met her?" Scottie asked the moment she entered the bedroom.

"No, but Finn keeps bringing me reports."

"Have you met her, Finn?" Scottie asked.

"Not formally. She's awfully content at that little table, and I think Iris is just letting her be."

"She's adorable," Scottie said. "And she fits in the chair as though it had been made for her."

"How did the gardening go?" Eli asked, not missing the dirt on her hands, nor minding it.

"I wanted a basket for Dannan and Corina, so I stayed out a bit longer. The weeds are trying to take over the beans, but I think I've gotten the best of them. Eli," she said, changing directions rather swiftly, "does it bother you that Iris hasn't brought Corina up here?"

"I thought I would meet her today," he replied, sounding only slightly disappointed. "And the day's not over yet, but her welfare is more important than my meeting her."

Scottie nodded, not surprised he felt that way. She knew he would love to see and meet her, but a too-thin, slightly bent, bedridden man whose hair needed cutting just now might be a little scary to Corina's small heart.

"I've got to clean up," Scottie announced, "and help with dinner."

"Coming to eat with me?" Eli asked.

"Absolutely," Scottie told him on her way out the door.

"Come in," Troy welcomed Dannan at dinnertime, having heard from Conner that he'd started the morning in a rough way.

"Thank you, Troy."

"Well, Dannan," Reese spoke from the doorway of the dining room. "I didn't expect to see you."

"Why was that?" he asked cautiously.

"You're certainly welcome," Conner put in, having come to his wife's shoulder.

"Yes, Dannan," Reese clarified, having heard the way she sounded. "I just assumed you'd be with the Petersons."

"Iris has given me an open invitation—I think I told you that—but I wanted to give Corina this first day on her own."

"Is it hard not to go?" Conner asked as they were each finding a chair in the dining room.

Dannan's smile was wry. "I'm just waiting for when I think she'll be napping. Then I'll check."

"That sounds like a good idea," Troy encouraged.

Reese had seen to another place setting, and just minutes later they had prayed and begun to pass the steaming dishes. It was a great meal—Reese could always be counted on for that—but as with everything else that day, Dannan's mind was half on Corina.

"Here you go," Finn offered, setting a cup of water next to Corina and gaining a shy smile. "Does your doll have a name?" he asked.

She gave a small shake of her head, and Finn just smiled at her.

It was only the three of them. Scottie dined with Eli, and Corina, happily situated on a box for height, remained at the worktable in the kitchen with Iris and Finn.

"These potatoes are good," Finn commented.

"Um hm." Iris' face was calm as she agreed, but Finn caught the pleasure in her voice.

Corina gave a small cough, and Iris came to complete attention.

"Easy now," she cautioned, leaning toward her. "Did it go down?"

Eyes streaming as she tried to catch her breath, Corina

coughed until she could find air and then sat still while Iris wiped her little face.

"Are you all right?" Finn asked.

She didn't respond but drank from the cup he offered. A little bit of a shudder, accompanied by a huge breath, lifted her frame before she took the spoon Iris handed her. The whole action made her look very tired and vulnerable.

When Corina started to eat again, Iris and Finn exchanged a look, their eyes silently communicating that Corina MacKay was a treasure.

"We have an early morning appointment with Douglas," Doyle informed Cathy when she stopped in to get his dinner dishes.

"Tomorrow?"

"Yes."

"Why so soon?" she asked.

"Well, Douglas stopped in on his way to see Eli, and I asked him."

Cathy looked at him. She had been resigned earlier, but now she wasn't sure about this.

"What's wrong?" Doyle pressed her.

"I'm not sure what we're seeing him about. Why don't you go on your own?"

"I thought you had questions."

He was right, she did. But at the moment she couldn't recall a thing.

"I'm not going to cancel," Doyle said, his voice calm and matter-of-fact. "If you remember by the morning, fine. If not, I'm sure we'll find something to talk about."

"Doesn't Douglas have better things to do than visit with us?"

Doyle was on the verge of telling her that Douglas had been very pleased about meeting with them, but someone was coming in the door. It took a while, and by the time he finished, Cathy was back at the house. Doyle was quite certain that the subject would resurface the moment he closed and went home for tea.

✵

"She's sound asleep," Iris informed Eli an hour after dinner.

"How did she do this morning? How did you do?"

"We got along just fine. She asked for Dannan when she grew sleepy but didn't cry for him."

"He'll be glad to know that. What did she think of the town set?"

"I don't have that out yet. Just a few toys at a time makes them all the more special."

Eli's smile for her was fond. "You should have married and had a family, Iris."

That woman only chuckled and reminded him it was time for Douglas to arrive. "I'll send him up" was her parting remark, leaving Eli on his own.

✵

"You're looking chipper," Douglas greeted when he gained Eli's room, shaking his hand as he always did.

"I knew you were coming," Eli teased, his Bible ready on his lap.

Both men valued these weekly visits. Eli was given a personal sermon, and Douglas had a student who was keen and hungry for God's Word.

"Did Scottie tell you about Corina and the bee?"

"As much as she could. She was feeling quite emotional."

Douglas nodded in understanding. "I'm still wondering about the way I handled it, but no one has expressed upset. At least, not yet."

"I think your comment, the one about how God feels when we sin, was very appropriate. I've only met Dannan a few times, and he doesn't seem the type to wear his feelings on his sleeve."

"I think you're right, but I wanted to be sensitive to the feelings of others as well."

"That's kind of you, Douglas, but the only person I would worry about in that situation is Dannan."

This gave Douglas pause, and after a moment's thought, he wondered if Eli might be right. Dannan and Corina were the focus just now.

A moment later, Douglas realized he didn't want to spend all his time with Eli on this subject. He opened his Bible and the men began.

Well over an hour later, as Douglas made his way downstairs, he heard Corina's voice. He knew he was always welcome in the kitchen and stepped through to say hello.

"Well, look who's here," Iris said to her charge.

"Hi, Corina," Douglas greeted her, glad to see recognition in her eyes.

"Tea," she said to him, handing him a small cup when he drew near.

"Thank you," Douglas just managed, wanting to laugh at her serious face. He noticed that her doll had tea as well, and it looked as if she had played in this spot all day.

"How is it going?" Douglas asked Iris.

"Very well. She's a good girl."

Douglas smiled down at the little girl, thinking it was quite true. Life had turned wrong side up for her, but as with most children, she was remarkably resilient.

"Thank you for the tea, Corina," Douglas said as he handed back the cup, stooping a bit to be at her level.

Corina looked up at him and began to speak. Douglas caught *Danna, dolly*, a word that sounded like *teepee, missus*, and even *Porina Joy*. Attending as best he was able, he smiled all the while.

"Did you get any of that?" he asked Iris.

"As a matter of fact, yes. Once you spend a little time with her, she's quite clear."

"What did she say?"

"She makes tea for Dannan and her doll, and he calls her Corina Joy and kisses her."

Douglas had to laugh. It all made sense now. He thanked Corina again for the tea, bid Iris a warm goodbye, and made for the door. It occurred to him that he usually saw both Scottie and Finn at the Peterson house, and neither had been in attendance. Nevertheless, it wasn't long before he was back on the green, a place he always used to remind him to pray for the folks in Tucker Mills, effectively putting the folks at the Peterson house in the back of his mind.

Dannan had not made it back to the house all day. He had

not planned it that way, but just about the time he was ready to peek in on Corina, he was needed across town. The visit had taken longer than he expected, and he knew when he had finished that it was much too late; she would have been awake from her nap.

But now it was finally time. Dannan knew he might be called away in the evening, or at any time during the night, but he planned to deal with that if and when the moment arrived. His long legs wasted no time gaining the Peterson home, and he knocked loudly on the front door.

Iris must have been expecting him because she opened the door, but the first person Dannan saw was Corina.

"Danna!" that little girl squealed as she ran for his legs. Dannan scooped her into his arms, having to restrain himself from squeezing the life out of her. His eyes closed as her little arms surrounded his neck, and his heart beat almost painfully. He finally shifted her in his arms to look at her face.

"How was your day?"

By way of an answer, she hunched her shoulders and smiled with her whole body, her little hands patting his cheeks before hugging his neck again.

"How did it go?" Dannan asked Iris, who felt her own emotions close to the surface.

"It went fine. She asked for you at nap time but fell asleep so swiftly that she wasn't upset."

Dannan looked back at Corina, who didn't appear interested in leaving his arms anytime soon.

"Why don't you bring an extra set of clothes tomorrow, Dannan?" Iris suggested.

"I'll plan on that, and will you please tell Eli that if he has time, I'll be up to see him when I come in the morning."

"I'll tell him. Corina didn't meet him. I'll let you handle that."

Dannan thanked her sincerely, instructed Corina to thank her, and then went on his way, holding tightly to the little girl. A part of him wondered how they'd survived the day. He wasn't actually sure, but he was thankful that they had.

"You can't do this every day," Iris, finding Scottie in the kitchen, told her in plain terms.

Scottie turned away from the worktable, where she was working on the cake for tea, and looked at her.

"I don't plan to, Iris, but I wanted to keep out of the way this first time. She's going to be a permanent part of our household. I have plenty of time to get to know her. Right now, she needs this time with you."

"That's the full reason?" Iris pressed.

"Iris," Scottie replied, growing a bit stern, "my heart is not made of stone. Don't you think I ache when I see that little girl? If it's selfish of me to keep my distance this first day to save my own heart, then call me selfish!"

Iris kept her mouth shut. She could count on one hand the number of times she'd seen Scottie grow cross with her or anyone else. Clearly this was sharply affecting the younger woman, and Iris had completely missed it.

"You let me know when you're ready to meet her," Iris said.

"I'll do that" was Scottie's reply, and that was the end of it.

"What's the verse tonight?" Dannan asked of Corina, putting her down a bit early for her sake as well as his own.

Corina's little face scrunched up with concentration for a moment before she said, "'Heavens delare the lory of God, and the firnament showdith his handiness.'"

Dannan, always delighted with her pronunciation, said, "I learned that verse when I was a little boy. You did very well."

"You know?"

"Yes, do you want me to say it?"

Corina nodded and watched his face as he recited from Psalm 19, "'The heavens declare the glory of God, and the firmament sheweth his handywork.'"

"Where's Mama?" Corina asked without warning, and Dannan wondered again what he should be saying. He improvised.

"She's with Papa."

Corina didn't seem upset or at all confused by this, but Dannan wasn't sure if it was the right thing.

"Time to sleep," he told her, watching as she climbed into bed. At the moment it felt like he'd been doing this for years. The brevity of the time was unreal to him. "Goodnight, Corina."

Her arms went around his neck when he bent to kiss her, and on impulse he decided to sit on the floor until she fell asleep. It didn't take long, and when she was out, he went downstairs to read in the parlor, or at least that was the plan. What he ended up doing was trying to pray, mostly asking God to help him in this new role as a father.

"You look distracted," Alison mentioned to Douglas after tea.

"I was just thinking about how we're doing as a church family. It's too easy to look good on the outside but still manage to harbor sin in our hearts."

"Did something in particular get you to thinking that?"

"I've been thinking about our hearts. You won't find our flock getting drunk and carousing around town, but you might find us unthankful, not humble, unforgiving, and forgetting to pray. All things that are so easy to hide if we aren't working to know each other and willing to be genuine about who we are.

"And I'm not talking about everyone else, Alison. I'm talking about the Muldoon family. Are we keeping the standard high, or have we let it slip just a little?"

Alison put her head on his shoulder, wanting to be close.

"We know when we sin," she said after a moment of quiet. "God doesn't hide His expectations from us."

"I wonder if there may be even just a shadow of turning in us, though."

"The heart can be a deceitful place, but if we treasure the Word there, God will show us where we're stained."

Douglas put an arm around her, adding a little more to what she said.

"We have to be on constant watch, Alison. We can't be lazy in any area, or Satan will gain a foothold."

"'Wherefore, my beloved,'" Alison quoted quietly from Philippians, "'as ye have always obeyed, not as in my presence only, but now much more in my absence, work out your own salvation with fear and trembling.'"

The two fell quiet with their thoughts for a time, but Douglas suddenly felt restless.

"Let's gather the kids," he suggested. "I want to talk to everyone and see how they're doing."

Alison went upstairs and Douglas headed outside. Within ten minutes the Muldoons were seated around the parlor, and the topic was holiness.

Jace put Valerie back into her cradle. For some reason, Maddie was exhausted. She had nursed the baby in bed and actually fallen to sleep. Valerie was asleep too, so Jace just moved her and climbed back into bed beside his wife.

"The baby!" Maddie started.

"She's back in her cradle."

"I'm sorry," Maddie said on a sigh.

"It's okay. Go back to sleep."

But that wasn't so easy now. Her heart had tried to leap from her chest, and she now felt wide awake.

"Jace?"

"Yeah."

"I figured something out."

"What's that?"

"I want control. I want God to do for me just as I ask. When I pray that we'll be here to raise Val, I *demand* it. And when I pray that Cathy will humble herself before God, I *demand* it. Douglas has talked about praying in God's will, but I haven't really taken it in. This is what he's talking about. I can ask, and I can ask in belief, but the ultimate choice is God's."

"And the choice to trust God is ours," Jace added, glad Maddie had told him what she was thinking.

"Yes," Maddie agreed on a sigh, feeling the fatigue roll over her again.

Jace was in the same state. Long hours in the fields had taken their toll. There was still much to discuss on the subject, but it would have to wait until morning.

"I've been thinking about God and death," Cathy told Douglas in the morning. He had come to breakfast at their house, and though it had taken most of the meal for her to admit it, she had remembered her question in the night.

"And how does it seem to you, Cathy? Is God in charge of it all or not?"

"I think He must be, but we always give Him praise. Why can we never blame Him?"

"I think we do blame Him," Douglas stated. "Every time we don't thank Him and recognize the sovereign work of His hand in our lives, we end up blaming Him and having the view that He's not doing His job.

"Now, Cathy," Douglas went on swiftly. "I don't think that's what you meant, so I won't go with that thought right now, but I will tell you that our only response to God can be thanks."

"Even when someone we love dies?"

"Yes, and the reason is all tied into who God is, how much we can trust Him, and how much He's in control."

"I know that He knows more than we do," Cathy said, "but it's hard to think that He would want His children in pain."

"It's how He gets our attention. If this old sinful world is too easy to live in, we might forget that this is not the final place."

"Eternity is hard to imagine," Cathy admitted.

"I think you're right. Everything here is so temporal. Everything here ends or dies. Life that goes on forever baffles the human mind, but we can trust what God has told us about that in His Word—"

"That trust in God's Son means eternal life with Him," Cathy supplied, telling both Douglas and her husband that she had been listening.

"And it also means we have a choice to make," Douglas

continued. "Do you think you know enough to make that choice, Cathy?"

"I don't know," she admitted, just as Doyle realized they were out of time. He had no choice but to mention that he should have opened the store ten minutes past.

"I'll tell you what," Douglas said. "If you think of anything else you want to ask, or if you just want to talk again, let me know."

The thanks Cathy gave Douglas was completely sincere. Things were not settled, but she didn't feel quite so adrift in her thinking. Doyle walked Douglas to the door, also sincere in his thanks. Doyle came swiftly back to Cathy's side, giving her a hug and then heading next door, his heart asking God to keep Cathy's heart hungry.

Nine

"Corina, this is Mr. Peterson." Dannan introduced her as soon as he arrived Tuesday morning.

The little girl's eyes were wide and solemn as she studied the man in the bed, but she didn't shrink back or try to hide.

"Please say hello."

"Hello." The little voice was soft.

"Mr. Peterson," Dannan prompted.

"Mr. Son," Corina tried, and Eli smiled in delight.

"It's nice to meet you, Corina. I hope you can come upstairs and visit me often."

Dannan spotted Iris in the hall just then and knelt down next to Corina.

"Why don't you go with Iris, and I'll come and say goodbye before I go."

When Iris appeared in the doorway, Corina went with her quite willingly, allowing Dannan to speak to Eli alone. The doctor found a seat—the very one Douglas used on Monday afternoons—and made himself comfortable.

"How are you?" Eli asked.

"I think we're doing all right. It hasn't been without adjustments, but we're managing so far."

"You probably didn't plan on being a father before you were married," Eli said, and even though it was not a comment Dannan expected from him, he replied.

"It's funny you should say that. I just began last night to think of myself in that way. I prayed about that very thing."

Eli nodded compassionately, quietly impressed with this man.

"I want to thank you," Dannan continued. "The house looks great. Corina's room is wonderful. I can't tell you how much I appreciate it."

"You're welcome. Scottie and Iris did the work. And that furniture was sitting in rooms here not being used by anyone, so your house is the best place for those pieces."

Dannan nodded, wishing he could find words that would truly describe how grateful he was.

"How are you liking the book?" Eli rescued him.

"I'm almost done. I should be ready to discuss it with you next week."

"Join Scottie and me for dinner. I'll tell Iris."

"Thank you, I'll plan on that."

Again Dannan fell silent as memories from the recent past surfaced. This was the man whose wife Dannan had admired. His heart had been in such turmoil since Grant's death that, for a time, Scottie had slipped away from his thoughts, but he still remembered standing in this room, learning she was Eli's wife, and working with all his might not to show his surprise.

"Scottie's around here somewhere," Eli suddenly mentioned, and Dannan eyed him. There was something in the older man's eyes that he couldn't quite read. He found it hard to believe that Eli would play games with him, but just for a moment, he wondered.

"I should be off," Dannan announced as he stood. "I've got patients to check on."

"Well, I'm glad you stopped."

"Thank you. You look like you're feeling very well," Dannan added on his way to the door.

"I am, thank you."

"I'll see you later."

"Bye, Dannan." Eli sent him off, relaxing his head back against the pillows Finn stacked high for him each day. A small smile played around his mouth. He had to be careful how he proceeded, but not proceeding was simply not an option. Dannan was the man he'd been hoping would move to Tucker Mills for a very long time.

∞

"It's hot for mid-June," Mrs. Greenlowe said to Doyle. "I don't like it this hot."

"It's a warm one," Doyle agreed. "What do you do to keep cool?"

"Oh, you know me, Doyle. I just complain and keep working."

The storekeeper couldn't help but smile.

"You haven't seen Reese today, have you?" Mrs. Greenlowe asked.

"No, ma'am, I have not."

"Good. I'm headed to the big house to pay her a visit, and I want her to be home."

"Going to surprise her?"

"That's the plan," Mrs. Greenlowe told him with pleasure. Just moments later, she was gathering her full basket and heading toward the door. Doyle went as far as he needed to watch which way she went. Sure enough, she walked in the direction of the big house.

ᘗᘐ

"One of my dresses is done," Scottie told her husband after breakfast. She was wearing an old one.

"How did it turn out?"

"Nice."

"Why aren't you wearing it?"

"I thought I would save it for services."

This was news to Eli, but he held his tongue.

"Eli," Scottie went on. "I want to take some of that fabric I bought and make a new dress for Corina. I haven't made a child's dress in a long time, and I think it would be such fun."

"I think that's a great idea, but I was still thinking you needed more than one new dress."

"I'll have two."

"You don't have another piece of cloth that would work for someone as small as Corina?"

"Oh, I guess I do." Scottie was surprised, not having thought of it herself.

"What's really bothering you?" Eli suddenly asked, and Scottie sat very still. Eli didn't press her but knew something wasn't right. He gave Scottie some time to reply, but when she continued to sit and look troubled, he began to worry. He wanted to know what was bothering her, but more than that, he wanted to rescue her.

"You don't have to talk about it right now, Scottie."

Wanting to unburden, Scottie looked at him but wasn't sure she had the words. She thought Corina MacKay was precious, but having her in the house was stirring up old, very unpleasant memories. This was not something Scottie had anticipated, and these recollections had taken her very much by surprise.

"I keep thinking about my past," was all Scottie could manage, pain covering her features.

Eli picked up her hand. "It will wait," he said softly.

Scottie nodded, relieved by that fact and thankful that her husband understood. Indeed, he did not press her about the subject again, and when she said she had work to do, he sent her off with a smile. She was not aware of the way he worried about her and even spoke to Finn when that man checked on him.

"Could it have something to do with Corina?" Finn asked once he'd heard him out.

"What made you ask that?"

"Iris said Scottie hadn't met her—didn't want to overwhelm the little thing."

If Eli hadn't seen his wife looking upset, he would have thought her only being kind, but this added to his worry. He usually felt better for having spoken with Finn, but not this time. He spent most of the morning worrying to God instead of praying, and feeling helpless for all the wrong reasons.

"Mrs. Greenlowe!" Reese stood in surprise in the yard when that lady walked up and found her working on the flowerbeds on each side of the front door.

"What are you doing weeding in this heat?" Mrs. Greenlowe demanded.

Reese smiled. "I didn't notice."

The older woman sniffed, trying not to smile.

"Come in," Reese invited, stepping toward the door, not willing to hear a negative word from her. To Reese's surprise, Mrs. Greenlowe willingly followed.

"Things look nice," the older woman commented, following Reese to the big parlor.

"Thank you. Have a seat."

"We don't have to talk in here, Reese."

"Of course we do," Reese teased her. "You don't visit often enough to treat this casually."

"Oh, go on, Reese. You don't want me hanging about the place."

"That's not likely to happen," Reese said dryly. "Now, tell me, Mrs. Greenlowe, what's in your basket?"

"Just things I picked up from Doyle," she said with a nonchalant air that didn't work on Reese.

Reese's brows rose, and Mrs. Greenlowe gave in.

"Look at these fabrics!" She leaned toward Reese in excitement. "Do you like them?"

"They're beautiful," Reese exclaimed, touching the top two.

"They're for a baby quilt! I'm going to start it this afternoon."

Reese smiled, her eyes full of teasing, and asked, "Whose baby?"

"Oh, go on with you, Reese. Stop teasing me or I'm going to leave."

"You can't do that before you see what I've been doing."

"What?"

Reese stood, and this time she led the way upstairs to a room she was preparing for the baby.

"Reese," Mrs. Greenlowe almost whispered as she crossed the threshold and stood very still. "It's beautiful."

Reese Kingsley had been busy. She was painting a scenic meadow on two walls of the smallest room upstairs. A few evergreens stretched to the ceiling, but most of the painting was full of leafy bushes and vivid bunches of wildflowers. Prairie grasses fell away almost like a path, and had it been a little more true to size, one would have been tempted to step through the wall.

"Conner thinks we're having a girl, but I still think it might be a boy. I didn't want it to be all flowers. If it is a boy, I might add a little water over here," she pointed to the edge on the right. "That way he can picture himself fishing when he can't really go to the pond."

Mrs. Greenlowe suddenly rounded on her.

"Why did you never tell me you could paint?"

Reese shrugged. "It never came up, and I hadn't done it in years, so I didn't know if I still could. And," Reese put in before Mrs. Greenlowe could go on, "the colors you chose for the quilt will be perfect in here."

The older woman couldn't say a word. It was impossible to complain, scold, or grumble when she was this pleased, and right now her heart was overflowing with contentment.

"I've got to get home," she announced, turning from the room and starting down the stairs. "This quilt isn't going to sew itself."

Reese trailed after her, not pressing her to stay. Not until they were at the front door did Mrs. Greenlowe stop and face her.

"You're doing a good job, Reese," she said swiftly, and she would have rushed out the door, but Reese was too fast. She gave Mrs. Greenlowe a hug, which was quickly reciprocated, and then stood at the door and watched her walk all the way down the green. At the moment, Reese was so excited to tell Conner about her visit she wondered how she would wait for him to come home for dinner.

At times, Lord, I can see every face, Scottie prayed, kneeling by her bed, her heart in agony. *I can see Marie's face and Sandra's. In my mind they're still little girls in the home, but it can't be true now.*

Scottie had to force herself not to imagine the worst. She desperately wanted to trust God for the past and for where these women would be now.

Wherever they are, Lord, whatever has become of them, touch their hearts and bless them, Father. Forgive them and save them, and let them find You. Thank You that you died for each heart there, even Matron and the other workers. Thank You for bringing me here and showing me Yourself.

Scottie couldn't manage another word. Tears poured onto the quilt where her face rested, trying to get past the pain of all those little girls who stayed behind on that day she went to the Peterson home.

It took some doing. She felt so heavy with the memories that she didn't climb into bed for a long time. When she did, it was to lie awake and stare into the darkness, her prayers continuing. There was no comfort in knowledge about the home because she had no answers, but comfort came from remembering who God was and how much He longed for hearts to turn to Him.

Scottie could think of nothing else to pray. Until she fell into a heavy sleep that lasted all night, she asked God to reach out in His saving way and bring those hearts to Him. And she didn't forget those under her own roof but prayed that Iris and Finn would believe and that she and Eli would be ever diligent in their example before them.

Thursday was as cool and rainy as Tuesday had been hot and sunny. Garden and field work were suspended all over Tucker Mills, and children, longing to run outside, lingered at windows and doorways wondering when the skies would clear.

Scottie was in the same state. Assuming she was going to

have time in the garden, she stood at the doorway to the kitchen and listened to the rain, thinking that even if it cleared, the mud would be impossible.

The fall of rain made a relaxing sound, and Scottie was in no hurry to move. A noise behind her made her turn. Iris and Corina were just coming in from the parlor.

"Hello," Scottie greeted, knowing that she could avoid this no longer. Indeed, she'd been keeping scarce all week. "I think you must be Corina."

"Yes, indeed," Iris spoke up. "Corina, this is Mr. Peterson's wife. This is Scottie. Can you say Scottie?"

"Sottie," Corina tried.

"That's right," Scottie praised her and smiled.

Liking this woman, Corina smiled back and stepped forward to show Scottie her doll. It was a doll that Scottie had made, but she admired it as though she'd never seen it before.

"Does she have a name?" Scottie asked.

"Porina Joy."

"That's your name. Is it your doll's name too?"

Corina nodded, and Scottie smiled at her. Corina moved a little closer and touched the fabric on Scottie's sleeve. Scottie glanced up at Iris, their gaze sharing in the surprise.

"You might remind her of her m-o-t-h-e-r," Iris said quietly.

"That would make sense," Scottie agreed just as softly, keeping still while Corina touched her sleeve. It was one of her old dresses, but the fabric was bright and fun, and Corina must have thought she could pull the flowers off. She fingered it a moment longer before looking into Scottie's face, her own a bit uncertain.

"Do you like flowers?"

"In my room," Corina said.

Scottie nodded, remembering the small patches of flowers

on the wallpaper. Scottie now understood her fascination with the dress. There was some resemblance.

"Your dress is pretty," Scottie complimented, watching as Corina's hand went down her front, smoothing the yellow pinafore that covered her blue and yellow dress.

"Can you say thank you?" Iris urged.

"San you." Corina looked into Scottie's face to speak and didn't look away. Scottie was so taken with the child's small face that she couldn't look away either. She had forgotten how clear and perfect a child's eyes could be. Corina's were a deep hazel, the white of her eyes so bright and perfect that Scottie felt lost in them.

"Did you want to take her up to see Eli?" Iris put in.

"I could do that," Scottie agreed, thinking she needed the distraction. "Would you like to go up and see Mr. Peterson, Corina?"

Corina nodded, but Scottie wasn't sure she understood. She half-expected her to change her mind somewhere on the stairway, but Scottie was wrong. The little girl held her hand and accompanied her as if climbing the steps was the most normal occurrence.

"Well good morning," Eli greeted when he spotted them. "How are you today, Corina?"

"I have flowers," Corina said, but her voice had dropped some, and she looked at Scottie, who had taken a seat on the bedside. That little girl moved to Scottie's side and stayed very close, even going so far as to lean against Scottie's leg.

"If the rain stops, you'll have to ask Scottie to show you the flowers in our yard," Eli said, trying to study his wife and talk to the little girl all at the same time. To the best of his knowledge, this was the first time Scottie had interacted with Corina.

"We'll plan on that," Scottie said to Corina. She then looked to her husband. "How was your night?"

"It was fine. Yours?"

"I think the rain woke me, but I went right back to sleep."

It was then that Scottie noticed something in Eli's eyes. Her brow lowered in question, but a small shake of Eli's head told her it would have to wait. Both adults looked down to see that Corina had spotted Eli's bookshelves. She hadn't moved from Scottie's side just yet, but her head was turned to study the full shelves.

"I have children's books," Eli told his wife.

"In here?"

"No. Try my mother's room. There should be quite a few." Eli then turned his attention back to Corina. "Do you like books, Corina?"

But that little girl didn't hear him. She was still studying the shelves and had even walked to the end of the bed, her doll hugged under one arm. She stood, a hand to the bedpost, and continued to stare toward the shelves.

"We'll head that way," Scottie suggested.

"But at some point you'll come back alone?" her husband asked.

"Certainly," Scottie told him, their eyes meeting as she tried to guess what was on his mind.

Eli didn't say anymore. He deliberated about giving her a hint, but the very person they needed to talk about was still in the room.

Ten

"Shall we read a book?" Scottie offered when they had found a fat stack of children's books in the late Mrs. Peterson's room.

Corina was swift to nod over this request, and Scottie, accompanied by Corina and all the books, went to the parlor to get comfortable. Both Finn and Iris came through at different times, but Scottie and Corina didn't budge from their spot in one corner of the sofa. They read through two books and were started on a third when Iris came to see if Corina needed to be excused.

Corina obediently accompanied her, and Scottie went to the window to see if the skies were clearing. Even in the rain she could see that the flowers in the yard were brilliant and knew that whenever she could venture forth with Corina, it would be worth the effort.

"Do you want her back?" Iris popped her head out of the kitchen long enough to ask.

"Actually, I have some things to get done. Will you please tell her we'll read again after dinner?"

With a swift nod, Iris disappeared back into the kitchen, and Scottie made a beeline for her husband's room.

"How are you?" Maddie asked of Reese, who had come to visit her at the farm. The women had just gotten comfortable in the parlor, Valerie in Reese's arms.

"I'm fine. A bit tired at times."

"What do you do when you're tired? Do you rest or push on?"

"I push on," Reese admitted.

"Do yourself a favor, Reese, and rest now. You won't have that option once the baby comes."

"I didn't think of that, but then I assumed I wouldn't be tired once the baby's born."

Maddie almost laughed before remembering that Reese had unbelievable energy. She did laugh, but at herself.

"Sometimes I envy you, Reese. I seem to be tired every day."

"Are you expecting again?"

Maddie opened her mouth to say no but stopped.

"What's the matter?" Reese asked.

"I was going to say no, but now I'm not sure."

"You think you might be?"

Maddie didn't speak; she was too deep in thought.

"How old is Val?" Reese asked next.

"She was four months last week."

"And you're still nursing, aren't you?"

"Yes."

Both women sat in silence, knowing it was possible but unlikely.

"That would explain the fatigue," Maddie muttered, her voice a little strange.

"Being the mother of a newborn would do that, Maddie," Reese said with compassion, almost sorry she'd asked. "I don't even know why I asked that."

Maddie looked into Reese's eyes and smiled. "I don't know why I'm so stunned. Even if I am pregnant, it's good news."

"Is it?" Reese questioned. "You didn't sound so sure a moment ago."

"Well, I guess I would be surprised, but not at all sorry. Jace and I have just assumed that Val would be the first of many."

"Conner's favorite passage these days is the one about children and a man's quiver being full of them."

"Where is that?"

"In the Psalms. Let me think—" Reese stared into space as Maddie went for a Bible.

"Do you remember where?" she asked, opening to that book.

"One-twenty-something," Reese guessed, and waited while Maddie began to search. It took some doing, but she eventually read from Psalm 127.

"'Lo, children are an heritage of the Lord, and the fruit of the womb is his reward. As arrows are in the hand of a mighty man, so are children of the youth. Happy is the man that hath his quiver full of them; they shall not be ashamed, but they shall speak with the enemies in the gate.'"

Maddie sat back, her face soft with a coming smile.

"I didn't know about those verses. It makes me wish I was expecting right now."

"Maybe you are," Reese reminded her, laughing a little over the chain of emotions from chagrin to pleasure. Maddie laughed as well.

"Well, if emotional changes in a matter of minutes are any indication, I'm probably carrying twins."

The women shared another laugh, and that was how Jace found them. He wanted to know what was so funny, but Maddie took pity on him, knowing it would not be news—even if she was only suspicious—that he would want to hear in front of company.

∞∞

"I couldn't ask you in front of her, but I'm wondering how you're doing with Corina in the house," Eli said, not wasting any time.

"I was a little tense until I met her, but it's better now."

"Why were you tense?"

"I was afraid I would be emotional in front of her and scare her."

"Are the memories still there?"

"Not if I keep busy."

"Are they about the orphanage?"

"Yes. They're not about the way I felt, never knowing from year to year what would happen to me and afraid of where I would end up, but of what might have happened to the other girls. I haven't thought about those years and all those other girls for a while now. Seeing Corina has brought it flooding back, and that's taken me by surprise."

Eli listened, waiting for her to go on.

"I think it would be worse for Corina. She knew her parents. The only life I'd ever known was at the children's home. I was afraid that just meeting her would be so crushing that I would sob, and that would have upset everyone."

"It was kind of you to hold off, but your feelings are just as important as Corina's."

"Thank you for that." Scottie looked grateful. "I just didn't know what to do. Iris was trying to press the issue, but I stood up to her."

"Good," Eli firmly agreed. "Iris means well, but you're not to be run over. I won't have it."

"Don't scold her," Scottie pleaded. "She just wants all of us to get along, and I'm sure we will."

"Did you read to Corina?"

"Two books, and we started a third. We'll go back to it after dinner."

Eli was pleased. His wife was smiling and relaxed again. Eli had spent a good deal of time that morning confessing to God how much he wanted to be in control and how worried he'd been. He wondered if Scottie might be doing better because he had chosen holiness over wanting his own way.

"I'm glad to hear you're doing better, but should those memories come back, tell me."

"I will."

"You know I pray," Eli added.

"And you know I need it," Scottie said with a smile.

They held hands like old friends, and for a moment Scottie wondered at the place God had put her. She couldn't imagine being anywhere with anyone else.

"That's a thoughtful look," Eli noticed.

"Just being thankful."

Eli squeezed her hand. "As am I, Scottie. As am I."

Their routine was more than a week old when Dannan went back to the Peterson house for his dinner and book discussion. He had seen Corina for a few minutes in the kitchen, but when he encouraged her to go back to her dinner, she did so without complaint.

Dannan took the stairs on quiet feet, his mind on the book

he was returning. He could have kicked himself when he walked into the room, took one look at Scottie, and had the content of the book fly from his head. Her face always beautiful, and she was downright distracting in a yellow print dress, her hair not under a bonnet but pulled up softly around her face in light red curls.

"Welcome," Eli greeted, reminding Dannan of the reason he'd come.

"Hello," the younger man responded, using Eli's presence to get his mind in order.

"Please sit here," Scottie invited, and Dannan was able to smile in her direction without having to look into those long-lashed eyes.

"Thank you." Dannan took a seat and found a small table placed in front of him. Finn had brought trays with the food, and after seeing to Eli, he made sure Scottie and Dannan had their dinner.

"Thank you, Finn." Eli smiled at the older man as he went on his way.

"I'll check back in a bit," Finn promised, heading out the door.

"Well, now," Eli began, smiling at Dannan. "Whenever anyone joins us for dinner, I ask him to pray. Would you mind, Dannan?"

"Not at all," the younger man said, bowing his head. "Father in heaven, thank You for this home and family. Thank You for the food and the generous sharing of that food. You have blessed us this day, Lord, and help us not to forget Your presence. In the name of Christ, I pray. Amen."

"Amen," both Eli and Scottie echoed, starting their meals. Dannan followed suit, and after just a few bites, Eli was ready to talk.

"So, tell me what you thought of *Ivanhoe*."

"I enjoyed it. I like the way Scott built the characters as well as the plot."

"What did you like the most?"

"Scott's attention to detail. It's interesting to be swept back to another time and place. As a doctor, I always wonder what strides were being made in medicine at that time and whether the people trusted doctors more or less than they do today."

"How often do you get called to help someone and find you don't know what to do?" Eli asked, having strayed rather easily from the book.

"It hasn't happened often, but it has happened—thankfully not since moving here."

"What do you do?" Scottie asked.

"I don't bluff, but neither do I admit it right away. I get very quiet while I work on my options."

"Which are?" Eli asked.

"Well, it all depends on how serious the situation is, but I have medical books I can read, and in Willows Crossing, I had a mentor in Dr. Collier. I consulted with him on more than one occasion."

"Did I hear Conner say that Dr. Collier trained you?" Scottie asked.

"In a way, yes. He was the doctor I worked with after my training."

"Where did you train?" Eli asked.

"At the University of Pennsylvania Medical School in Philadelphia."

"We've gotten off the book," Scottie said quietly to her spouse.

"Yes, we have," Eli admitted. "Do you mind, Dannan?"

"Not at all."

"How did you choose that school?" Eli went right back to the topic of medicine.

"Their reputation of excellence. Dr. Collier graduated from there and sent me off with a letter of recommendation."

Eli seemed fascinated, and truly Dannan didn't mind, but the discussion never did arrive back at the book. By the time Eli was ready to question him, Dannan had to excuse himself to get back to work.

Scottie wanted to laugh at the irony. Eli finally had someone to talk books with, but he'd spent all his time on Dannan's training. She wanted to laugh but didn't. Eli had been having too fine of a time.

"Corina, I said no," Dannan repeated when she didn't seem to hear him.

Corina looked up, her face turning stubborn.

"I know you're hungry," Dannan said, meeting her gaze, "but I don't have all the food on the table yet, and I want you to wait."

Dannan was tired and hungry as well and could feel his temper rising. His brows rose, telling Corina he was waiting for an answer, but she turned away from him. Dannan's jaw tightened as he went down on one knee to confront her at eye level.

"Did you hear me tell you to stay out of the bread?"

Her lip quivered, and Dannan did everything in his power to remember what Grant would have done in this situation.

"I don't want you to cry," Dannan directed softly, schooling his features but refusing to allow her willfulness. "Did you hear me?"

"Yes," Corina said, lip quivering some.

"We will eat very soon, and you will not cry or touch the food until we sit down."

The contents of the pot on the stove began to boil, and Dannan had no choice but to stand up to stir it. He had no more done this than Corina began to cry. As though her heart had been broken, she put her hands over her face and began to sob.

Dannan did not immediately move. His head went back for a moment, frustration filling him. Taking a few moments to calm down, Dannan moved the pot to the table and went to Corina. He took her in his arms and sat down with her in his lap.

"Corina," Dannan spoke softly. "Listen to me. Corina?" he tried again.

When the words did not work, Dannan rocked her a little bit and prayed. He thought about how little of this type of behavior there had been. He did not want to make excuses for sin, but she had been amazingly well behaved since arriving in Tucker Mills.

Corina's crying was stopping, so Dannan used his handkerchief to dry her face and wipe her small nose. She looked at him with a miserable, wet gaze, and Dannan's heart felt as though it was breaking in two.

"Let's eat," he said hoarsely, unable to utter another word. Tears had clogged his throat, and he couldn't even pray. He prepared Corina's plate, and as soon as she was done eating, put her to bed. She was asleep within seconds of lying down, but Dannan did not leave the room. He knelt by the side of the bed and prayed. His heart heavy with his cousin's loss and his new job as father, he begged God to give him the strength and to raise Corina as Grant would have done, believing that man to have been a very fine father.

It was a painful time on the floor of Corina's room in the dark. Just thinking about Grant's tender way with Corina brought Dannan's own tears.

"This book is called *Old Dame Trot and Her Cat*." Scottie held the book out for Corina, who was cuddled against her side on the parlor sofa. Scottie had been busy all day with no time to read, so they were getting a late start. Iris warned them that Dannan might be along any moment, but Scottie said they would get in as much as they could.

"'Here you behold Dame Trot, and here her comic cat you see. Each seated in an elbow chair as snug as they can be,'" Scottie read, holding the book in such a way that Corina could see the funny pictures. Corina smiled at the picture of a cat in a red dress and another of the cat sitting by the fireplace in a chair as a person would.

Scottie read slowly, making the story last as long as possible. When the kitchen door opened, she glanced up and found that Dannan had come in the back way.

"Look who's here," Scottie said to Corina.

"Danna!" the little girl looked delighted to see him but didn't leave Scottie's side.

"Hello," Dannan quietly greeted his little charge, not aware that Scottie and Corina had become so close. He took the chair closest to him in the room and tried not to show his surprise. This was the first time in almost two weeks Corina hadn't run to him at the end of the day.

"We can finish tomorrow," Scottie said, her eyes shifting between the two.

"I'm not in a hurry if you have time, Mrs. Peterson," Dannan said.

"She Sottie," Corina told him.

Scottie smiled, and Dannan had to smile as well.

"She calls you Scottie?" Dannan asked.

"Everyone calls me Scottie."

"Sottie," Corina said again, looking completely content at her side.

Dannan could not hold the huge smile that spread across his mouth. He was just short of laughing when Scottie, also smiling, dropped her eyes and went back to the book.

It didn't take ten seconds for Dannan to know that he should have gone back to the kitchen with Iris or upstairs to visit Eli. The longer he listened to Scottie and watched her interaction with Corina, the more trapped his heart felt. Her voice and manner with Corina was so tender that had Dannan not known better, he would have taken the two for mother and child.

The book was done in rhyme form, and Dannan tried to attend. However, whenever he did that, he began to listen to Scottie's voice and found that doing so took his mind to a bad place. Dannan tried to let his mind wander to other things, and it must have worked. Before he realized it, the story was done.

"Did you thank Scottie?" Dannan asked, coming to his feet as Corina came to him.

Corina turned to do the honors, and Dannan said, "Let's go thank Iris too."

Dannan held out his hand to Corina. They were headed toward the kitchen when Finn came from Eli's room.

"Dannan," he called from the open hallway upstairs. "Can you see Eli a moment?"

His tone was lost on Dannan, who started that way with Corina, but Scottie caught it.

"Dannan," she said his name softly and spoke when he turned. "Corina should stay down here."

Dannan's eyes shot up to Finn and finally saw what Scottie had caught.

"I want you to go and see Iris," Dannan instructed Corina, putting her down and ushering her that way before taking the stairs two at a time. Scottie followed behind Corina to quietly explain the situation to Iris and then went back to the parlor to wait. She sat so she could see her husband's door, knowing it would be closed but feeling better just keeping watch.

❦

"It came on suddenly," Finn explained because Eli had no breath. "It's just like last time, the attack that was over before you got here."

Dannan was bent over the bed, his stethoscope moving over Eli's chest. Finn had moved him off the headboard a bit, and Dannan listened to his thin chest rattle. Dannan, however, was more interested in Eli's face. His eyes were calm, but his lips were growing purple. Dannan put a hand under his back and lifted him slightly. The rattling eased some, and Eli's chest rose for the first time since Dannan entered the room.

"Better?" Dannan asked.

Eli gave a small nod, and the younger man continued to hold him up even when his arm began to pain.

"Finn, try putting some pillows right here."

The men worked on either side of Eli, and not many minutes later, the bedridden man tried a few words.

"Better," he said with a wisp of breath. "Thanks."

"Just rest," Finn cautioned.

"Scottie," Eli tried.

"Just as soon as you're stable," Finn promised.

Dannan knew it was not his imagination that Eli relaxed as soon as Finn assured him that he would get Scottie. He was at an awkward angle, but his complexion was clearing, and in a few more minutes, he was able to speak.

"What's causing these episodes?" Eli asked.

"There are a few possibilities," Dannan said, "but I want to do some reading before I answer."

"You're supposed to grow quiet and think about it," Eli teased.

Dannan smiled. "That's the last time I answer questions about my work."

Eli closed his eyes with a small sigh. These sessions, where the very air was robbed from him, were taxing. He also hated the thought of Scottie waiting in the parlor. He knew she worked hard not to worry, but he was also certain that she would not go about her business until she had news.

Eli was on the verge of dropping off when Dannan asked how he was doing.

"Better. A little sore, but breathing."

"Do you want Scottie now?" Finn asked.

"Do I look sick?" Eli asked, giving Dannan a glimpse into the relationship he had with his wife.

"Just a little pale, and you're not in your usual place against the headboard."

Eli thought about it. "Let her come."

Dannan didn't ask if he should stay. He was going to continue to keep an eye on this man until he was sure there was nothing else to be done. Backing away from the bed when Scottie came swiftly inside, Dannan retreated only as far as the foot.

"How are you?" Scottie asked, having wasted no time sitting down and reaching for his hand.

"Better," Eli assured her. "How are you?"

"Just concerned about you."

"It was like last time, but I think it might have lasted a bit longer."

Scottie reached up and smoothed his hair. "You look tired."

"I am. I think I might just sleep and not worry about tea."

"What if you wake in the night and feel hungry?"

"I'll use the bell for Finn."

Scottie studied his face. Finn had finally cut Eli's hair, so it wasn't wild around his head, but his dark beard made his pale cheeks and forehead stand out. Scottie wanted to fret over him but knew he would allow no such thing. Still holding his hand, she turned to Dannan.

"Do you know why this happens?"

"Not yet. I plan to look into it."

"You'll be back tomorrow?" Scottie checked.

"Or in the night if you need me."

"Dannan," Eli began, but then glanced at his wife. "Thank you" was all he managed, not willing to say anything that might make her worry. "Stay for tea, Dannan," Eli said next. "I'm sure Iris has already served Corina, and she always makes more than we need."

"I'll just head down and do that," Dannan agreed, "and then I'll be back up to see you before we go."

Scottie thanked Dannan as he left the room and then turned back to her husband.

"He's a fine man, isn't he?" he surprised her by saying. She thought he would be ready to talk about the way he was feeling.

"He is," Scottie agreed, "but I must admit that Dannan's not really on my mind right now."

Eli smiled, a smile that Scottie misunderstood. After all, her husband never wanted to give her reasons to worry. Had Scottie but known it, Eli's smile was about something else entirely.

"Why don't you head down and have your tea?" he suggested.

"I'm not very hungry."

"But you will be later, and Iris will want to come up and see me. She can't do that unless she knows Dannan and Corina are taken care of."

Scottie agreed, telling him she would be back up as soon as she could.

As Scottie left, Finn came back to the room. He had been waiting in the hall. Stopping by the bed, he fixed a stern eye on his employer and did not mince words.

"This sick, and you're still plotting and planning for the future."

"Ah, Finn," Eli replied, smiling without remorse. "You know me so well."

Eleven

Dannan and Corina left the house a little early on Saturday morning for their walk to the Petersons' house. Dannan had not been called on in the night, but he'd been awake some, thinking about Eli. As the two walked on this particular day, Corina was ready to chat.

"We have tea," she said. Dannan thought she might be talking to her doll, but he still answered.

"You have tea at the Petersons'?"

"My doll."

"That's nice of you to give tea to your doll. What else do you do?"

"Read boos," she told him, her word for books.

"With Scottie?"

"Sottie."

Dannan smiled and just listened for a while. Corina chattered away about the little table, and having dinner, and then seeing flowers in the garden. She had her own pronunciations for most of these activities, and Dannan couldn't stop smiling.

"Who zat?" Corina suddenly asked.

"I don't know," Dannan had to tell her as the man walked past and bid them a good morning.

Corina rattled on about something else, but Dannan didn't

catch it all. They were almost to the house when Dannan asked, "Do you help Iris in the kitchen?"

"I dry," she said.

"The dishes?"

"Pups."

Dannan knew that she was not drying small dogs; he felt it fairly safe to assume that Iris gave her the cups to dry. He praised her being a good helper and encouraged her about trying to make her bed that morning. They arrived at the house a moment later, the door opened by Iris.

"Come in, come in," she invited. "Eli tells me you want to see him."

"Yes, I do. Corina, I'm going upstairs to see Mr. Peterson. I'll come and see you before I leave."

The word "leave" caused her to possessively wrap her arms around Dannan's leg. He bent and gave her a hug before taking the stairs. He found Eli in his usual position, Finn and Scottie standing nearby.

"Good morning," Dannan greeted, his eyes taking in Eli's wife and man before fastening on the bedridden man.

"Hello," Eli greeted, looking quite chipper. "How was your night?"

Dannan smiled. "I think *I* need to open with that question."

"It wasn't the most restful, but I'm not complaining."

"Did you have trouble getting comfortable, or was your breathing an issue?"

Dannan was aware that Scottie was slipping from the room, but he had made up his mind to keep his heart in check and managed to keep his attention on the patient.

"I think I was just sore."

"You were a little labored about two o'clock," Finn put in,

having closed the door and resumed his position on the other side of the bed.

"Well, let's have a listen," Dannan suggested, and Eli began to open his shirt.

Dannan took out his stethoscope and went to work. Everything sounded calm this morning, but Dannan was a little concerned over the bruising on Eli's chest. He kept listening with the instrument to his ear, but his mind was on those marks.

"Why are you so bruised?" he finally asked, straightening up to full height.

"I've always bruised easily. Finn couldn't be more gentle, but sometimes I bruise during my bath."

"This one's awfully dark," Dannan said and pointed to a very purple bruise on his upper chest.

"I started to tip over on the edge of the bed, and Finn had to catch me."

Dannan nodded. He knew the man wasn't being harmed, but bruising could indicate a more serious condition. Dannan was actually relieved to hear the explanation.

"How does he sound?" Finn asked, his face reflecting the concern he felt.

"Better. I'm still not sure why his breathing deserts him so fast, but I'm going to keep looking into it."

Eli was righting his clothes by this time, and Dannan was putting his instruments away. He took a moment to check Eli's pulse and then looked at Finn.

"Should it happen again and you can't find me, lift him as we did last night. Putting him flat on his back might make it worse, but try different positions."

Finn was pleased to get this information, always happy to see to Eli's needs. Finn would have seen Dannan all the way downstairs, but Eli detained him.

"Please shut the door," Eli asked.

Finn did as he was asked but only stared at Eli when the door was shut.

"It's going to happen one of these days, Finn, and it won't be your fault. You've made it your job to keep me alive, and you've got to realize that you've taken too much on yourself. If you can't find Dannan, and you can't make my breath come back, you know I'll be in a better place."

Finn's eyes closed for a moment. The thought gave him such pain that his heart squeezed in his chest. He stood very still by the side of the bed, the years he'd been here all a blur in his mind. He opened his eyes long enough to meet Eli's gaze before going down to tell Scottie she could come up.

"I've kept my sermon short today so we could have a time of sharing," Douglas told his flock. "Maybe you've been battling with sin and can encourage us with the way you're staying strong. Or maybe you're having a struggle that's not resulting in victory, and you covet our prayers. Either way we would like to hear from you. You can step to the front or stay where you are."

This said, Douglas stood quietly and waited for someone to respond. He didn't wait long. Nate Peternell stood to his feet but stayed in the pew.

"I think most of you know that my father is dying. He's very ill, and probably won't be here for Christmas. It's hard to get time to visit him in Worcester, with my needing to stay and run my business here, but that's not the toughest part. My father won't discuss spiritual issues at all." Nate had to clear his throat and take a moment to compose himself.

"He and I exchange letters every week; my mom writes them for him. We talk about so many things, but God is not on the list. I will be honest and tell you that my heart is beginning to grow heavy and discouraged.

"Part of me thinks I'm out of time and I have to speak to him about life in Christ, even if he doesn't want to hear it. The other part thinks that I don't want to end my father's days on earth with aggravation and possible alienation, not to mention my last memories of him being in a quarrel."

Again Nate composed himself. "Please pray that I'll be wise about what to say and that I will trust God to save my father as He saves me. And if any of you have had similar experiences and have words of advice for me, I would certainly welcome them."

"Thank you, Nate," Douglas said from the front. "We will pray for you and Mr. Peternell."

The room grew quiet again until Conner stood.

"I did battle with sin recently," he whispered, "and it was all about my trust in God. I was plagued for a time about losing Reese in childbirth. I discussed it with Troy, who challenged me by reminding me that this is when our faith is defined.

"I was all ready to talk to Dannan, to gain some type of assurance that Reese is healthy and the risks are low, but then I realized that I don't want peace from that source. I want peace because of God's character. I want peace because of who God is, how much He loves me, and His perfect plan for my life.

"I don't have a specific promise that Reese and the baby will be well, but I do have several promises from Psalm 34." Conner bent his head to read from his Bible. "'I sought the Lord, and he heard me, and delivered me from all my fears. O taste and see that the Lord is good: blessed is the man that trusteth in him.'

"I know I will be tempted to fear again, but I want to keep fighting, and I want to keep remembering God's promises for me and for those I love. And I wanted my church family to know that I'm fighting the battle with sin."

"Thank you, Conner," Douglas said, his heart blessed by the sharing of these two men. And that was not all. Before he brought the service to a close, a total of seven folks shared from their hearts. Some needed prayer, and some were battling strongly. Douglas was renewed in his belief that God was at work in this small body of believers.

Taking a moment to look at the verses that Conner had just shared, Dannan didn't see Corina move. One moment she was next to him, and the next she was gone. He glanced around and then stood, spotting her in the back row with Scottie. Their heads were close together, and they seemed to be in deep conversation. Dannan approached but didn't interrupt them.

"Iris?" Corina was asking.

"She's not at my house today. She'll come tomorrow when you come."

"Finn?"

"Finn is at home, taking care of Mr. Peterson."

"Mr. Son."

"That's right. Now, tell me, what are you going to do today?"

Corina talked about her doll and tea, and something about flowers. Scottie sensed someone's presence and looked up to see Dannan. She raised her brows in question, and Dannan tried to fill in.

"She was quite taken with the flowers at your house, and we don't have many. She wants flowers around our house, and I keep telling her we'll plant a few someday. Every day she thinks we're going to do this."

"I can help with that, Dannan," Scottie offered. "We've so many that could be thinned and shared from our yard. Why don't Corina and I work on that this week?"

"Are you sure?" Dannan checked.

"Yes. Just give me an idea of where you want them."

Dannan smiled and nodded at his charge.

"Corina will show you. I somehow think she has this all figured out."

Scottie looked back down at Corina with pleasure and then said she had to be on her way. "I'll see you tomorrow, Corina. Bye, Dannan."

The small family told her goodbye, did a little more visiting, and then headed home. They'd not been asked to anyone's home this day, but Dannan might have been surprised to learn that he was actually the topic of conversation before the day was over.

Dinner with the Muldoons had been delightful, but as soon as Conner and Reese had a moment alone, Conner had a question for his wife.

"Do you think Dannan might be a bit taken with Scottie?"

Reese looked at him, her brow furrowed. "What have you seen?"

"Just a bit of interaction at the meetinghouse."

Reese looked troubled and then only thoughtful. "Scottie has been turning heads in this town forever."

"Even as a child?" Conner looked shocked.

"Her face has always been beautiful, and then all those curves developed. On top of that, she couldn't be sweeter."

Conner looked even more concerned. "You make it sound like it's all right."

"I didn't mean to," Reese said. "Dannan might be tempted in a direction that makes sense to me, but I wouldn't agree with his giving in to temptation."

"What about Scottie? Do you think she would encourage such a thing?"

Reese nearly laughed before saying, "If I was forced to hazard a guess, I would say that the ways between men and women are a complete mystery to Scottie Peterson. Old Mrs. Peterson kept her very protected from the time she came to live with them, and right after she died, Scottie and Eli were married.

"I'm certainly not privy to everything that goes on in the house, but I know theirs is not a romantic union—one of love and caring I'm sure, but not romance."

Conner didn't comment, but Reese could see that the subject was still on his mind.

"Will you speak to Dannan?"

"I don't know. If I've misunderstood, I don't want to put thoughts into his head."

"No, you're only willing to put them into mine," Reese said dryly.

"You're right. I did do that. I know that everything I see from now on will be filtered through a bias." Conner picked up her hand. "I'm sorry if it's ruined anything in our friendship with Dannan. I've not decided he's guilty, but I had to talk with you."

"It's all right. I don't think anything is ruined, and I'll certainly pray for him and for you. Maybe you're supposed to speak to him."

Conner nodded, unable to completely reject the idea but certainly not sure how to proceed.

"I got a letter from Paige Nunley this week," Maddie told Cathy. The Nunleys lived in Boston, and Maddie had worked for their family before marrying Jace.

"What did she have to say?"

"She's met someone."

"At her age?"

"She's 18," Maddie explained, shifting the baby against her breast; the women were alone in the kitchen.

"What does her family think?"

"She doesn't say. She wants me to come and visit with Val, but I told myself the last time I went that I wouldn't return without Jace."

"Maybe you can go right after planting in the fall," Cathy suggested.

"Maybe," Maddie agreed, still wondering whether she was expecting. Jace knew of her concerns, and he'd been as excited as she knew he would be, but she wasn't willing to discuss it with anyone else.

"I did something last night," Cathy suddenly said.

Maddie's brows rose and she waited.

"I prayed," Cathy said.

"In what way?" Maddie asked.

"I told God I believe in Him, but I'm not sure it's the same as you and Doyle."

"What happened that you did this last night?" Maddie's heart had sped up a bit, but she worked to stay calm and ask the right questions.

Cathy shifted a bit in her seat before saying, "I don't know if I can explain it."

"Where were you?" Maddie tried another tack.

"In bed."

"What were you thinking about?"

"Mostly Doyle."

"Were you scared?"

"No, just feeling left out."

Maddie didn't quite know how to respond to this. In a big way Cathy was left out, but that had been her choice.

"So what did you do?"

"I told God I wanted to believe in Him the way you and Doyle do, and suddenly I did. My heart just knew that He died for me, but I'm afraid that wasn't enough."

"Have you told Doyle?"

"No."

"Why not?"

"I want to wait and see if it's real."

"How will you know?" Maddie had to ask.

"He'll see a difference in me like I have in him."

Maddie was so full of emotion she couldn't speak. Cathy took this as a bad sign.

"Is that the wrong way to do it?"

Maddie laughed a little at her aunt's worried face and startled her sleeping daughter.

"No, Cathy." Maddie rocked the baby a little. "I'm just so emotional right now that I don't know what to say."

"Don't you start us crying," Cathy commanded, sounding more like herself. "Doyle will want to know what's going on, and I'll have to explain."

"I won't say a word," the younger woman agreed. "But you need to keep me informed."

"I will."

Silence fell in the kitchen. The men did not interrupt them, and the baby went back to sleep. Maddie tried to take in this news while Cathy continued to wonder if her newfound faith could be this real.

"How are you doing with Corina in the house?" Eli asked Scottie in the middle of the week.

"Fine."

"No more memories?"

Scottie thought about this. "I guess I expected to see myself in Corina, but it hasn't happened. She's so secure in her relationship with Dannan, and she's already so comfortable in this house and at the meetinghouse. I wonder if she cries for her mother at night or when she's alone with Dannan, but it doesn't happen much here."

"Did you ever cry for your mother?"

Scottie shook her head. "Few of us did. We knew from the moment we understood anything that there was no mother or father to cry for. Those words weren't even used. If a girl grew attached to one of the workers, she might ask for her, but they were too busy to be kind so that wasn't likely."

"Were all the girls born there? I can't remember if you've said."

"Most were, but my memory right before I left was that older girls seemed to be arriving. No one older than ten or so, but certainly not babies."

"But Corina doesn't make you think of those times? It's not worse for you?"

"No. These days when I look at her, the girls' home doesn't even come to mind."

"I'm glad," Eli said sincerely, knowing how torn he'd be if Scottie couldn't deal with Corina's presence in the house. "Now—" Eli made a swift topic change. "I think we need to discuss the Fourth of July."

"There's nothing to discuss," Scottie said, coming to her feet and moving around the room. Straightening the blanket and some books that didn't need straightening, Scottie resolutely avoided her husband's eyes.

"I want you to go," Eli started again.

"Why? I've never gone before."

"But you could have. You should have, even. You don't have to stay all day—just go for the speeches and the food and then come back and tell me all about it."

Before Scottie could frame a reply, Iris came to the door.

"Scottie, Corina is looking for you. She said something about flowers."

"Tell her I'll be right down," she told the cook and then turned to Eli. "I have to go."

"Isn't that convenient," Eli teased, his eyes sparkling with suppressed mirth.

Glad to be released from this topic, Scottie exited without further comment.

Scottie and Corina didn't start out until Thursday morning that week, but both were ready for some serious gardening. Eli did not want Scottie carrying all the flowers herself, so when she and Corina had thinned many blooms and a bush and placed them in baskets and pails, Ollie Heber loaded them into a wagon and dropped them off at Dannan's.

Scottie and Corina walked there, and just as Dannan had

said, Corina seemed to know exactly where she wanted them. The little girl had a special fondness for flowers at the front door, so they spent a long time in that spot, Corina getting muddier with each moment. Corina was so excited that Scottie didn't know when she'd had so much fun.

"Well, now," Dannan suddenly spoke from behind them about midmorning. Corina ran to him with a squeal of delight.

"Wait, Corina," Scottie called. "Don't touch Dannan."

Dannan caught her muddy hands before they could wrap around his pant leg. He bent low and kissed her forehead.

"Why don't we hug after you've washed your hands?" Dannan suggested.

"We plan flowers," Corina's words tumbled out. "A rush and a tree."

Dannan looked to Scottie for clarification.

"She thinks the goldenrod looks like a small tree, and we did bring one bush."

"Well, things look nice," Dannan complimented, liking this scene way too much and having to fight his emotions.

"Thank you," Scottie spoke sincerely. "We'll be done shortly."

"Okay." Dannan inched toward the door. "I'll get out of your way."

"Bye, Danna." Corina waved him off, looking completely delighted with the day.

Dannan slipped inside the house and sat in the first chair he came to. Being around Scottie Peterson was not getting easier. He needed to get over to the Pazan house, but he took a moment to pray, asking God to remind him of verses that promised He would be with him every step of the way.

ಌೋ

The Fourth of July in 1840 was on a Saturday, and the celebration on the green was the talk in every corner of town. The Reverend Mr. Sullins had been asked by the committee to read the Declaration of Independence. There had been much debate among the committee members as to when this reading should occur, but those who believed the reading should be before dinner and not after won the day.

Food tables were lined up end to end, all shapes and sizes, and food arrived in an abundance for the feast. Folks who lived on the green left their hot dishes in the kitchen until the ceremonies were over, but folks on the outskirts, such as Jace and Maddie, brought breads and salads that didn't need to be kept warm.

Maddie had spent all week thinking about Cathy. They hadn't seen each other, and Maddie hadn't spoken of the conversation to anyone, not even Jace. Jace had Valerie in his arms, and Maddie delivered the food. The moment she was finished arranging her dishes, however, she began to search for her aunt.

"Are you going to be all right?" Troy asked of Reese. The two were standing in the kitchen at the big house.

"Yes, why do you ask?"

"It's awfully warm and humid today, and you look a little pale."

"I'm a redhead, Troy. I always look pale."

Troy only studied her.

"If you keep this up, you'll have Conner worried."

"That's not my intent, but it is warm out."

"We'll put our quilt under a tree."

Noise from the green could already be heard, so Troy decided to act.

"Show me which one we're taking, and I'll go make sure we get shade."

"All right," Reese agreed, sounding only slightly resigned. She gave the quilt to Troy and almost let him get out the door.

"Troy," Reese called his name.

He stopped and looked at her.

"Thanks."

Troy didn't speak. His smile said it all.

"How are you doing?" Maddie asked Cathy as soon as she tracked her down.

"Fine."

"Have you told Doyle anything?" Maddie clarified with Cathy, who, being on the committee, was still helping to organize.

"No, and Doyle hasn't noticed."

"Cathy," Maddie shared, deciding to be blunt. "Doyle might not be that observant. You might just want to tell him what's been going on."

Cathy thought about this for a moment, even knowing she didn't have time to stand around.

"On Sunday," she declared. "If he hasn't noticed by tomorrow night, I'll say something then."

Maddie, now doubting whether she'd handled this well, only nodded. She wished she'd told Jace. He might have told her to encourage Cathy to talk to Doyle no matter what. At the same time, it seemed to Maddie to be good thinking, and even an act of faith on Cathy's part, for her to want Doyle to notice. A new creature in Christ was a different person; changes should be evident.

One of Maddie's temples began to ache. It was too late to

change the past, and today she wanted to enjoy and pray for the wonderful people of Tucker Mills. Hoping to do just that, Maddie moved to find her husband and daughter.

"Tell me something, Scottie," Reese asked when she'd joined them on their quilt. "Do you usually come to this celebration?"

"This is my first time," she admitted.

"Why is that?" Conner asked.

"Eli's mother never came, so I didn't, and then when she died and Eli and I married, it bothered me to leave him for so many hours."

"And today?" Reese pressed.

"Eli wanted me to. He said he's been sorry all these years that I didn't think I could go."

"Are you glad you came?" Troy asked.

Scottie didn't immediately answer, causing the older man to smile. He thought he'd heard reticence in her voice.

"It won't be long, Scottie," Reese reassured her. "The speeches never last long, and once the picnic begins, it's easy to slip away whenever you want."

Scottie thanked her and remembered what Eli had requested. He would be curious about the speeches, who was there, and what she ate. She realized now that he'd known exactly what he was doing.

Twelve

Dannan walked toward home, a drooping child in his arms, his heart at peace with the way the picnic had gone. He'd fought his emotions and natural desires; he'd fought hard. Not once did he search Scottie Peterson out with his eyes or have special thoughts about her. He spotted her a few times, but his eyes didn't linger and his mind didn't fantasize.

The fellowship during the course of the day was extremely sweet, and with only one minor injury during the townball game, Dannan had enjoyed a day off. The food had been a feast in every sense of the word, and after Corina played herself into exhaustion, Dannan decided to head for home.

Corina didn't wake while he washed her face and hands or when he changed her into her nightdress. She was as limp as her cloth doll by the time her head touched the pillow, and Dannan did not hear from her until morning.

How are we doing on hospitality?

The question rolled around in Scottie's mind all the way home from the meetinghouse. Douglas had asked the question at the beginning of the sermon, not preaching on it but simply taking some time to remind everyone what a vital and important command hospitality was in Scripture.

Never before this day had Scottie considered that she might need to do things differently. Always she had assumed that a bedridden husband made biblical hospitality impossible.

And it wasn't as if no one visited, Scottie heard herself rationalize. *Eli has company every week.*

Even as she said this, Scottie realized she never did; she never had anyone over. She took a moment and thought about trying to have folks into Eli's room and nearly shook her head. There wasn't much room. And Eli's leaving the bed was not an option.

Scottie was home without even noticing the distance, and as usual, she headed right for Eli's room. Her feelings and thoughts were totally foreign to her, and for the first time seeing him was not a comfort. What if her questions made her sound disappointed in him? The thought was heartbreaking to her because it was so untrue.

"How was your morning?" Eli asked as soon as she entered, his eyes seeing immediately that something was on her mind.

"It was enlightening." Scottie said, taking her seat on the bed.

"And upsetting?"

"A little, because I feel as though I've missed something all these years."

"What?" Eli asked, his voice patient.

Scottie hated that he had to coax it out of her, but she was still working to find the words.

"Douglas mentioned hospitality, and I think I could be doing a better job."

The uncertainty in her eyes surprised him. Scottie was never afraid to talk about an issue with him, but clearly she feared something right now. Thankfully, she continued.

"I feel as though my thoughts are going to give you the wrong impression—that I'm disappointed in my life."

"I do not believe that would be my first thought."

"Or disappointed in you," Scottie went on.

"My mind wouldn't entertain that idea either."

Scottie nodded, relief showing in the way she held her body. Eli watched her nod a little and then begin.

"You have company every week, but how do I offer hospitality to others and not leave you out?"

"That's a good question," Eli complimented her. "Are you thinking about other families or women friends?"

"I haven't gone that far in my thinking yet. I just know that I could be doing better but don't know where to start."

Eli's head went back against his pillow, his eyes on the ceiling. He was thinking about her question but also about some aspects of his own personality that entered into all of this. He knew right then that there were things he needed to confess to his wife, but he wanted to find the words. For the moment, he ended with a suggestion.

"Why don't you join Douglas and me for our session tomorrow? I think he might be a big help to us."

"You don't mind?"

"No. I think it's just what we need."

More relief bowed her shoulders, and Eli knew he was going to have to fix this. It hadn't occurred to him before today that this was a problem, but right now he could see it as plain as day. He picked up his wife's hand.

"Isn't it a sweet thing when we're convicted of something and God gives us a chance to change?"

Overrun with conflicting emotions, Scottie didn't have words and only nodded her agreement.

"I'll get dinner now," she said after a few moments of silence.

"Are you too tired?"

"I am tired, but I'm hungry too. I suspect you are as well."

Eli didn't detain her, but his mind went back to work on the issue the moment she left. He wasn't sure how it would all work out, but he was clear on a few things: He was the leader of their home. He was the head of their small family, and his selfishness had gone on long enough.

"I prayed to believe," Cathy said to Doyle at bedtime Sunday. She was sitting on her side of the bed, her back to her husband, not even turning when she heard him move to face her. "I asked God to help me believe like you and Maddie do. I told Him I'm a sinner only He can save, and He helped me."

"When was this?" Doyle asked, staying still and waiting for her to turn.

"A week ago."

Doyle was stunned. Cathy had been working hard at understanding Scripture for months now, but he didn't think she'd come to this point.

"Did you feel like you couldn't tell me?"

"I wanted you to notice."

"I'm sorry I didn't, Cathy," Doyle wasted no time in saying. "That was wrong of me."

Cathy finally turned. "Maybe you didn't notice because there's been no change."

"Is that what you hoped I'd see?"

Cathy nodded.

Doyle went and sat beside her. He put an arm around her shoulders, and Cathy leaned into him.

"Do you suppose it was real, Doyle? Did I really believe?"

"Right now we're going to operate under the belief that you did, but I can tell you some things you can watch for."

"All right."

"A repentant heart and a hunger for the truth of God's Word."

"Is that all?"

"Those are huge, Cathy," Doyle said.

"I just thought there would be such a long list."

Doyle thought about that for a moment.

"I can tell you one other thing, something Jace shared with me on Sunday," Doyle continued. "He said too many folks think they can make Christ their Savior but not their God. They think that a one-time prayer experience and regular church attendance are enough, but the Bible says that we're like slaves to a master, the most wonderful Master in the universe, but still a master. The giving up of our will, of expecting to have our way, and of being in control are some of the things God expects from us."

Cathy looked thoughtful over this but not rebellious. She was not a person who liked being told what to do. She was capable and strong, and in the past quite certain her sin was not serious enough to condemn her.

"And that's how I'll know," Cathy spoke, almost to herself. "My heart will be changed."

"Exactly."

Cathy suddenly smiled, but Doyle didn't see it. It was true that he hadn't noticed, but Cathy had noticed all week. The changes were small, but they were very real.

Putting both arms tightly around her husband, Cathy wished that she had told him a week ago.

⚭

Dannan headed to the Peterson house alone on Monday morning. He had been called out at four o'clock in the morning, and by the time he'd returned, Iris had already left for work, naturally taking Corina with her.

Dannan knew he could go about his day, but not seeing Corina at all in the morning felt wrong to him. She was a wonderful little person to start the day with, and Dannan missed her. On top of that, Corina had been struggling lately with a few things, and Dannan wanted to make sure she remembered the precautions they'd been talking about.

"Well, Dannan," Finn greeted that man. "Come on in. Your little miss is helping with the baking this morning."

"That's fine timing on my part. Maybe she'll share."

Dannan made the kitchen in time to see the first pan of cookies go into the oven. Corina watched from a distance and clapped her small hands when Iris turned to her with excited eyes.

"Someone to see you, Corina," Finn announced, and Corina threw herself at Dannan.

Dannan scooped her up and held her close for a long time. He stood in the Peterson kitchen, the morning sun streaming through the window, and just let himself enjoy the feel of those little arms around his neck.

"Danna?" Corina pushed away enough to see his face. "Read boos."

"You want to read books?"

The wispy bits of hair around her ears bounced as she nodded.

"We'll do that when we get home tonight. I have to work right now, but I wanted to see how you were, and to remind you to eat what Iris gives you and be thankful."

"San you," Corina said.

"That's right. When I see you later today, you can tell me what a good job you did."

Again the nod, and Dannan kissed her cheek. She wanted to show him something with the tea set, but as soon as this was accomplished, Dannan went on his way, first giving Iris a word of thanks. It was never easy to leave Corina, but seeing how happy she was and knowing that Iris' care of her was excellent, gave his heart a good deal of peace.

"I think I found a mistake." Scottie sat at her desk in the parlor at midmorning, speaking out loud to the empty room. She double-checked the books she was working over and then checked them again. As soon as she was sure, she headed up to see Eli.

He was reading a book when she arrived but set it aside as soon as she came into view.

"What's up?" he asked.

"I think we've made a mistake," Scottie sat so that he could look at the account book with her. It was the book where they recorded all the transactions with their rental houses and two fields. It was the way Eli's mother had made a living, and she had handed these properties down to her son. Eli had waited only a month after marrying Scottie to teach her every aspect of the system.

"Look at this rent payment at the Cole house." She pointed with the tip of her pencil. "They don't pay as much as Bentzens do, but that's the number entered. We're off by at least two dollars."

"Not we," Eli said, studying the line. "That's my hand-writing."

Scottie took time to look. Their penmanship was very similar, and she honestly hadn't noticed.

"Well, anyway," she said, dismissing it as unimportant, "did we make a change that I've forgotten about?"

"No, I must have entered it wrong. Where else are we off?"

Scottie walked him through the places she'd found, and in less than 30 minutes, all numbers were back on track.

"What would I do without you?" Eli asked when she closed the account book.

"Have mistakes in the book, I expect."

Eli only laughed and went back to his reading, and Scottie went downstairs to check on Iris and dinner.

"Sorry I'm late," Dannan apologized to Reese when Troy showed him in from the front door.

"Not at all," Reese replied. "You've been busy lately, and we've missed you."

"Thank you." Dannan took a seat and filled his plate from the dishes passed his way. "How did you fare at the picnic, Reese? I noticed you stayed in the shade."

"I did fine. It was warm, but I felt pretty good."

"She probably stayed under the tree to humor me," Troy put in.

"And me," Conner added.

Dannan had to smile. For a moment he wondered what it would be like for Reese to have two people fussing over her, and then he realized she was one of the most relaxed, calmest hostesses he'd ever encountered. She was an excellent cook, and her baked goods were delicious. She never rushed about but sat down and ate with her guests, taking their compliments in stride.

"What month are you due, Reese?" Dannan asked when he realized he didn't know.

"October," Reese told him, thinking nothing of this. Conner, however, kept his eyes on their guest. When Dannan didn't do anything but nod, Conner wanted him to know he could say more.

"Do you have concerns, Dannan?" the big man asked.

"No." Dannan was truthful. "She's large, but I think it's easy to assume that's because the baby is."

"Do you enjoy delivering babies?" Troy asked.

"Always," Dannan said with a smile.

For several minutes, Conner battled with worry. It was so easy to expect God to fall in line with the will of man and not be as concerned about the will of God.

"I don't get fearful," Reese suddenly shared, "but I think I've accepted the fact that it's not going to be a fun time."

"It's going to be what it's going to be," Troy put in, at times fighting his own battle of worry. "We'll make sure Dannan is close by and leave the rest in God's hands."

No one commented further on the subject as they continued the meal. What Troy said was true, and he had put it so nicely.

"I asked Scottie to join us today," Eli explained as soon as Douglas arrived in his room and found both husband and wife.

"Oh, I'm glad," Douglas said sincerely. "How are you, Scottie?"

"I'm doing well, thank you. How about yourself?"

"I'm well. A little sore after that fifth horseshoe game at the picnic."

"You kept winning," Scottie reminded him.

"Yes, and I don't know why, since I don't play very often."

"Which explains why you're sore," Eli added dryly.

"Exactly," Douglas agreed, just as dryly.

Eli laughed at him before getting to the point.

"When Scottie came home on Sunday," he explained, "she had a question for me. I didn't have a great answer and hoped you could help us."

Douglas turned to Scottie.

"Ask away," he encouraged.

"It's about hospitality. I'm not sure I'm doing a good job."

"Before you answer," Eli cut back in, "I have something I need to say to you, Scottie. I wanted to do it in front of Douglas so he could hold me accountable."

Scottie only stared at her spouse.

"I've been extremely selfish, just expecting you to be at my beck and call. I could have suggested that you have someone over, but I always wanted to be a part of things. I always expected to have you to myself."

Scottie had all she could do to keep her mouth shut. This was the last thing she'd expected from Eli.

"I'm not saying that I actually thought of you having someone over and kept the idea to myself, but the fact that it never occurred to me tells me how self-centered I've been."

"Eli," Scottie began, but he put a hand out to her. Scottie took it and remained quiet.

"You're going to try and defend me, and I don't want you to do that," Eli said with kindness, but his voice was also firm. "I'm glad you brought this up. I need to change in this area."

Scottie looked uncertain, but Eli squeezed her hand and looked back to Douglas. "Can you help us?"

"I think so," Douglas started. "First of all, I can't tell you how much I appreciate your willingness to be obedient in this. Biblical hospitality is vital to a church family, and I think there might be some ways you can do it. I have some suggestions for you if you'd like to hear them."

"Please," Eli said, more than ready to do the right thing.

"Scottie, your main job is Eli, and that will limit you some, but what if once a month you had some other women in for afternoon prayer or even to visit or sew? And Eli, I can think of several couples who would do very well joining the both of you for a meal here in your room. You don't object to that, do you?"

"Depending on how well I know them, it might be a little odd, but I could get over that."

Scottie suddenly sighed, and Eli turned to smile at her.

"She was worried," Eli explained to Douglas.

"I was," Scottie admitted. "I just didn't think along those lines. It's really quite simple."

"And never forget, Scottie, that God knows your heart. You don't have to do this every day or even every week. I think it should be as often as you can. We're without excuses if we aren't diligent in this area, yet your situation is unusual.

"My suggestion is that you ask God to help you think creatively. Ask Him for ways you can have someone here, someone who fits in with your life as well as Eli's. It would be a blessing to all involved."

The Petersons thanked Douglas before they opened their Bibles to 1 Timothy and 1 Peter to spend some time looking at important verses about hospitality. The three then prayed together that God would open doors they had never seen. By the time the pastor left, Scottie and Eli were very excited.

"Thank you." Scottie's relief was palpable as she sat in her usual place on the bedside, smiling hugely at him.

"Thank *you*," Eli said right back. "God laid it on your heart, you listened, and I get to reap the benefit."

It was a warm, special moment. The two smiled, acknowledging their shared affection, before Eli said he was weary. Scottie left him to rest but found she wasn't the least bit tired. Energized by the thought of opening their home, Scottie got more done that afternoon than she had in a long time.

It had all been so normal. The day had been winding down for Scottie. Tea was over and Finn was readying Eli for the night. And then without warning, Finn was running from the bedroom, saying he had to find Dannan. Eli's breathing was labored, and nothing he attempted would ease it.

Scottie sat with Eli until the men arrived, but now, for nearly 30 minutes, she had sat in the parlor, eyes on the stairs. Even knowing that Finn and Dannan were at Eli's side, Scottie begged God to take care of her husband.

"Dannan." Eli whispered the doctor's name as soon as he had breath, the color of his face still bluish.

"Give yourself time," Dannan cautioned. "Just take it easy."

Eli's head moved restlessly, and he struggled on.

"There is no time," he gasped. "One of these days I'm not going to make it."

Dannan nearly interrupted him, but the older man's eyes

found his, and the gaze was so intense that Dannan couldn't speak.

"I waited a long time for you to come. She won't understand."

Dannan now frowned in confusion, but Eli went on.

"I've watched you fight it and knew you were the one. You must understand, Dannan, that she won't understand."

"Mr. Peterson," Dannan had to break in. "What are you talking about?"

"Scottie. When you start to show interest, she'll only be confused, but you must persevere. You're perfect for her."

Dannan could not believe his ears. He looked to Finn, thinking that man could explain this irrational behavior, but Finn only smiled at him in kindness and understanding. Dannan looked back down at his patient, his mouth slightly agape.

"Don't try to figure it out. We might still have time to speak again, but I had to be sure you knew."

"Mr. Peterson," Dannan began, well and truly humiliated. "I'm sorry about what I've felt. When I first saw Scottie, I had no idea she was married."

Dannan stopped when Eli gripped his arm. It was not a harsh grip; indeed, the man was quite weak, but it still stopped Dannan's words.

"You must be holy before God with your thoughts and actions, but never mistake the facts: Scottie will be a widow someday, and when that happens, you must act. You must make it known that you will love and cherish her."

Dannan had all he could do not to shake his head in amazement. Eli held his eyes a bit longer and then relaxed back, his arm dropping. Dannan's heart pounded heavily, thinking he'd lost him, but Eli was just spent. Dannan could relate. He could have used a chair himself.

Keeping still, trying to hold him so he could breathe, Dannan took some time to let Eli's body rest back against the bed, watching his breathing all the while. When it seemed that he was comfortable, Dannan pulled the chair up and sat close. He checked Eli's pulse and then looked to Finn.

"Can you tell me what that was about?"

"Just as he said." Finn's voice held no censure. "He knows he'll be gone and that you would be perfect for our Scottie."

"You knew about this?" Dannan pressed him.

"Yes."

"Did you try to talk him out of it?"

"Out of talking to you? No. Out of dying? Yes. But that has nothing to do with you and everything to do with him. He always just hears me out because we both know he won't have control over that."

"Could it be the breathing?" Dannan couldn't let it drop. "Is his mind cloudy right now?"

Finn actually smiled. "He's not been at all cloudy when he speaks to me about it."

Dannan found this made it no easier. These two lived together. They could both be off the deep end.

"I need to get Scottie," Finn announced, adjusting the covers a bit before exiting.

Dannan let him go without another word, but that didn't mean that he didn't have plenty to say. At the moment, however, he just had no idea with whom he could share.

"How was your night?" Scottie asked, having gone to Eli's room as soon as he was awake in the morning. He had not awakened the night before, but her own sleep had been intermittent at best.

"I think well." His voice was gravelly, and while he tried to clear his throat, it didn't help. "I feel worn out."

"Yesterday was a big day," Scottie reminded him, smoothing his hair a little.

Eli looked at her. Her hair was down, strawberry blonde curls falling around her face, and she was still in her robe, quite clearly worried about him.

"I'm getting sick," he told her, feeling the heaviness in his chest.

Scottie picked up his hand.

"We both hate it when you get sick."

"Me most of all," he teased a little, and even though Scottie smiled, she could hear what Eli was feeling. His voice seemed to come from his chest, deep and strained.

"I'm going to get dressed and start your breakfast."

"What will Iris say?"

"She'll scold me, and things will feel normal."

Eli smiled at her candid reply as he studied the concern in her eyes and wished that he could comfort her. His being sick took a toll on each of them, but at the moment there was little he could do about it.

❧

"May I come and see you after work tonight?" Dannan asked of Conner as soon as the bank opened on Tuesday morning.

"Of course," Conner agreed. "Come for tea."

Dannan glanced at Corina, who stood just a few feet away. "It's rather private."

Conner nodded. "Come for tea anyhow, and we'll disappear into my study as soon as the meal's done."

"Thank you," Dannan said and moved on his way. He wanted

to get Corina dropped off and check on Eli, but he'd made the stop at the bank because he knew he had to speak to someone.

Dannan went through the motions of routine. He left Corina with Iris, telling her he would be back to say goodbye, and then he took to the stairs, his mind still reeling with the events of the evening before. All of this, however, fell away the moment he saw Eli. His breathing was labored, and his eyes were closed as he lay back against the pillows. Finn had propped him up some, but he was not in his usual position.

"Mr. Peterson?" Dannan softly spoke his name. Eli answered but did not open his eyes.

"Hello, Dannan. I fear I'm getting ill."

"I can see that," Dannan acknowledged as he rummaged in his bag for his stethoscope and put the instrument against the older man's chest. The sounds coming to Dannan's ear were not encouraging.

He listened in silence for a few moments, glancing up when Scottie came to the door.

"Oh, Dannan, I didn't realize you were here."

"I just arrived," the doctor answered without taking his concentration from Eli.

The door had been left open, and this time Scottie did not give them privacy. She stood in the doorway, out of the way but watching carefully. Her heart was not bolstered by Eli's stillness or the severe look on Dannan's face, but when her eyes met Finn's, that man gave her a small smile.

It reminded Scottie to trust. Finn had watched Eli in this state dozens of times through the years. If he could muster a smile for her, she could keep trusting in her God.

Thirteen

"Go up," Scottie commanded quietly to her cook. "I'll stay with Corina."

Iris hesitated, but Scottie could see how much she wanted to see Eli. The older woman was worried sick. Scottie wasn't feeling at all good about Eli's condition and didn't want to leave his side, but she also wanted Iris to have some time upstairs. It was good to have Iris leave the kitchen without another word.

Corina was thankfully oblivious to their conversation and was quite content to move from her little table to the shelf in the buttery Iris had cleared for her and back again, talking to her doll the whole time. The little girl had been outside with Iris earlier, and Scottie knew from the droop of her small shoulders that getting her to sleep after dinner would not be an issue. Scottie thought about offering to read her a book but then realized that when Iris came down, it might delay her return to her husband's room. Seeing how content Corina was at the moment, Scottie wasn't willing to take the chance.

Dannan was not prepared for how swiftly Eli went downhill.

He had made him as comfortable as he could manage with plans to check back at noon. In those short hours, Eli's breathing worsened until it could be heard all over the room.

Scottie was very close, moving only when Dannan needed the position, and Finn was in his usual place. Dannan didn't try to communicate with his patient, but he was not pleased.

"Is he coughing?" Dannan asked of Finn.

Finn gave a small shake of the head, and Dannan, aware of Scottie's presence, didn't comment or let his expression give him away. Eli was growing weaker by the hour, and Dannan seriously began to wonder if he might lose him.

"Mr. Peterson," Dannan called, finally waking him. "Can you hear me?"

Eli stirred, his breathing raspy. His eyes opened slowly and spotted Finn.

"Dannan is here," the caretaker told him.

"Dannan?" Eli rasped.

"Right here. Can you hear me?"

"Yes."

"I need you to cough, Mr. Peterson. You've got to clear your lungs."

The effort completely taxed Eli. He coughed weakly, and Dannan began to pray in earnest. This man was not going to make it if they couldn't get him in a better position to cough.

"I want him to sit up more," Dannan instructed Finn, and then to Scottie, "and bring a pot of strong tea with sugar, no milk."

Delighted to have jobs, Scottie and Finn fell to their respective tasks. Moving in the gentle way that was second nature to him, Finn's powerful arms lifted, shifted, and adjusted until Eli was sitting up higher. Feverish and miserable, Eli only laid his head back as soon as he was able.

He'd been settled in place for a few minutes when Scottie

arrived with the tray. Finn coaxed some tea into Eli, and he made an effort to sit up and drink more.

"Scottie?" Eli whispered when he found air.

Scottie moved so she could see him and tried not to look as concerned as she felt.

"I'm here," she said, picking up his hand.

Eli stared at her, wanting to say so many things, but his body wanted only to lie back and sleep.

"Cough if you can," Dannan instructed, and Eli did his best. Indeed, Eli attempted everything Dannan told him to do, but he was weakening swiftly. Iris arrived with beef broth and more strong, sweet tea for him to drink, and when Dannan spotted his daughter in the hallway, he went out to her. Dannan picked her up and walked a few paces away from the door.

"Mr. Son sick," the child said.

"Yes, he is. We can pray for him."

"I pray," Corina said.

"Yes, you do, and when we pray, we can trust God for Mr. Peterson."

The sweet, trusting little face that looked up into his was too much for Dannan. He tucked Corina's head under his chin and just held her close, hoping she would always be a child who loved to be cuddled.

"Do you want to bring her back?" Iris was suddenly there asking, obviously returning to the kitchen.

Dannan looked at the older woman and thought of Reese.

"I can take her to the big house if you'd like, Iris. Reese will welcome her."

Iris gave a small shake of her head.

"I want her with me" was all Iris would say, taking Corina's hand when Dannan put her down. Dannan sent her off with a wave and resumed his position in the sickroom. To his intense relief, Eli's eyes were open, and he looked a bit more alert.

"How's the breathing?" Dannan asked.

"Better," Eli whispered. Dannan thought it might be somewhat improved but not enough to raise his hopes. He glanced at Finn and Scottie and saw that they both drooped in their chairs. Dannan decided to step in.

"Go and get something to eat, both of you," he commanded. "Eli and I will talk about books."

Scottie looked to her husband, who gave a weak nod, and Finn followed Scottie from the room.

"I meant it," Eli got out, the moment the others were free of the door.

Dannan took a seat and looked at him sternly.

"You are very unwell," he started, but Eli was not done.

"All the more reason," he began and then panted.

Dannan was ready to argue with him but knew that would have been wrong. Eli was an older man in the faith, and on top of that, he was probably dying. Much as Dannan wanted to argue, he held his peace.

"Your hand," Eli was running out of strength fast, but Dannan did as he was asked, putting his hand out so Eli could take hold of it. "I need to know you'll try."

"Try what?"

"To have a life…"

Dannan didn't want to say it, but he could see that Eli was desperate to hear the words.

"With Scottie?" Dannan asked.

Even in the hand that held his, Dannan felt Eli relax. To be understood was all he needed. Dannan wanted to remind his patient that there were no guarantees Scottie would want anything to do with him, but something more pressing was on his mind.

"I want you to fight this," Dannan instructed, his tone firm. "You're talking like you're already gone, and I won't have it."

Eli could not lift his head from the pillow, but he nodded, his eyes watching Dannan's face. Dannan looked right back. He had not known this man long enough, and he didn't want to lose him. He racked his brain to make sure he hadn't missed anything, but pneumonia was tricky. Some had it for weeks, walking around coughing and feeling miserable. Others, especially those in a bedridden state, could die within days of the first sign. Dannan did not want Eli to be in the last group, but he was not sure any of them had a choice.

"How about some more tea?" Dannan offered.

Eli drank to please him, sensing in his heart that he was not going to recover from this. He did not want to break Scottie's heart, but he couldn't remember feeling this poorly before. His lungs had filled on other occasions but he hadn't been feverish and achy. When Dannan ordered him to cough, it was almost more than he could bear, but he made the effort, never wanting the younger man to believe he'd given up.

When he couldn't hold his eyes open any longer, he fell into a deep sleep. Dannan checked his lungs and pulse and then stepped out into the hallway. Scottie was just coming up the stairs.

"How is he?"

"Asleep."

"But how is he, Dannan?" she repeated.

"Not good," that man told her quietly and watched as her eyes filled. When she spoke, however, her voice was steady.

"Tell Finn I'll be in my room. I want him to come for me the moment Eli wakes."

Dannan nodded and watched her go along the landing and slip swiftly into the last door. Dannan stood there, not to listen but because he couldn't move. The last person he wanted to see leave the earth right now was Eli Peterson.

"I don't know how long I'll be," Dannan told Reese when the day began to end and he knew he would need to find a place for Corina for the night. "I planned to meet with Conner tonight, but that will have to wait."

"How bad is he?" Reese asked.

"Bad. He's so weak that I wonder if something hasn't been brewing for a while now."

"How is Scottie?"

Dannan only gave a small shake of his head; it was all he could manage. He knew it was not his place to say the things he'd overheard, but it went beyond that. Remembering how much she hurt right now was almost more than his heart could take.

"You've been warning me for years," Dannan had heard her say to Eli. *"But you were never supposed to get this sick."*

"My mother," Eli got out, *"said I never did as I was told."*

Scottie had tried to smile, but it was a very crooked one, and a tear slid down her cheek. Remembering it now made Dannan's heart feel tight in his chest.

"The time doesn't matter, Dannan," Reese assured him. "We'll keep her as long as you like. Do you know if Douglas has been given word?"

"I don't, but I'll go there next and make sure."

Not only was Douglas thankful to hear of the news, he accompanied Dannan back to the Peterson house. Eli was sleeping, his breathing labored, and after speaking to him and gaining no response, Douglas just prayed quietly by his side, hoping Eli would catch some of the words.

"Is there anything I can do?" he then asked of Scottie.

"I don't think so, Douglas. If he wakes, I'll make sure he knows you were here."

Douglas thanked her for that but did not rush away. He stayed for almost two hours and spoke with all of them. Eli did not wake before he left, but Douglas said he'd be back in the morning.

By morning it was too late. Elias Peterson died just before dawn. His wife, completely crushed and lost, was at his side.

Dannan counted the bells that rang Wednesday morning and learned that he'd been far wrong about Eli's age. He figured him to be a man in his mid-forties at least, only to learn that he was 35. On further reflection it wasn't surprising, considering how he'd spent most of his life, unable to be robust and hearty in his lifestyle. At the same time, it caused Dannan to wonder again how Eli and Scottie came to be married.

As soon as the thought came to mind, Dannan realized he didn't want to think about it. He was weary from a sleepless night and planned to catch a quick nap before going to get Corina. It took longer than he expected to fall asleep, but he did so praying for Scottie, Iris, and Finn. The next few hours and days would be an especially painful time.

"I should help," Scottie told Finn, her hands shaking so much that her teacup clanked back into the saucer.

"You should not help," Finn argued. He was against Scottie being involved in the laying out of Eli Peterson, his voice resolute but not unkind. "It's the last thing Eli would have wanted."

Scottie looked away in an attempt to compose herself. Finn studied her profile. To his amazement, he found he was dealing with Eli's death quite well; the preparations he and Eli had made for many years were indeed helpful. But Scottie now being so completely on her own was something his heart was fighting. There had not been a thought or an idea that Eli had not shared with him, including his desire to see Scottie happily married to Dr. Dannan MacKay. Tomorrow would not be too soon for Finn. Watching her look so lost and uncertain was proving to be the real test of his heart.

"You didn't have that type of relationship, Scottie," Finn tried another tack, his voice still gentle. "No one could have taken better care of Eli than you did, but not in that private way. Iris and I laid out his mother. Eli didn't even want you to have to do that. I'm sure he would not want this for you."

Iris had held her tongue up to this point, not wanting to make things any harder for Scottie than necessary, and Finn had always had a way with their mistress. But now she spoke.

"The next few days will be draining enough without adding this to your load, Scottie. Half the town will be coming through the front door, and you'll have to be in the center of it all. Save whatever strength you have for that time."

Scottie nodded, tears still clogging her throat. Knowing she'd have to stay busy to survive, she finished her tea and stood.

"I'll be in the garden. Please come for me when you're done."

Iris watched Scottie walk out the door. She didn't know about Eli's plans to see Scottie married to Dannan, but outside of that, her thoughts almost mirrored Finn's. It was harder to see Scottie looking so bereft and alone than it was to say goodbye to Eli.

"Thank you for coming," Scottie said over and over the next

day. Iris had been correct. An amazing number of townsfolk came to view Eli's body, and Scottie sat in the accustomed place by the casket, Iris and Finn at her side. The burial would follow the viewing, Douglas would be speaking at the graveside, and then folks were invited to the big house for a meal.

Scottie felt as if she were dreaming. Every time she looked at the casket, she expected to see Eli wake up. The longer she sat there, the more she realized that wasn't going to happen, but it still hurt her heart to see his casket lowered into the ground and know it would be covered with dirt.

She heard little of what Douglas said, her mind still telling Eli he wasn't supposed to get that sick, and he certainly wasn't supposed to die. Not until the end, when Douglas reminded the crowd that God had a plan, did Scottie snap out of her daze.

"Eli would have wanted me to remind you," Douglas spoke kindly, "ours is a God who can be trusted because He holds all things, even life and death, in His sovereign hand."

How could you forget that, Scottie? she asked herself. *Eli and his mother were the very ones to teach you that you're safe in God's hands because of your trust in Him. And Eli's not in that bed anymore. Would you really wish him back?*

The tears that came to her eyes as she stood for a few minutes more by his grave were a mix of sorrow and peace. For a few hours there she had done nothing but think of herself. She was ready to throw off the mantle of that burden. This wasn't about her. This was about a man who had trusted God and who had gone home to be with Him at the time God appointed.

Scottie was able to accompany Reese and the others to the big house, looking forward to seeing everyone and thanking them again for all their support. She had done that at home during the viewing but had only been going through the motions. Now her thanks would be heartfelt.

She didn't kid herself about the future. She knew tears would come in the days ahead, along with much adjustment and hurt, but the Savior who had determined that it was Eli's time to leave the earth was just as able to care for her, no matter what the future held.

"Did you want to come tonight and see me, Dannan?" Conner asked when the men had a moment alone.

Dannan thought about it. He was tired, but he suspected that getting Eli's words off his chest might help him to sleep better.

"I think I might. Is Reese up to more company after this mob?"

"I'll check with her, and if she needs to rest, I'll come to your house."

Reese was fine with the company, but as it turned out, Corina needed to be in her own bed and at an early hour, so Conner came to Dannan's house. The two men settled in the parlor to talk.

Conner listened quietly as Dannan told him what Eli had said, even including the exchange he'd shared with Finn, and then sat in stunned silence.

"Your silence actually encourages me," Dannan admitted when Conner did not speak. "I'm glad I'm not the only one surprised by this."

Conner shook his head a bit. "And this was what you were going to talk to me about when Eli grew ill?"

"Yes. I feel almost cheated that he's not here to continue the discussion, but as soon as we had a few minutes alone, he brought it up again."

"What did he say then?"

"He wanted assurance that I was going to take it seriously."

"How did you assure him?"

"I didn't really. He said he wanted me to have a life and then ran out of words. I put Scottie's name in where he wanted it, and he relaxed as though the weight of the world had been lifted off his shoulders."

Conner thought about this for several minutes.

"It's funny, Dannan, but in truth I don't think Eli did anything wrong. He might have been trying to control things a bit beyond his grasp, but clearly he wanted to see Scottie happily married and cared for, and he thought you were the man."

Dannan sat quietly, so Conner asked another question.

"So, do you think you're the man?"

"I think falling for Scottie would be easy, but that doesn't mean she'll want me in return."

"So you haven't fallen for her?" Conner had to ask.

"I won't tell you that I'm not attracted, but I've been fighting it since I found out she belonged to Eli Peterson."

Conner was well and truly pleased with this information and suddenly knew exactly why Eli wanted him for Scottie. Beyond his belief in Christ, Dannan MacKay was a man of honor. He was also the perfect age for Scottie. The two of them could provide siblings for Corina.

"What are you thinking about?" Dannan asked.

"Many things," Conner replied, admitting only so much. "But mostly I think Eli might be right. You're perfect for Scottie."

"Which means what?" Dannan asked, his brows raised.

Conner opened his mouth and then closed it. The two men ended up laughing a little.

"It's not that easy, is it?" Conner said.

"It's not easy at all," Dannan corrected.

"Be that as it may," Conner said, bringing the discussion to a close and allowing Dannan to seek his rest. "If God wants the two of you together, there will be a way."

Dannan would not have believed that he could sleep after such a discussion, but he was wrong. He thought about it and prayed about it the entire time he was readying for bed, but sleep claimed him the moment he grew comfortable on the mattress.

"Good morning," Dannan greeted Iris when she opened the Petersons' front door the following morning. "I didn't want to assume that you were up to this. Once again, Reese has offered to take her."

"I knew you were going to say that," she said, her voice and face normal. "I would have sent Finn to look for you if you hadn't come within the hour. Come in here, Miss Corina," Iris commanded, turning to the little girl. "You and I are going to bake bread today."

Scottie chose that moment to come through. She greeted Corina but then waited for Iris and the little girl to move toward the kitchen before speaking to Dannan.

"I don't know if I thanked you," Scottie began. "You stayed so long, and I know Eli appreciated it."

"You're very welcome. How are you doing, by the way?"

"I'm keeping busy," Scottie half-whispered, smiling, but her eyes showed the hurt.

"Let me know if you'd rather not have Corina around right now. I mean, Iris seems to enjoy it, but if you'd rather not…"

"Not at all," Scottie assured him. "We have to get back to normal as soon as we can. She's so sweet, and both Iris and Finn have already grown so attached."

"Is Finn still here?"

"Oh, yes. When both he and his house are ready, he'll move his things. I imagine he'll still take at least some of his meals here."

"I didn't realize he had a house." Dannan found it so easy to talk to her.

"Yes, it's right on the green, about five doors down from the bank. Mrs. Peterson bought it with him in mind after he came to work with Eli. No one's in it right now, and it probably needs a bit of paint and freshening up. Finn's not in any hurry to move from here, so for now we'll stay as we are."

"Big changes can be hard."

"It's the small changes I worry about," Scottie admitted and then caught herself. She hadn't realized before how easy it was to talk to Dannan MacKay. She looked up at him, a bit surprised, and since Dannan noticed everything about her, he mentioned it.

"Are you all right?"

"Yes, but I just realized I must be keeping you."

Dannan shook his head. "I'm just glad to know you're doing well. I'll be praying that it gets easier instead of harder."

Scottie nodded, and Dannan noticed that she glanced up the open stairway and hall to Eli's closed door. Dannan didn't know what to say. His own heart was very affected by all of this, and it was all too easy to imagine how Scottie must be feeling.

"If you want another book," Scottie offered, brightening, "I hope you'll come and choose one."

"Thank you. I would enjoy that. Maybe not right now, but sometime."

"Finn could take you up," Scottie said, her eyes growing a bit guarded, and Dannan knew that she wasn't ready to enter Eli's room.

"I'll just plan on that in the future."

"Do you read often?"

"Always. Anything I can get my hands on."

"You could go now," Scottie began, but Dannan stopped her.

"After our book discussion from a few weeks ago, Mr. Peterson sent *Gulliver's Travels* with me. I'm still working on that."

"I'd forgotten about that. Have you gotten to the part where he's in the farmer's house and describes the cat as looking three times larger than an ox? I don't know why, but that scene is very real to me."

"I'm just past that," Dannan admitted, realizing for the first time that she probably read as much as Eli did. Dannan didn't let himself speculate too long but plunged ahead with his next thought.

"I don't wish to overstep, but since you've read it, maybe we could discuss it when I'm done."

"I would enjoy that," Scottie replied, completely unaware of her effect on this man. "You could join us for dinner. Iris and Finn would enjoy it as well."

Dannan had all he could do not to smile in delight. Instead, he gave a calm nod with his head.

"I'll let you know when I'm done."

Scottie said they would plan on it, and Dannan made his exit. Scottie went immediately about the business of working on the dress she planned to make for Corina, glad she still had that to do.

Dannan walked on a cloud all the way back to town, telling himself to go very slow but not listening all that well.

Fourteen

Scottie had barely started the third page of the book when Corina's head fell against her arm; the little girl was fast asleep. Scottie shifted her so she could be comfortable on the sofa and then studied the child's beautiful face, wishing her own sleep would come as easily.

Eli had been dead for six days. He had filled Scottie's mind and thoughts all day and at any time she could not sleep in the night. She hadn't expected this but now recognized that she should have. Her days had been built around him and now he was missing.

Even Finn was out of place. He had not spent every waking moment in Eli's room but certainly much of his time. To have him in the kitchen, parlor, and garden so often only served to remind Scottie all the more that her husband was gone.

She wanted to cry again. She had done little else in the last six days. Scottie let her head fall back against the sofa, tears making her throat ache.

Maybe Corina has the right idea, she thought to herself. *Maybe I just need a nap.*

"How is she?" Finn asked from his place at the worktable. Iris came back from peeking out the kitchen door to report.

"They're both asleep."

"Good," Finn said. "Scottie's pale these days, and she has shadows under her eyes."

"She cries when she doesn't think we see."

Finn only grunted, thinking he'd done the same thing. Eli's closed door was a constant reminder. And it wasn't as if he could avoid the upstairs. His room was right next door, the first one at the top of the stairs. Eli's was next, with marvelous windows that had allowed him to see out into a world that was no longer his. Old Mrs. Peterson's room was next, and then a very small bedroom. The last one on the landing was Scottie's.

Finn's new routine was difficult as well. He had his chickens and the cow and pig to see to, but where in the past he'd always rushed to get his chores done and get back to Eli, he now found they took little time at all. He tried to stretch them out, making them last as long as he could, but the milking and feeding took only so long.

"More tea?" Iris asked, and Finn pushed his cup that way.

"Thank you," he said quietly, but Iris didn't answer. She was in her own world of pain, feeling that things were never going to be normal again. Taking care of Eli had been the focus of her life for years. She hadn't doubted Finn and Scottie's abilities, but she took great pride in knowing how Eli liked his food and what all of his favorites were.

Crying didn't come easily to her, and she thought the constant headache that recently plagued her might be rooted in that. Finn had mentioned that Scottie was looking pale. Iris' own mirror told her she was in no better condition.

"Go ahead and cry," Finn suddenly ordered, getting to his feet. "I'm going to check on the animals."

Iris didn't reply and neither did she cry, but she appreciated his words. Not a demonstrative man, Finn still knew she was hurting—even without the tears—and that meant a great deal to her.

Dannan thought he would see so much of Scottie. He was going to finish the book and then have dinner at the house to discuss it. He didn't reckon on being so busy that he didn't have time to read or the fact that he would come and go to get his daughter but see no sign of the mistress of the house.

On top of that, he missed Eli Peterson. He'd not known that gentleman for very long, but his presence had had a profound effect on Dannan's life. He wanted to speak to Eli again, not just about the things he'd said concerning Scottie, but also about books and the life he'd known. A case like his was fascinating to a doctor, but Dannan's interest was beyond medical. From the first time he'd met Eli, he was impressed with his attitude toward his situation. Eli was not bitter or angry about being in that bed. Dannan was certain that from a spiritual standpoint, he could have learned much from that man.

Having just left Corina at the Peterson house a week after Eli's death, Dannan's heart was a bit heavy as he walked away. He had some ointment he needed to prepare and at least two patients to check on, so he tried to get his mind back on work, but all the time he wondered what the next days would look like.

Dannan was in his workroom preparing medicine. At a time when the practice of purging, puking, and bleeding was much too common, Dannan had been trained to use specific medicines for specific needs, hoping to move away from mineral remedies that often brought such harmful effects.

Dannan had known some success with salves to cleanse wounds. The ointments helped fend off infection, but not all of his patients would listen or agree. A book on United States flora had been very helpful, and Dannan had started a small garden as soon as he'd taken over the house, also growing things in the window of the workroom.

He enjoyed the experimental side of medicine but at times missed Dr. Collier's input. That man had great experience in this area, and Dannan had learned much from him. In the midst of his work, Dannan had an idea. He wrote down the ingredients for a mixture he thought might be used to treat burns.

Dannan didn't have two of the plants needed to make it. Rather than try to obtain them, he opted to write to Dr. Collier and get his opinion. Dannan was in the midst of this letter when someone came looking for him.

For a moment Dannan understood why some doctors only studied treatments. Interruptions at times like this could be frustrating. But the little boy—less than five years old—who had almost severed a finger—got Dannan's mind back on track. He would never want to leave his life of helping people who needed his skills as a physician.

"You look tired," Conner commented to Dannan when he arrived for dinner. He'd been tempted to go to the Petersons' but didn't follow his heart.

"I am a little."

"Busy schedule or busy thoughts?"

Dannan looked up into Conner's knowing eyes. "Both, I think."

Conner didn't comment, but he'd certainly been praying for the other man. He still remembered Reese's reaction to the news and knew that her face mirrored his own response when Dannan had shared with him.

"Eli told Dannan he was the one for Scottie?" Reese clarified, her mouth open a bit. "He said those very words?"

"Yes. Dannan thought he'd misunderstood, but Eli brought it up again before he died."

"Poor Dannan." Reese's face was filled with compassion. "It must have been dreadfully awkward."

"Yes, and I assume Eli was desperate. Here came Dannan on the scene, perfect in Eli's eyes, and at a time when he felt like he was slipping away."

"And he was," Reese whispered, looking distressed.

Conner wished he'd kept his mouth shut.

"We'll pray for him," Conner encouraged. "He's thinking well about it, and who knows, when all is said and done, maybe Scottie will agree with Eli."

Reese nodded in agreement, liking this idea, her face showing her thoughts.

"What are you thinking?" Conner asked.

"Just that they would be perfect for each other," Reese admitted.

"Reese Kingsley." Conner tried to sound stern with his whisper. "We are not going to get involved."

Reese tried to look innocent, but she liked the idea so much—Dannan and Scottie—that it was hard to pretend she felt otherwise.

"I have to get some sleep," she told her husband as she began to brush out her hair.

Conner would have pushed the point, if only to tease her, but he knew she wouldn't do anything rash. At least he hoped she wouldn't.

"Are you coming in?" Reese was suddenly in the hall, looking for her husband and Dannan. "Dinner is on the table."

"We're coming right now," Conner assured her, only just realizing that he'd been standing there in deep thought, Dannan staring at him.

"You'll have to tell me what that look was about," Dannan remarked to his host as they moved to the dining room.

Conner nodded, knowing it was only fair. "Just as soon as I get a chance," the banker promised, and the men went in to dinner.

"Come in," Douglas called quietly to whoever was knocking on his study door, his handkerchief in his fist.

"Papa?" 14-year-old Joshua ventured as he opened the door.

"Hi, Josh," Douglas said thickly, and the young man came all the way inside and shut the door. He walked until he stood opposite his father's desk.

"You look like you've been crying," Joshua said quietly.

"I have been," Douglas admitted.

"Mr. Peterson?" the pastor's son guessed.

Douglas nodded, his heart squeezing some. He had not been prepared to lose Eli, and although they usually had only one visit a week, it was a precious time for Douglas. His week now felt incomplete without it.

"It was so fast," Joshua reflected.

"I think so too. I wish I had stayed a little longer that night. He didn't wake up, but I would have wanted to be there had I realized how swiftly he was going downhill."

"Do you think about him in heaven?"

"A little. I can't picture heaven, so that's hard to get my mind around, but I'm thinking of him standing before he kneels at Christ's feet." Douglas smiled a little. "That makes me envy him."

Joshua laughed a little, and Douglas asked if he needed something.

"Mama wants to know if you're hungry. She said you didn't eat much dinner."

"I am a little, but I'll wait for tea. Thanks, Josh."

"I'll go tell her and come back."

"Why will you do that?" Douglas asked.

"Because you need someone with you right now," the young man said simply.

Douglas could only nod, needing his handkerchief again.

Dannan found Corina on the sofa next to Scottie. Scottie was reading to her. It was a scene that was bittersweet to his heart. He had come to the kitchen door and into the house that way, thanking Iris and telling her he would see himself out.

"Hello," Dannan said quietly when Scottie came to the end of the page. "This looks fun."

"It is," Scottie said, closing the book and smiling down at Corina.

To the adults' surprise, that little girl frowned up at her.

"Corina." Dannan's voice was firm. "I want you to thank Scottie."

A mutinous expression crossed her face, and Dannan's brows rose in warning, a warning Corina didn't heed. Corina climbed from the sofa, frowning first at Scottie and then at Dannan.

"I apologize," Dannan told his hostess. "Clearly Corina and I have something to discuss when we get home."

"It's all right," Scottie said swiftly, coming to her feet. "I think she's tired."

"If that's the reason, it's not all right at all," Dannan countered quietly.

Scottie blinked. "What do you mean?"

"Only that fatigue is not an excuse for treating someone poorly."

Scottie stared at him, not sure what to say.

"We'll see you tomorrow," Dannan said, not really taking in Scottie's reaction in his need to get Corina out the door and home. This was not acceptable behavior from her, and he was already trying to figure out just how he would explain that.

"You were not thankful to Scottie," Dannan said, wasting no time but starting the conversation the moment they were in their kitchen. "You were cross with her." From his kneeling position on the floor, Dannan stopped and studied the child's face. "Do you know what I'm talking about?"

Her lip was beginning to quiver, but she still said, "Sottie read boos."

"Do not cry," Dannan said firmly, and even though tears clung to Corina's lower lids, she did not weep. "Yes, Scottie does read books to you, and when I asked you to say thank you, you would not do it."

Corina's eyes could have swallowed her face as she looked into Dannan's disapproving countenance.

"I want you to be thankful. Do you understand?"

Corina nodded.

"So the next time I ask you to thank Scottie, what are you going to say?"

"San you."

"That's right. You will not act like that again."

The eyes were almost more than Dannan could take, but he remembered Grant and didn't soften.

"Why are we thankful, Corina?" Dannan asked, his voice losing some of its firm edge.

Corina didn't answer.

"We have such a great God." Dannan told her, knowing it would be some time before she knew that for herself. "We need to be thankful to Him all the time and also to those He puts in our lives. Like Scottie."

"Sottie read boos," Corina repeated, and Dannan looked at her lost little face and wondered if he'd made any ground at all.

"Come here," Dannan sat down on the floor, and Corina wasted no time climbing into his lap. Dannan hated having to scold her, and he wished he knew why she'd reacted the way she did, but he couldn't wait to address the issue until he figured that out.

"Are you hungry?" Dannan asked after pressing a kiss to her small, round cheek.

The little head bobbed against him, and Dannan realized he was proud of her. She hadn't burst into tears, and even when she hadn't answered his question, she hadn't done it with a rebellious look on her face. He didn't know how much had actually gotten through, but he hoped they were off to a good start.

Corina was asleep before Dannan remembered the letters he'd picked up from Doyle. He settled in the parlor, shifting the candle close so he could read, and settled back to hear from his family. He started with the one from his mother.

> *Do you have any idea how much I pray for you? I think that you and Corina are on my heart constantly. Do you remember those first years of poor health? I fought against God for a time, so sure He would want me up and around and then so angry to learn that He had another plan. I still wish I could do my own laundry and paint the house, but in truth my schedule leaves much more time for thought, and you just about fill mine.*
>
> *I will not overburden you with questions, but do write soon and tell us how you are both doing and if Corina is still enjoying Iris.*

Dannan put the letter down for a moment and thought about what a blessing Corina was in his life, and what an equal blessing it was to have Iris. Iris had been wonderful for Corina. And it hadn't been that long. So much had happened in the last month, but the stability Iris offered was a constant source of comfort.

Dannan finished his mother's letter and then read the one from his uncle. They both had much the same words, so Dannan wrote only one letter back. He was able to be honest about how he was feeling and all the changes that had gone on and wrote of his appreciation for their prayers.

He ended the letter with a special word of thanks to his uncle, who had sent him to Iris. Dannan knew he would not have been able to manage without her.

"Dannan, how did you learn so much about parenting?"

It was the next morning, and Scottie had waited only until Iris had taken the little girl into the kitchen to ask. Before she had done that, however, Dannan had asked Corina to thank Scottie for reading to her, and she had complied.

"You mean what I do with Corina?"

"Yes."

"I just try to remember everything Grant did."

"Grant was Corina's father?" Scottie clarified.

"Yes."

"And he expected her to do well, even when she was weary?"

"He did. He knew it was his responsibility to see that she was rested, but we can't always control how much sleep we get or even how much we can give our child. To lower the standard on the premise of fatigue is a poor idea."

Scottie had nothing to say. She didn't disagree; she'd just never considered this issue before. Dannan took her silence as dissent and questioned her.

"If you feel I've been unjust, I hope you'll tell me."

"I wasn't thinking that. In truth, I hadn't considered this before, and I'm just going over all of it in my mind."

Dannan left her with some time of silence, but he wished very much that he knew what she was thinking.

"It was out of character for her," Scottie finally said. "Is there room in one's parenting to account for that?"

"That's an excellent point, and I think you're right—there is room. If she was a little older, I might be able to explore that with her. At this age she probably can't articulate to me what was going on, so I have to assume, as you did, that she was tired. Until something else comes to light, I have to train her from that standpoint."

"But it's still a sin?" Scottie double-checked.

"Unthankfulness is always a sin."

Again Scottie stood and thought about this. There was certainly no argument she could offer; it was just taking some getting used to.

"Just so you know," Dannan put in, "I took her home, talked to her about it, fed her, and put her to bed. She slept all night, and when I told her at breakfast that she would thank you when we got here, she agreed without hesitation."

"You must have spent a lot of time with your cousin and his wife."

"Until I moved here, I just about lived at their house." Dannan's voice had dropped. "Grant, Annie, and I never ran out of things to talk about, and one time, when Grant was feeling uncertain about the future, he told me he would count on me to take care of Annie and Corina if anything ever happened to him."

Just the words made Dannan's heart squeeze. It was the last thing he had expected, but it was all too real. Annie had been taken as well, and he was now a father.

"I won't keep you any longer," Scottie said, realizing how long they had been standing there and wondering yet again how easy he was to talk to.

"I'll be off," Dannan agreed, "but if you have any other thoughts on the issue, I'd like to hear them."

"All right. How is the book coming?"

"A little slow right now. I hope to have it done next week."

"Good," Scottie said, and Dannan exited on that note. He was halfway down the green before he stopped trying to figure out what she meant by that word.

Early the next week there was an early morning knock on Dannan's door. Dannan opened that portal to find Finn on his step.

"Good morning," Dannan greeted the man.

"Good morning, Dannan. I've a message from Iris and Scottie. Iris is under the weather, but Scottie said to bring Corina along anyhow. She'd be happy to have her."

"Thank you, Finn. Should I check on Iris? Is she quite ill?"

"No," Finn answered with a smile. "She said you would ask that and to tell you she'll be on her feet in no time."

"Well, keep me informed, and if you think she needs something, don't hesitate to let me know."

"Will do," Finn agreed. "I'll see you at the house."

Dannan thanked him and went back to readying himself for the day. He found he envied Corina a bit. She was going to spend the day with Scottie.

∞

"Now, let's see, Corina—" Scottie had stopped on the green, her small companion stopping with her. "Here is the big house, but where is that block?" She dug into her basket, which was nearly full of Eli's town set. Scottie had things to do, but today she was ignoring her own agenda.

The two had ventured out to match the town set with the actual houses and shops along the green. So far they had seen the bank, Shephard Store, the Commons Meetinghouse, and the blacksmith's shop, and they were now standing at the big house.

"Look at the little windows." Scottie showed Corina. "They're all in the right places."

"Flowers!" Corina exclaimed, looking at the tiny front door and then up at the house.

"I see that."

"Well, now," a voice joined in as Dannan came upon them. "This looks fun."

"Danna!" Corina greeted him with pleasure.

Dannan swung her up into his arms and smiled at Scottie.

"We're matching the town set," Scottie explained, holding out the block that matched the Kingsley house. Dannan took it from her hand.

"This is amazing," Dannan said as he studied it. "Who did these?"

"Eli couldn't remember. His mother had them done after he became bedridden."

Dannan looked into her eyes. They were only a little sad.

"How are you?" he asked, thinking again of how much had happened in such a short time.

"Lonely," she admitted. "There's so much to be done at the house today, but I'm ignoring it all and using Corina as the excuse."

"Maybe that's for the best."

Scottie's head tipped a bit to the side. "Do you always think about what's best for others?"

"Always," Dannan answered, a small twinkle in his eye.

"Allaas," Corina said, and Scottie's mouth opened.

"Is that what she's saying? *Always?*"

Dannan laughed. "I say it all the time."

"Iris and I have not been able to figure it out."

"In what context does she say it?" Dannan asked, realizing how swiftly she'd picked it up.

"Oh, I don't know." Scottie thought. "I guess when Iris might say, 'You like cookies, don't you?' Or something like that."

Dannan laughed again. "That's exactly the way I would use it." He turned to look at Corina. "Are you my *always* girl?"

Corina smiled, hunching her shoulders with pleasure before repeating, "Allaas."

Dannan kissed her cheek and set her back on her feet.

"I have a patient to see, so I'd better keep moving" Dannan said, forcing himself to leave when he could have easily joined them for the day.

Scottie and Corina bid him goodbye before continuing their tour. They saw the covered bridge, two more houses, the schoolhouse, and even Dannan and Corina's home. They ended at the Peterson house just in time for Scottie to go inside and put something together for dinner.

Fifteen

"I have to talk to you," Reese said urgently to Conner.

Conner willingly followed his wife, who had taken his hand and was leading him out of the kitchen to the back stairway. It was a narrow space for Conner's size, but Reese had only gone up a few steps before stopping to look at him. Conner shifted his body as far as he could to one side so the light could show on his wife's face.

"Have you talked to Dannan again about Scottie?" Reese whispered.

"No, has something come up?"

"They're perfect for each other," Reese said seriously. "You must tell him that."

Conner couldn't stop his smile. It was so unlike his wife to voice this type of romantic opinion or to have anything to do with matchmaking.

"Am I being laughed at?"

"No," Conner quickly schooled his features, but Reese did some shifting of her own, allowing the light to catch Conner's face. "Reese," he said as soon as she did this. "What is going on?"

"I saw them on the green. They stood for a long time in front of the house and talked, Corina in Dannan's arms." Reese's breath caught a little. "So many memories came rushing back. You came into my life so suddenly, and I knew a love I'd never known. I want that for Scottie. I want her to let Dannan love her."

"Come here." Conner reached for her.

Reese let herself be swallowed in his huge embrace, wanting to cry but knowing she would have to explain to Troy if she did.

"Conner? Reese?" the couple heard, and Conner released her.

"I'll go put dinner on," Conner offered. "You come when you're ready, and when Troy leaves, I'll stay for a bit."

"All right."

Conner kissed her tenderly, his hands holding her face.

"Eli just died. For Scottie's sake we can't rush this, but I think it's going to be all right."

Reese nodded, hoping it was true. Conner left the stairway then, and Reese joined the men a short time later. True to his word, Conner stayed after dinner, but Reese had no more words; all she could do was cry in her husband's arms.

"Feeling better, Iris?" Dannan asked on Wednesday when he joined the Peterson household for dinner and that lady answered the door.

"I am, sir, thank you. Have a seat," she invited, and the meal began.

Dannan hadn't done this too often when Eli was alive, so he didn't know if things seemed normal or not, but the three occupants of the Peterson house appeared to be doing very well. Indeed, Scottie started talking about the book Dannan was reading, and along with the delicious meal, the time simply flew.

Dannan was surprised to suddenly see Iris refilling coffee cups and offering pie. A moment later, Scottie asked him if he wanted to choose another book.

"Only if you don't mind," Dannan answered.

"Not at all," Scottie replied honestly. She just didn't want to accompany him.

"Go on up," Finn said, his voice a bit low.

Dannan exited the room, Corina on his heels. He didn't try to stop her and knew that she trailed him up the staircase. Dannan let himself into the neat room and could see that it had been cleaned from top to bottom.

"Boos," Corina said, spotting the shelves, but Dannan didn't answer. He was suddenly seeing Scottie all over again. It was in the last hour of Eli's life. Heartbroken and weary, she held his hand and spoke.

You mustn't go, Eli. I need you here. How will I do things without you? Nothing will ever be the same. Please don't leave me, Eli. Please don't ever leave.

"Danna?" Corina tapped his leg.

"Yes, Corina."

"Mr. Son?"

"Corina," Dannan replied. He couldn't take her questions just now. "Have you looked out this window?"

Taking the red herring, Corina went to the window to peek out. Dannan headed for the shelves, not wanting to take any more time. Knowing there was little here that he didn't want to read, Dannan simply selected a book, barely glancing at the title. Just seconds later, he had Corina by the hand and was taking her back out the door, closing it softly in their wake.

Dannan had placed his satchel in the parlor when he arrived and now set the book next to it. When he joined the family in the kitchen, no one asked about the book, and Dannan didn't comment. It looked as though it was going to be an awkward moment, but Corina rescued them all by asking a question about candy. Iris was swift to answer, and Scottie and Finn, smiling at the interchange, finished their tea.

As soon as Dannan could take his leave, he went quietly on his way.

Scottie was on Dannan's mind the next morning, so it was with great regret that he dropped Corina off without seeing her. She wasn't usually in the kitchen when he went in that way, but he had been hopeful. Not until he was letting himself out the kitchen door did he remember the garden. Going to the high gate, as high as the fence itself, he found it ajar and peeked in. Scottie was working over a tomato plant. Dannan slipped inside and greeted her.

"Good morning," she said in return, but her voice was quiet and she kept at her work.

"How are you?" Dannan asked quietly, and hearing the concern in his voice, Scottie turned away from the plant to face him.

"I'm staying busy," Scottie answered, the thought flitting through her mind yet again that she could always share her thoughts with this doctor.

"It helps, doesn't it?"

"Sometimes."

Dannan nodded, his eyes betraying his thoughts for just a moment.

"Dannan," Scottie began cautiously. "Sometimes you get a look in your eyes that I can't read. Do you pity me?"

"Never," he told her sincerely, telling himself to be more careful.

"What is it I'm seeing?" Scottie pressed, and Dannan was struck for the first time as to how innocent she truly was.

"It's caring," he began, but Scottie only stared at him, and Dannan stopped. Without thinking, he added, "Eli said it would be like this."

"Like what?" Scottie asked, her face open.

"That you wouldn't understand," Dannan opted for complete honesty, unaware of how thin the ice was.

"Eli talked to you about me?" Scottie's eyes grew with the question.

Dannan nodded his head yes, suddenly sorry that he'd even come to the garden.

"About what?"

It never occurred to Dannan to lie to her, so he admitted, "About your lack of experience concerning the ways between men and women."

Scottie didn't know when she'd been so embarrassed. The emotions in the garden had gone to a dangerous level, and neither person was thinking before speaking.

"He wouldn't do that," Scottie stated flatly, anger evident in each word.

"What do you mean?" Dannan's voice grew a bit silky—not a good sign.

"I don't know why you would say such a thing," Scottie accused. "Eli would never."

"So I'm lying to you?" Dannan suggested, his face showing his surprise.

"It's good to hear you admit it!" Scottie shot back at him, and Dannan's face flushed with anger.

"I'm leaving now," he said quietly.

"Good!"

Dannan exited swiftly, and Scottie stood alone, her chest heaving with irritation and hurt. She stood for a long time and stared at the gate, ready to give Dannan more of her mind, but she was quite alone.

The longer she stood still, the more confused she became, but it didn't change how hurt she felt. Her anger starting to cool, she went back to work, asking herself how she could have been so wrong about Tucker Mills' doctor.

"Scottie," Iris called, coming to the garden before the younger woman was finished. "Finn isn't back from Doyle's yet. Do you have time to gather eggs?"

"Yes, I'll do it," she answered, her voice calm now but her heart still troubled.

"Are you all right?" Iris asked, not missing the droop of Scottie's shoulders.

"Yes," Scottie lied. "I'll get those eggs right now."

Finn had been keeping chickens in the pens at the back of the property for as long as anyone could remember. It was his little escape from his duties indoors, and he loved it. The only hitch in the system was Governor. Governor was a cantankerous old rooster that knew he ruled the coop. He was tolerant of Finn and Scottie, but that was as far as it went. Given a chance, he would peck or spur anyone who forgot that he was in charge. He allowed Finn and Scottie to collect eggs, but he was ever watchful, and they had to be quick about it.

In Scottie's distraction, she forgot this. She moved slowly, stopping at one point to think about everything Dannan had said. She had just collected the last egg when Governor struck.

His aim was swift and sure, and without warning, Scottie had been spurred on the back of the hand.

Scottie just managed to keep the eggs in her apron and press the back of her hand into the cloth as well. It throbbed painfully, and she aimed a kick at the rooster before hurrying toward the door. Having no choice but to "knock" with the toe of her shoe, Scottie was glad to see Iris just moments later.

"That was fast."

"Governor got me." She hurried to the table, and Iris unloaded the apron's contents into a basket.

Corina was quiet, but her small face was watchful as the women settled the eggs and then inspected Scottie's hand. The cut was deep, ugly, and jagged. Scottie began to wash it.

"Where is that salve you use for cuts?" Scottie asked.

"We're out."

"Are you sure?"

"Let me wrap that so you can go get some from Dannan."

Scottie looked at Iris oddly.

"What's the matter?"

"Are you sure we don't have any?" Scottie questioned again, not aware of how strange she sounded or looked.

"Quite sure." Iris' voice had grown impatient. "Now, go before that has a chance to get infected."

Scottie knew there was nothing to argue over. Iris wrapped her hand tightly, but blood was already leaking through. Scottie took off her soiled apron, held another cloth to her hand, and started toward the green.

Dannan heard the door. He wasn't ready to see anyone at the moment but knew that when someone walked in without knocking, he needed medical attention. He headed that way, coming up short when he found Scottie.

"I'm not ready to talk to you right now," Dannan wasted no time saying.

Looking vulnerable and uncertain, Scottie stared at him for a moment before turning for the door. Without thinking, she reached for it with her injured hand.

"Stop."

She heard the quiet command behind her but didn't turn. She heard Dannan's steps but stayed still until he came and took her arm. He unwrapped her hand and wasted no time.

"Come to the workroom."

His voice was quiet, but Scottie didn't hesitate to follow him to a room off the kitchen. Dannan told her to sit on the high stool and then stood before her to work.

"This is going to burn," Dannan warned.

Scottie shook a little when the brown liquid filled the cut. He hadn't been joking. It felt like fire.

Dannan's work was thorough. He cleaned and inspected her hand with minute care, using the salve Iris had been out of and then wrapping it expertly for healing.

When he was through, he didn't let go, but held her hand and studied her bent head.

"I would never lie to you," he whispered.

"Somewhere on the walk over here I figured that out," Scottie whispered back, raising miserable eyes to his. "But if you didn't lie, that means my husband talked to you about me, and that cuts my heart to the quick."

Dannan nodded.

"Why would he do that, Dannan? What was he thinking? What did he say?"

"I don't think you want all the details right now, Scottie, but I will tell you that he did it because he loved you so much."

Tears filled Scottie's eyes. She felt so betrayed by the man who had always had her best interests in mind. It made no sense.

"What did he expect you to do?" she finally asked.

Dannan hesitated, not wanting to baby her but already sorry for what he'd revealed. He opted to repeat himself, "I don't know if you want to know that right now, Scottie. Your grief is so fresh."

Scottie wanted to argue but hesitated. She had spoken without thinking too much today and was paying for it. Scottie slipped off the stool and looked up at Dannan.

"I'm going home now. I said things today that didn't need to be said, and now added to my grief is confusion about Eli. I'm going to want to know what he said, but not today."

"I'm sorry also," Dannan had to say. "I should never have opened my mouth about our conversation. I respect your right to know what Eli said, Scottie. Just let me know when you want to know."

"Thank you, Dannan."

"Here." Dannan stopped her. "Take this salve, but try to keep that hand dry for a few days. If it starts to bleed again when you unwrap it, come back to me so I can wrap it."

"Thank you, Dannan."

"On second thought, leave it wrapped until Saturday morning, and then I'll check it when I drop off Corina."

Scottie agreed and started toward the door.

"I thought Finn took care of the chickens," Dannan commented, trailing her.

"He usually does, but Iris needed eggs."

Dannan nodded and then picked up her hand. "This is going to throb some, but if the pain suddenly becomes worse, tell me."

Scottie nodded and stood still. Dannan still had her hand.

"Maybe you should tell me now," Scottie said.

"If you want me to, I will."

Scottie bit her lip. She was seeing it again, the look that had caused her to question Dannan in the garden. Suddenly she was afraid. Eli was right: She was ignorant of the ways between men and woman.

"Did you know that I was born and raised at a home for girls?" she suddenly asked him.

"No, I didn't."

"I don't remember seeing a boy until I was ten. There was some type of traveling peddler who came every few months to the orphanage, but no boys."

Dannan nodded, his face open, but Scottie suddenly reclaimed her hand. She folded her arms over her chest and looked embarrassed.

"I don't know why I told you that."

"I'm glad you did," Dannan encouraged, and for a moment Scottie couldn't look away from his eyes.

"I'd better go," she finally forced herself to say. "Iris will think I've fallen into a hole."

"I'll see you Saturday."

Scottie walked back down the green, wishing she understood what was going on inside of her. It was the kind of thing she would have rushed home to discuss with Eli. Her heart clenched painfully when she remembered he wouldn't be there.

It was evening, and Corina was in bed before Dannan had time to think about the morning. Scottie had no more left when Dannan had been called upon to set a bone, a broken leg that took some doing. The rest of his day had been just as busy, but now in the quiet of the parlor, Dannan closed his eyes with regret.

Scottie's grief over Eli was just a few weeks old. He'd never intended to put such a burden on her. He'd hoped someday to tell her of his conversation with Eli but certainly not this soon.

And where did they go from here? Part of him hoped she would ask questions soon, and part of him wanted to put it off for months. Dannan didn't know when he'd felt so drained. If Corina hadn't already been asleep, he might have gone to see Conner. Of course that would mean explaining everything that had happened, and he was too tired for that.

Dannan planned to pray and read, but he fell asleep in the chair, not even aware when the candle sputtered into darkness.

"Finn?" Scottie waited until they were alone the next morning to speak to him in the parlor. Iris and Corina were in their usual places in the kitchen.

"What is it?"

"Did you know that Eli had talked to Dannan about me?"

"Yes," the older man answered without even hesitating.

"Do you know what they talked about?"

"Yes. How did you know about it?"

"Dannan mentioned it, but not the specifics."

Finn nodded. He had wondered at her quiet the day before.

"Does Iris know?"

"No."

Scottie eyed him. It wasn't fair to ask, but she was going to. "Can you tell me?"

"Dannan didn't want to?"

"He said he would whenever I was ready."

"And you're ready now?"

"I don't know."

"If you want to know, Scottie, then ask," Finn said simply, "but ask Dannan. I think it would be best."

Scottie had to agree. It would be less embarrassing with Finn—he was family—but in all fairness to Dannan and Finn, she had to finish that conversation with the doctor.

"Someone's a bit teary today," Iris observed to Finn and Scottie as they relaxed after dinner with their tea. "I had rather hoped you-know-who would join us."

"I can read to her until she sleeps," Scottie volunteered.

"And fall asleep yourself?" Finn teased her.

"I might," Scottie smiled.

"How is that hand today?" Iris asked, spotting the wrap and remembering.

"It hurts some but hasn't bled through. Dannan said he would check it in the morning."

"Danna?" a wounded voice suddenly inquired. The older woman took Corina up and cuddled her close, kissing her small cheek.

"There's a dear," she comforted. "Just as soon as Scottie has finished her tea, she's going to read you a book. Won't that be nice?"

Corina nodded against her, and the three adults could see that no book would be needed. By the time Finn and Scottie had drained the pot, Corina was asleep in Iris' arms.

Alone in the parlor on Saturday morning, Dannan was pleased

with the progress of Scottie's hand. The bleeding had not started again, and it looked as if there would be no infection. Dannan recleaned the wound, used the salve, and replaced the bandage with a fresh one. The moment he was done, Scottie spoke.

"So Eli spoke to you about how unfamiliar I am with male-female relationships. What did he expect you to do about it?"

Dannan's heart sank. She wasn't supposed to be this direct.

"Dannan?" Scottie pressed him, and he vowed once again never to lie to her.

"He wanted me to marry you."

Scottie could not keep her mouth shut. Her lower jaw dropped, and it remained that way. Dannan looked at her as his thoughts raced. It took some time before he thought of something to say.

"Can I explain a few things to you?" Dannan began, but his voice enabled her to speak.

"Was he serious? He could be a terrible tease," Scottie said, her eyes begging Dannan to tell her it was all a joke.

"Listen to me, Scottie, Eli knew that sooner or later he was not going to make it. He wanted to know you would be cared for."

"But I have Finn and Iris."

"Yes, but he wanted more for you, I think."

"Why are you so understanding, Dannan? You must have been horrified, if not repulsed."

"Not at all," Dannan said quietly.

Scottie stared at him, suddenly feeling bold. "Tell me what you're thinking."

"Eli knew some things," Dannan admitted.

Scottie's gaze was direct. "What things?"

The room had suddenly become very warm to Dannan, but

he answered. "He was very intuitive, Scottie. You must have known that. He could tell what I was thinking."

"About what?" Scottie asked cautiously, wondering if she was as ready for this as she thought.

Dannan took a breath. "If you recall, I had no idea when I first met you that you were a married woman."

Scottie looked confused.

"In front of Shephard Store," he prompted, and her face cleared.

"When I poked you in the head."

"Yes."

"What did my marriage have to do with that?"

Dannan's collar felt as though it was strangling him, but he made himself keep on.

"I'd seen you at the meetinghouse but never talked to you. Thinking you were single, I was attracted to you."

Scottie's heart did something it had never done before. There was a sensation of pain, but it was too pleasant to be described as painful. She stared into Dannan's handsome face and at the same time tried to read what she was feeling inside.

"Scottie, are you all right?"

"I don't know," she admitted.

"I want you to know what was said, but I don't want you to be horrified at the thought that I expect this of you."

"That's what I said to you," Scottie said.

"But I wasn't horrified because of what I was feeling. I was horrified at how you'd feel about his talking to me." Dannan paused. "And I was right."

Scottie felt helpless. How did she explain something of which she had no understanding? She wasn't horrified by Dannan, not at all, but it was true that another marriage had never entered her mind.

Scottie was on the verge of trying to say just that to Dannan when Finn came their way, Corina in his wake.

"How is the hand?" he wished to know.

"Danna!" his daughter squealed as she ran to him.

The next few minutes were taken with conversation about Scottie's hand and Dannan saying goodbye to Corina yet again. Scottie would spend the rest of the day talking to Dannan in her head, quite certain that she would never be able to share all she was thinking.

Sixteen

"We need to finish our conversation," Dannan said to Scottie as soon as the service ended on Sunday morning and they had a moment together. Corina was at the end of the pew, standing near Alison, who was holding Jeffrey in her lap.

"I've been thinking the same thing, but I'm afraid I won't know what to say."

"I hope you'll say whatever you want, whatever you're feeling," Dannan encouraged her.

Scottie nodded but had to look away to ask, "What happens next, Dannan?"

"What do you mean?"

Scottie couldn't answer. This was the very thing she feared: his not understanding her when everything she was experiencing was so new, coupled with the fact that she had been a married woman such a short time ago.

"This I know," Dannan said, feeling the room grow more empty as folks exited. He lowered his voice some. "We're friends. We've been friends through all of this, and we'll keep on in that way. If something else comes up, we'll talk about it."

The sigh that lifted Scottie's chest was real. He had understood her enough to give her an answer she could live with.

"Thank you, Dannan. I hope you know how much I appreciate you."

"Always."

The word made Scottie smile. That smile did things to Dannan's heart, even as he reminded himself that there were no promises here. This was new territory for Scottie. She might learn that she did not want to marry again. She also might not know anything about her feelings for a long time.

Corina appeared in their midst a moment later, and before Dannan picked her up, he thanked God for Iris Stafford and her job at the Peterson house. Without that woman's connection to his daughter, his contact with Scottie would be very limited.

Even as he and Corina went on their way home, it was wonderful knowing that he might see Scottie the very next day.

Sunday noon found Jace, Maddie, and Valerie at the big house for dinner. They were the only family visiting on that day, and the conversation was sweet.

"What is the most challenging part of your faith in Christ?" Conner asked Jace.

"Probably remembering to be thankful. In those first few weeks and months, I was thankful with every thought and breath, but we're finding it easy to take God for granted."

"And if you had told us at the time we came to Christ," Maddie put in, "that we would not be as excited a few months down the road, we would have argued with you. But we both can grow discontented if we don't remember what we've learned from God's Word."

"It's about the hard work," Jace continued. "At first it's so easy to praise God and be obedient. When time passes and the same is required, that's when the first temptations to complain and be unthankful visit."

"And if you don't fight them," Troy agreed, "they become all too commonplace."

Valerie slept during their meal, and the afternoon turned into a long one. Not until the men went to the office to look at a book Troy had purchased did the women retire to the large parlor with the baby, giving them a chance to visit.

"Are you expecting?" Reese asked first.

"No," Maddie answered with a sigh. "I was somewhat disappointed, but things are busy right now, and we're all right with waiting. How are you feeling, Reese?"

"I'm feeling well," Reese confirmed, holding Valerie in her arms. "A bit emotional at times, but not too tired."

"How do you do in the heat?"

"Some days I get so little done. It can be frustrating."

"How many more weeks to go?"

"About 12. It feels like a long time."

"Well, you look great—your color and everything."

Reese looked down at her very round stomach. She needed only one arm to hold the baby because she fit on the top of her stomach so well. Reese studied the baby's face, still drowsy with sleep, and coaxed a small smile from her.

"Every time I see Val or Corina, I want a girl," Reese told her guest.

"They're fun little people."

"Is Val five or six months?"

"Right in between," Maddie answered. "I just remembered I wanted to see the baby's room. Did you finish the wall?"

"I did." Reese answered with pleasure and stood. "Come up and see it."

To the women's surprise, the men had beaten them to the room. Conner and Troy were showing the room and Reese's wall mural to Jace. Both Randalls were sincere in their praise of Reese's artistic abilities. Reese only smiled and thanked them quietly, but the pride she saw in Conner's eyes made her heart swell with contentment.

Sunday had turned into Scottie's day alone. Iris had not come on Sundays since Eli and Scottie were married, and although Finn took his meals with them and worked around the house and yard, he now lived in his own home on the green, so she didn't see him on Sundays either.

Not until she had the house to herself did Scottie think about the fact that up until now, she had been rarely alone. This had never bothered her, and since Eli's death, she was actually enjoying this day of solitude in her own home.

Today, however, was a bit different. Today she was getting ready to go into Eli's room for the first time since she'd cleaned. Scottie was not sure she was altogether happy with her husband. It was too late to speak to him in person, but she thought she might feel closer to him if she went into his room. And in her hurting mind, she thought that feeling closer to him might help her to accept that he'd felt a need to talk to Dannan.

She had so many questions for Eli Peterson. What had his view of her really been? Had he thought her helpless? Had she not known him as well as she thought?

Without warning, Scottie realized how much Eli had been able to control from his bed. It wasn't a bad thing—after all, he had rental properties to manage. But Scottie suddenly realized that the entire household had revolved around him. He was her husband. Wasn't that the way it was supposed to be? And he couldn't have survived without Finn, so Finn's life had to revolve around Eli. And what would they have all done without Iris?

Without even realizing it, Scottie had made her way to Eli's room. She stood by the bed, tears pouring down her face, trying not to feel so lost.

"Maybe you were right," she whispered to him. "Maybe I do need a keeper, but you've made me feel a little bit defective, Eli. You've made me feel as though the only way someone would want me is if you asked him to marry me."

More tears found their way down Scottie's face, but she felt better. Voicing those thoughts actually lifted some of the load. She did not have to have Eli physically present to know he would say that was the last thing he intended, but Scottie wasn't sure if it still might be a bit true. Another marriage had not been on her mind and probably wouldn't have been if not for Dannan's words.

"I'm Your child, Lord," she said, still speaking out loud and to the one Person she needed to talk to most. "I have value in You. Right now I feel bruised and discarded. I know Eli would never have deliberately hurt me, but he has hurt me. You had a plan here. Maybe Dannan shouldn't have spoken, but he did, and I must trust that You're still in control."

Thinking about Dannan caused fresh tears. He had said he was drawn to her, but Scottie didn't really know what that meant right now. She was desperate to talk to someone about it, but just thinking of asking Dannan made her blush.

Reese came to mind without warning. Since she was married earlier this year, she might well remember what her courtship looked like.

Scottie suddenly stopped. *Is Dannan courting me?* The word had never come to mind before, and for some reason it put a new face on all of this. There was so much they didn't know about each other. *But isn't that what courtship is about? Finding out about each other?*

Scottie suddenly shook her head and moved toward the door. She had to get out of that room, and she had to stop thinking about Dannan and Eli. She would find time tomorrow to go and see Reese, but for the moment she would go on a walk and try to empty her mind of questions she could not answer.

"Danna, where's Mama?"

Dannan stopped what he was doing at the dining table in the parlor and looked down at the little girl at his knee.

"Do you remember what I told you about your mama?"

"She died. Papa too."

Dannan could only nod.

"I miss Mama," Corina said with dry-eyed seriousness.

"I miss her too," Dannan whispered, his own eyes growing moist.

Corina studied him before patting his knee and saying. "Danna sad?"

"I am sad, Corina. I'm sad when people I love die."

"I love Danna," the little girl said, and Dannan's heart couldn't take anymore. He put his arms around Corina, held her in against his chest, and silently begged her to stop talking. She was too little and vulnerable, and all he could think about was how ill-equipped he was to be her father.

"Where's my doll?" Corina asked, and Dannan began to breathe again.

"I don't know. Why don't you look in your room?"

"You too," Corina directed, climbing from his lap and taking his hand.

"Okay, here we go," he agreed, knowing she wouldn't catch the weary hurt in his voice. They trooped up the stairs together, and Dannan managed to make a boisterous game out of finding the doll.

He would have willingly admitted to anyone who asked that he had a double motive. He hoped Corina would fall asleep right on time tonight. He was ready to be alone.

ࣲ

"Do you have time for a visit?" Scottie asked Reese when she answered her front door Monday morning.

"Of course I do. Come in, Scottie."

Reese led the way to the parlor. She could see that while Scottie took a seat, an action that was completely normal, there was something on her mind.

"How are you?" Reese asked in her open way.

"I'm not sure. You're going to think I'm losing my mind, but I wanted to ask you some questions about courtship."

Reese laughed. "I won't think any such thing, and besides that, last year at this time I was in the midst of courtship, so you've come to the right place."

"That's what I thought," Scottie confirmed, but she just sat there. Reese waited, but Scottie was clearly at a loss for words.

"Has someone caught your attention, Scottie?"

"I don't know. I just feel so awful. Eli's death is so recent, and do I have any right even talking to you about this?"

"About what?" Reese asked, already quite sure who the man was but wanting to give Scottie a chance to talk.

"It seems that Eli spoke with Dannan about me. And not just about me but about marrying me. I'm not very happy about

Eli doing that, but now Dannan has spoken up, and it seems he is a little interested in me."

"And you're not sure what to do?"

"That's right. I haven't been close to a lot of men, just Eli and Finn, and there was nothing romantic about that."

"But with Dannan it's romantic?"

"I don't know. I'm not sure what it is."

"And Dannan hasn't said?"

Scottie thought about this. There had been lots of words between them, but emotions had been high, and she wasn't sure she had taken them all in. She had a sudden awful thought that she shared with Reese. "What if Dannan wants a marriage like Eli and I had? Do you suppose that's what he's thinking?"

"Like an arranged marriage?

"Yes."

"I would be surprised if he was thinking that, Scottie." Reese put it as delicately as she could manage, not wanting to remind Scottie of her husband's bedridden state.

"But he might," she argued. "I'm sure he wishes Corina had a mother."

Reese knew this was not what Dannan had in mind, but she didn't know if she was the right person to tell Scottie.

"What does that look on your face mean, Reese?"

"I don't think that's what Dannan has in mind," Reese went ahead and said, "but he should be the one to tell you."

Scottie looked appalled by the very idea. She even came to her feet. "I can't, Reese. I can't ask him that. What if that isn't what he's looking for? How humiliating for both of us when he has to tell me he doesn't want that kind of marriage."

Reese stood and went to her. She was inches taller but bent enough to put her arms around Scottie Peterson and hug her.

"It's too soon for your heart, Scottie. You've just lost Eli, and now you're trying to take this in."

"Dannan was sorry," Scottie said, just holding tears. "He didn't mean to say all that was said, but now I know that they talked, and I can't stop thinking about it."

"Here." Reese took her to the sofa and sat beside her. "There are some things you need to know. I can't tell you all of Dannan's intentions because I don't know them, but I can tell you something about Dannan MacKay.

"He would never willingly hurt you. His heart is extremely tender and kind. You know that he was attracted to you before Eli died, but did you also know that he fought that in his heart?"

"He told me he'd been drawn to me."

"Good. Well, he also shared some of his struggles with Conner. Dannan knew it was wrong to have special thoughts of you when you were married. He is a man of honor, Scottie. He is not a man who would play games with a person's heart or treat her feelings with little regard. And he's still in his own time of grief. I think there's still a good deal of shock over Grant and Annie's death, not to mention in becoming a father."

Scottie nodded. Her emotions had run wild, and she hadn't completely considered Dannan's feelings in this. "Dannan said we were friends, and we just need to proceed from there."

"I think that's a good plan, but probably harder to carry out than talk about."

"I've already proven that," Scottie agreed.

"Why don't you come to dinner on Sunday? I'll ask Dannan and Corina too. It'll just be the six of us."

"Will Dannan know I'm going to be here?"

"I'll tell him."

"What if he'd rather not come?"

Reese looked into the other woman's face and thought about how similar their childhoods had been.

"We've both been abandoned by people who were supposed to love us, haven't we, Scottie?"

The smaller woman sighed. "We certainly have."

"I think it makes trusting harder."

"It must, since I assume that Dannan can't admit his true motives to me and doesn't even want to be around me when he's already talked about the attraction."

"I'm not trying to throw the two of you together or play matchmaker, but I thought if you could spend some time here, it might help."

Scottie thanked Reese and accepted the offer. She had to stop herself from double-checking with Reese about whether Dannan knew. She would work on trusting.

"Would you like some tea?" Reese asked, thinking they both needed a cup.

"I would, but to be honest, I don't want Iris asking too many questions, so I'd better get home."

Reese didn't press her, and after seeing her to the door, she encouraged Scottie to come anytime. Reese watched her walk away and began to pray.

"Scottie was here today." Reese had walked Dannan outside after dinner to talk. She had asked Conner if she should tell Dannan about the visit, and he'd told her yes. She had waited until Troy and Conner returned to the bank, and they now stood on the stone path that led to the front door.

"Is she all right?"

"Mostly, but she's rather torn."

"About what?"

"Many things, but one that she mentioned is that you might be seeking a marriage of convenience."

The look on Dannan's face caused Reese to put a hand over

her mouth so she wouldn't laugh out loud. Dannan slowly shook his head, his face amazed.

"Eli said she wouldn't understand, and I really didn't get it until right now."

Reese's look was one of compassion, but she didn't try to advise him. She knew she'd said enough.

"Thanks, Reese," Dannan said with a quick hand to her arm. "I can't tell you what a help this has been."

Reese hoped he was right. Remembering her conversation with Scottie from that morning, she started to pray again. If Dannan's plan was to woo and win the Widow Peterson, she wasn't sure if he truly understood the task that was before him.

Scottie stared into the darkness and wondered if she would ever sleep through the night again. Finn and Iris liked to tease her about napping with Corina, but in truth, she hadn't slept well since Eli's death, and napping was about the only thing that got her through.

For a few days she had forced herself to stay awake, leaving Corina alone on the sofa, but that only made her so tired she could barely function. She had ended up making so many mistakes in the account books she knew she couldn't afford that.

But the nights were so lonely. The house was large and empty, and even if she'd wanted to talk, there was no one down the hall to oblige her.

Scottie gave up after an hour and lit the candle on her bedside table. She read her Bible for a while, amazed as she always was at Joseph's willingness to trust God. Eventually, Scottie felt her body grow tired. She blew the candle out and asked God to give her Joseph's faith, marveling as she fell asleep that he kept on no matter what was put in his path.

"Is there anything left to eat?" Dannan asked as he slipped into the Peterson kitchen two days later. "I was going to join you today but got called to one of the outlying farms."

"Was someone hurt?"

"The woman was in hard labor, but she got through it."

"Boy or a girl?"

"One of each."

Iris' smile was huge when she invited him to have a seat and began to fill a plate. "Coffee, Dannan?"

"Please."

"Where is everyone?" Dannan asked after Iris handed him a fork.

"Finn went home to work on a project, and Scottie fell asleep on the sofa with Corina."

Dannan stood and went to the door. He peeked out into the parlor and came right back.

"Is that normal?"

"It is since Eli died. I'm not sure she's sleeping at night."

"She's here all alone, isn't she?"

"Yes, but she says she's not afraid."

Dannan didn't comment. He ate every bite on the plate and the pie Iris served him as well, and then he told the cook he would be in the parlor. He slipped into that room and onto the other end of the sofa. Scottie had curled into the corner with Corina's head in her lap. Dannan sat on the other end, not even needing to shift Corina's feet, and stared at them.

It wasn't every man who could watch a woman be another

man's wife and then have the chance to have that woman as his own wife. Scottie Peterson was very special. She had put her husband's needs ahead of her own and been a helpmate to him in every way. And she had been happy; he had seen that every time he was here.

Dannan's heart wanted her to have that same happiness with him. He wanted her to be Scottie MacKay and to care for him as she had Eli. In the same way, he wanted to cherish her every day and have her be his very own.

Dannan was studying her face, thinking about how beautiful she was, when Corina shifted around a bit and Scottie woke. She took a moment to see him.

"Hi," Dannan said softly.

"I didn't see you."

"I haven't been here too long."

"Did Iris feed you?"

"Yes, thank you. Are you sleeping at night?"

Scottie made a face. "Not very well. I tried to skip the naps, but I still wake up and end up too tired during the day."

"Are you nervous about being here alone?"

"No." She looked surprised at the very thought. "But sometimes it would be nice to have someone to talk to."

The image this created for Dannan was purely intended for a married couple. He thought about how sweet it would be to share a bed with your wife and have companionship just inches away.

"What are you thinking about?" Scottie asked in a way that was becoming familiar.

"I'll tell you sometime," Dannan stalled, "but right now I have to get back to work."

Scottie looked disappointed, which gave Dannan pause. He didn't want to leave her with questions about his motives.

Scottie saw him look at her and waited.

"You look beautiful," he told her sincerely.

The surprise on Scottie's face made Dannan smile.

"What did you think I was thinking?"

"I don't know," she admitted. "Just not that."

Dannan smiled again but didn't linger. Reese had told him that Scottie was coming to dinner on Sunday, so he knew he had that to look forward to. At the moment, it was the only thing that made him willing to leave.

Seventeen

"Did I see Dannan headed this way after dinner?" Finn asked Scottie later that day as she helped him make some repairs on the chicken pens. The chicks were getting out and disappearing.

"Yes. Iris said he had a delivery to make, but she still fed him."

"Did the two of you talk?"

"A little."

"I mean, did you get to ask him your questions?"

Scottie looked across at him. "How much do you know, Finn?"

"As far as Eli is concerned, he talked to me about everything. You and Dannan are another matter."

"So you knew that he talked to Dannan and what he was going to say?"

"I was there."

Scottie hesitated. Finn had much on his mind but waited for a question.

"Do you think Eli trusted me?"

"With all his heart."

"Even to take care of myself?"

Finn smiled. "Now that's where Eli struggled, Scottie. He

wanted so much to know that you'd be looked after. He even doubted his God at times, and you know how strong his faith was."

"Why did he worry about me?"

Finn's eyes were fond. "You don't know what we all saw when you came here. You don't know how we all lost our hearts to that shy little girl who came into our midst."

Scottie said on a sigh, "I miss Eli so much." She didn't want to cry but felt as though she could.

"Of course you do."

"But then how can I be thinking about Dannan?"

"Scottie, it's normal and right that you would want a fine man like Dannan. Eli shouldn't have interfered. Dannan would have found a way on his own. But your feelings are normal."

"Why did Eli do it?"

"Like I said, Scottie, he was still trying to take care of that shy little girl."

Scottie looked thoughtful and a little unhappy.

"Don't withhold your forgiveness, Scottie. Your Bible teaches otherwise."

"You're a fine one, Irv Finnegan." Scottie sprang on him without warning. "Saying *Eli's God* and *my Bible*. They could be your God and your Bible too!"

Finn's eyes twinkled.

"And don't be smiling at me," she went on fiercely. "I know the promise you gave Eli, and I've yet to see you at the meeting-house!"

"You're right," Finn agreed, as calm as ever. "I did promise, and I'm working on it."

Scottie gave a single nod of her head and did not press the matter further. She had plenty more to say but knew that no amount of words would sway the man. She also knew that the promise had been between Finn and Eli, and that Finn, sooner or later, would be true to his word.

∞

"I've learned so much," Cathy shared with Douglas and Alison before they even sat down for Sunday dinner. "I never really read the Bible before, and I can't believe what I've missed."

"Well, you and I did read," Doyle amended, "but not with any depth of understanding."

"I can see the changes in you," Douglas told Cathy. "You were guarded before, but that's all gone."

Cathy looked pleased and peaceful, and the smile in Doyle's eyes was impossible to miss.

"Come to the table," Alison invited, knowing it was going to be a great afternoon.

∞

"How are you?" Dannan asked of Scottie at the big house, his first chance to speak to her that day.

"I'm fine. How are you?"

"I'm fine, thank you. How is the back of your hand?"

Scottie showed him. There was a scab now, long and jagged, but healing was coming along nicely.

"It looks good," Dannan said, having taken her hand. "It must have been the good doctoring."

Scottie tried not to laugh at Dannan's innocent eyes but failed. Dannan watched her, smiling at how relaxed she seemed. The last time they spoke he'd not been able to say all that was on his mind, and he hoped that no walls had come up between them.

"Sottie!" Corina cried, suddenly there and throwing her arms around Scottie's legs. Scottie reached down to hold the little girl's face in her hands, and the two smiled at each other.

"Where is that little girl?" Troy's voice came, and Corina's eyes got huge.

"Mr. Roy! Hide!"

For everyone but Scottie this was old stuff. Troy played hide-and-seek with Corina on a regular basis. At first Corina tried to hide behind Scottie's skirt, but the closer Troy got, the more excited she became. She scurried from the entryway into the parlor, giggling all the while.

"Come in," Reese greeted from the door of the dining room. "Troy will find Corina in about two seconds, and they'll join us."

"Sit here," Conner invited when Scottie entered the large dining room. She hadn't been in this room recently and had forgotten how lovely it was. Reese's dishes and flatware sparkled in the sunlight streaming through the windows, and although there was no fire burning in the fireplace, the mantle—with a family portrait hanging above—gave the room a homey feel.

The six of them were all seated a short time later, Conner and Reese taking the ends and Dannan and Corina on one side with Troy and Scottie across from them. Reese had prepared ham and corn chowder with biscuits. The bowls of vegetables that she put on the table were mouthwatering and plentiful.

Dannan served Corina, and when everyone's plate was ready and they had prayed, Conner asked Troy to share about the letter he'd received from his daughter, Ruth.

"They had a bit of excitement in downtown Linden Heights last week," Troy began, his eyes twinkling. "It seems that one of the town constables was in the bank to settle a matter with his account when he dropped his weapon and it discharged. No one was harmed, but the bank had several customers right then, mostly women, and the shot, along with the screaming women, gave another officer the impression that the bank was being robbed. Complete panic broke out before the sheriff stepped in and sorted things out."

"And was your daughter there at the time, or did she just hear about it?" Dannan asked.

"She heard about it, along with the entire town. She wrote that folks were in and out of the bank all day, just wanting to see the bullet hole and hear what happened firsthand from the tellers."

Even Conner and Reese, who had already heard Troy read the letter, laughed all over again. The story caused Conner to think of one of his own, and for the next hour, the men regaled the company with banking stories.

The stories made the time move swiftly, but Dannan was still constantly aware of Scottie's presence and wished he could talk to her alone. Not until Conner went with Reese to get the dessert and Corina climbed onto Troy's knee did Dannan have an opportunity to speak quietly across the table to her.

"Are you sleeping any better?"

"No, but I'm going to fight it this week and try not to fall asleep with Corina."

"Do you want me to give you something?"

Scottie looked surprised. "Every so often I forget you're a doctor."

Dannan laughed a little.

"What would you give me?" Scottie asked now.

"A glass of whiskey would work, but you don't drink."

Scottie knew she was being teased. Her hand came to her mouth, but her eyes were brimming with suppressed laughter.

"What?" Dannan asked, his eyes a study in innocence.

Scottie didn't have to answer. Conner and Reese were returning with coffee and dessert, and since Reese's pies were not to be ignored, private conversation was momentarily put on hold. Not until they were settled in the parlor did Dannan have a chance to question Scottie again. She declined something to help her sleep and was still wanting to ask what he had in mind when Troy suddenly spoke.

"Is it story time?" he asked of Corina.

"Boos!" she cried with delight and rushed toward the bookshelf in the corner. Several children's books hit the floor before she found the one she wanted, but Troy was ready and waiting.

Corina, however, had other ideas. Without even glancing at the older banker, she headed for Scottie's lap. Scottie looked surprised as well, but Corina didn't notice.

"I do believe I've been replaced," Troy grumped quietly, but he was smiling.

"Do you mind?" Scottie asked, even as Corina climbed up with the book, not even aware of the confusion.

"Terribly," he said, his attempt to look offended not working at all.

"I think this is a daily occurrence, isn't it, Scottie?" Dannan checked.

"Just about," she agreed, opening the book.

What happened next was not something Scottie had planned on. She read to Corina, keeping her voice low so the others could talk, and as usual, the little girl was soon asleep. In spite of her own best efforts, Scottie dropped off too. The book still in her hand, she didn't stir even when Reese took it from her and covered her with a light quilt.

"She's not sleeping at night," Dannan told the others when Reese sat back on the sofa next to Conner.

"Did she tell you this?" Troy asked.

"Iris was the first to mention it, but Scottie and I have talked about it."

"Is that normal, or has it just been since Eli died?" Conner asked.

"Since Eli's death. She usually naps with Corina but just told me today she's going to try and fight that."

"In some ways it feels as though Eli has been gone for months," Reese commented, thinking that having Scottie with them on a Sunday was not something that would normally have happened.

"I'm sure it does for her too," Conner agreed.

Scottie stirred a little then, and Conner suggested they move to the small parlor to visit. No one argued. The idea of waking Scottie, who would already be embarrassed by the act of falling asleep, didn't appeal to any of them.

"How are you?" Dannan whispered to Scottie when her eyes opened.

She frowned at him, trying to understand why he was in her parlor, when she remembered where she was.

"Oh, no, Dannan, did I fall asleep?"

"Yes, and Corina just came to find me, so you must have been out pretty hard."

Scottie put a hand to her face and made herself stand up. She felt fuzzy and disoriented and wanted to shake it off as soon as possible.

"I actually dreamt," Scottie admitted, "that you asked me to marry you so I could be a mother to Corina."

The moment the words were out of her mouth, Scottie's eyes flew to Dannan's in surprise.

"I can't believe I said that." She stepped away from him a bit. "I'm sorry." Scottie would have walked from the room, but

Dannan moved so she would have to go around him. Scottie eyed him warily but didn't speak.

"Let's just be sure we have this one thing straight," Dannan said slowly, doing an amazing job of keeping his feelings in check. "If it comes to the point that I ask you to marry me, it won't be about Corina."

Scottie wanted to question him but didn't. Later she would wish that she had because she thought about the statement for the rest of the day.

"I can't get over the change in both of them, but especially Cathy," Alison pointed out to Douglas when their guests were gone. "I've always liked and enjoyed Cathy, but there wasn't a lot of warmth there. Now she's overflowing with warm-heartedness."

"And the way Doyle looks at her," Douglas mentioned, his own eyes smiling with fondness. "You can tell that he's fallen in love all over again."

"Jace and Maddie must be thrilled."

"We're having our own little revival," Douglas said. "We need to work hard as a church family to be ready for these blessings from God."

"And for the challenges and questions from folks like Cathy."

"She's got some good ones," Douglas agreed with a huge sigh. "I can't remember the last time I was so tired after dinner."

Indeed, Douglas looked as though he could fall asleep in the chair he was sitting in, but his youngest had other ideas. Jeffrey, awake from his nap and ready to go, chose that moment to look for a grown-up playmate.

"May I mention something to you?" Conner asked Dannan at the door much later that day. Scottie had left, and Troy was treating Corina to one last game of hide and seek.

"Certainly."

"Scottie has no awareness of you as a man right now. You're going to have to take it slowly."

Dannan nodded. "I've noticed that. She looks at me with friendship and a bit of confusion, but that's all."

"I'm glad to hear that she considers you a friend. She needs that very much right now."

"I think so too, but don't think it's all for her. On my part, having Scottie as a friend is a very rewarding thing."

Conner nodded and then had a heart-sinking thought. "Scottie is going to believe that we've all plotted against her." He shook his head a little, knowing this wasn't the case. "I hope when all is said and done that she'll be your wife and we can spend a lot of time laughing about all of this subterfuge."

Dannan only quietly nodded and thanked his host, realizing he was ready to go home and think for a while on his own. He gathered up Corina and headed that way, forgetting until he got there that she'd had a nap and was ready to play.

On Monday morning Scottie walked up the steps to the Cole house, planning to collect the rent, her mind not on the task. Nothing had changed in this area of her life. She and Finn had taken turns collecting the rent money for years, but now Eli was not there to go over the books with her. She didn't fear making a mistake, but it was something they had usually done together and one more thing to remind her of his absence.

Scottie felt her heart grow heavy. She didn't want it to be this way. She had always prayed for each of their renters as she made the collection, and now she was caught up in herself.

"Scottie!" Mrs. Cole said, glad to see her. "Come in a moment."

"Thank you, Mrs. Cole," Scottie said sincerely, only just remembering to pray for her.

"How are you?" Mrs. Cole asked, looking concerned.

"I'm coming along," Scottie said truthfully. "There are things to keep me busy, and that's a great help."

"Will you be raising my rent?" Mrs. Cole blurted.

In her surprise, Scottie took a moment to respond but then kept her voice kind.

"I have no plans for that, Mrs. Cole. And if ever I had to do that, I would give you at least six months' warning."

The renter was so relieved she suddenly sat down. Scottie stared at her, not having expected this at all.

"We've appreciated your prompt payments all these years, Mrs. Cole. I would not want to lose you as a renter."

"Thank you, Scottie." That woman gathered herself and offered tea.

"As a matter of fact, I can't stay, but we'll plan on it another time."

"Thank you, Scottie."

Scottie went graciously on her way, determined to collect the other two houses swiftly and make her way home to do something quiet.

She arrived home to find Iris busy in the kitchen, Corina at her side. Scottie had gotten up early that morning and done the washing and dusting. When collecting the rents, Scottie usually wasted no time adding the amounts to her account book. But this morning she told herself there would be time to go over the books later. Right now she just wanted to work in the solitude of her garden.

"I want you to know that we have plotted against you just a little bit," Dannan said without preamble, very ready to have everything out in the open, even knowing that some things would need to wait.

"What are you talking about, Dannan?" Scottie asked. They were once again in the garden.

"I'm talking about the fact that I went to Conner when I was having feelings for a married woman, so we talked about you. He said something yesterday about you not knowing about our subterfuge, and I found myself uncomfortable with the fact that you might not realize we've talked about you. I don't want secrets between us."

Scottie nodded. Her first reaction was unease in knowing she'd been discussed. She then realized she'd talked to Finn about Dannan, and wasn't that the same thing?

"You have to have someone to talk to," she said reasonably, and not until then did Dannan realize he'd been holding his breath.

"Who do you talk to?" Dannan suddenly asked.

"Lately, you and Finn."

"Does it help?"

Scottie's smile was a little crooked. "Sometimes it just makes for more unanswered questions."

"Give me one, and I'll try to answer it."

Scottie had been kneeling on a burlap sack. She now pushed

to her feet and worked to remove the dirt from her hands, all the time her mind racing.

"Even if you've already answered this, I need you to answer again."

"All right."

"What went through your mind when Eli said that to you about me?"

"I didn't take him seriously. He was very ill. He could barely breathe or talk, and I thought his mind had slipped a little."

"What about when you realized he was serious?"

Dannan smiled and tried to make light of it. "I thought we decided on one question."

"Why don't you want to answer?" Scottie asked, and Dannan knew the smile hadn't worked.

"When people are at different levels with their feelings, it gets a little tricky," Dannan began. "This is all so new for you, Scottie, but you've been in the periphery of my mind for months. To share my feelings when you're feeling nothing of the sort is not fair to either of us. You'll only feel pressure, and I'll only feel rejected."

"Why do you understand people so well?"

"They're my business, Scottie. On a good day I can give aid to a person's body; on a great day I can give them peace of mind about their body no matter what I was able to do for them physically. I learned early on that treating a person's ailment is only part of the job. If you don't know anything about him, it's much harder to meet his needs."

"And who meets your needs, Dannan?" Scottie asked the question and then felt embarrassed. She looked down before saying, "You don't have to answer that."

"I might not have to answer, Scottie, but I do have to say that you're one of the kindest persons I've ever known."

Scottie's head came up. "Thanks, Dannan."

Dannan smiled into her eyes and said he had to be going. The smile stayed in Scottie's mind until Finn came looking for her.

"You're a bit warm," Iris said to Corina when that little girl climbed into her lap just a few hours after Dannan dropped her off. "Do you feel all right?"

Corina didn't answer but snuggled closer to her caregiver. Iris would have thought nothing of this had it been after dinner when Corina's little system usually ran out of steam, but this was too early in the day.

Iris didn't know where Finn was at the moment, but as soon as he showed up, Iris would be asking him to look for Dannan.

It hadn't worked. Scottie had been completely ready to stay awake, but Corina had been so ill, and Scottie had nodded off before Dannan showed up to take his daughter home. Now it was the middle of the night, and Scottie was wide awake. She was weary and a little bit anxious with the questions and new ideas running through her mind, bringing her no end of confusion.

Scottie's mind went back to her evening. Iris and Finn had gone on their way, she'd had her tea and cleaned the kitchen, and then she'd realized how long the evening was looking. Without giving the idea too much thought, Scottie decided to go for a walk. She didn't get very far, however, before she spotted a young couple walking by the millpond.

Standing near a tree, embarrassed to be caught watching, she observed as they held hands and even stopped for occasional kisses. The man's tenderness was obvious from a distance, and the woman's head was tipped back almost constantly to look into his face.

Scottie had eventually walked home, her heart in a quandary. She had been sleepy at the normal time, but then awake in the wee hours, her mind running with everything she'd seen.

It took some time, almost two hours, but at last Scottie fell back to sleep. However, before that happened she had made plans for the next day, and she fervently hoped that Reese Kingsley would have more time to talk.

Dannan went to Corina's room early on Wednesday morning. She was still warm but hadn't been sick to her stomach in the night. Tea had not stayed down, and it had looked as though the night would be a sleepless one. But Dannan had been the only one awake. He'd checked on Corina every few hours, not able to sleep deeply.

Dannan went quietly from the room, thinking to sleep a bit longer. He dropped back off, hoping that when he didn't show up at the Peterson house, Iris would assume Corina was still ailing.

"I keep catching myself worrying," Scottie admitted to Reese. "I try to get my mind busy with other things, but it doesn't last very long."

"What's bothering you the most?"

"All the things I don't know. It seems obvious to the rest of the world but not to me."

"What exactly?"

"The private things, Reese. The first time you had your monthly flow, were you embarrassed in front of Conner?"

Reese smiled and put a hand on her round stomach before admitting, "I haven't had it yet."

"Oh, that's right," Scottie recalled softly, her voice sounding a bit discouraged.

"But I do know what you mean," Reese added swiftly. "It is a little odd when you're just trying to imagine it, Scottie, but by the time you marry, you're comfortable and in love, and those small things become normal very quickly."

"Do they really?"

"Yes. Since the second month of this pregnancy, I've had to relieve myself more than I thought possible, and Conner just teases me about it. It's not embarrassing at all."

Scottie nodded, trying to see herself in the same role—and failing.

"I guess it's pretty obvious that Eli and I didn't share such things. I kept to my room, and Finn took care of his needs."

"It might be obvious, Scottie, but it's also not something that I think anything about. You were Eli's wife in the ways he needed you to be, and likewise he was your husband in the way you needed."

Scottie knew this to be true, and she wondered why she'd never thought of it that way before.

"Tell me something, Scottie," Reese asked. "Did you ever long for children?"

"No," Scottie said honestly. "It never occurred to me. I guess the Lord just brought me contentment on that issue."

Reese was ready with more questions, but someone was at the front door. Reese went that way and came back with Dannan.

"I'm sorry to do this to you, Reese, but you're closer than Iris at this time of the day, and I've got an emergency."

"It's fine, Dannan; just put her on the sofa."

"Hi, Scottie," Dannan greeted as he put his sleeping daughter down. "I'll be as fast as I can."

"Don't worry about it, Dannan." Reese saw him on out the door and returned to the parlor. The women continued to talk but didn't have much time. Corina woke, looking as miserable as she felt, and after Scottie took some time with her, she went on her way.

Eighteen

"Are you free to join me for dinner on Sunday?" Scottie asked of Alison Muldoon.

"We are, Scottie," Alison agreed with pleasure. "Let me just make sure Douglas hasn't asked someone here and not mentioned it. Have a seat and I'll be right back."

Scottie sat in the Muldoons' empty parlor, thinking that her heart needed this so much. She had caught herself just in time. Mired in her own thoughts and consumed with Eli's loss and her confusion over Dannan, she had almost forgotten that her mind would just keep going to the wrong place until she put something else there.

When she'd walked down the green from the big house and looked over to see the Muldoons, it was perfectly obvious to her what she must do. And not just this Sunday, but often, opening her home to the families she knew.

"He said yes," Alison spoke as she entered the room, Douglas at her heels.

"We are so glad to see you, Scottie," Douglas added, taking a nearby chair. "How are you?"

"Some days I do better than others," she answered honestly.

"I've been praying for you. I miss Eli so much; I can just imagine how it is for you."

"It's hardest at night when I can't sleep."

"Have you always been like that, unable to sleep?"

"No, it's just recent."

"What do you do?"

"Sometimes I worry and fret, and sometimes I go ahead and put a light on so I can read and pray."

"Are there verses that are a particular comfort just now?"

"Not specific verses. I'm studying in Genesis, marveling over Joseph's willingness to trust God in the most awful situations. He's been such an example to me. He says openly that he fears God, and then when his brothers fear his retribution, Joseph's answer to them in Genesis 50 is such a peaceful one about God intending only good for him."

"That's amazing, isn't it?" Douglas agreed. "So many years had passed in a place of spiritual desolation, and yet he feared God."

"I can't claim anything so horrendous as what Joseph went through," Scottie said with a small shake of her head. "Yet sometimes I feel sorry for myself in such a way that you would think I had been cast out."

"I'll remember that when I'm praying for you, Scottie, but I must tell you what an encouragement you've been to me through all of this."

"How is that?" Scottie asked, confused because they hadn't spoken recently.

"Your presence on Sundays, and the fact that you stay now and visit with everyone. I think it would be easy to dash home and be on your own, but you don't do that, and that lifts my heart.

"And now your hospitality to us. You are a blessing to us in so many ways, Scottie. Eli never had anything but praises for you, and I can see why."

"Oh, my," Scottie whispered, her heart working to take it in. "It never occurred to me that you and Eli would have discussed me."

"He loved you and wanted to take such good care of you. Your welfare was everything to him."

"Thank you for telling me," Scottie said sincerely. "I can't describe to you what it means."

Douglas didn't linger but left the women to visit. Scottie didn't stay overly long either—she had work to do—but Douglas' words had been a comfort to her heart. Scottie thought about their conversation all the way home.

"She's had a little bit to drink and even a small piece of bread," Reese explained when Dannan returned.

Fever-bright eyes, glazed and miserable, stared at Dannan's face, and Dannan had to smile at her.

"She's certainly not herself," he agreed with a small laugh, even as he pressed a tender kiss to her small, warm cheek. "I think we'll head home and hope we can stay there. Thanks so much, Reese."

"My pleasure. Bye, Corina. I hope you feel better."

Corina's small hand lifted in a wave, and Reese's heart melted a little.

"How's Scottie, by the way?" Dannan asked as he walked toward the door.

"She's asking good questions and doing lots of thinking."

Dannan nodded, knowing that he couldn't ask but oh-so-curious to know what the women had talked about. Dannan took Corina home and settled her back into bed. She fell instantly asleep, and Dannan was glad. It was the best thing for her right now, and maybe if the house was quiet, he could figure out his next move with the Widow Peterson.

Scottie heard the knock on the door Sunday morning but dismissed it. No one ever came to the house this early in the day. Not until it sounded a second time did she head that way.

"Hillary!" Scottie said in surprise. "What brings you out so early?"

"My family is sick," she told Scottie. "Mother, Josh, and Marty all have come down."

"I'm so sorry to hear that, Hillary. Tell them we'll do this another time."

"All right."

"Wait a minute, Hillary," the older woman added, stopping her. "I'm going to send food with you."

Hillary tried to protest, but Scottie would have none of it. Taking a few minutes to package everything up, Scottie walked back to the Muldoon house with Hillary to deliver the meal. It certainly wouldn't be the same as having company, but Scottie was delighted to do this. She walked home with a light heart and sweet knowledge that she had helped in a small way.

Sunday was the first day Corina seemed to be feeling completely herself. Dannan had kept a close eye on her for a few days, and she was now her chipper little self. She was even a bit wiggly during the sermon, and twice Dannan had to tell her to sit still. He wasn't at all surprised to see her on her feet as soon as the service ended, heading over to see Jeffrey Muldoon—one of her favorite people—who was seated on Hillary's lap.

Dannan kept an eye on her but also came to his feet. He spotted Scottie in the back pew, eyes on her Bible, and went that way.

"How are you?" he asked, sitting down right next to her.

"I'm fine. Is Corina feeling better?"

"Yes. I think she's completely back on her feet."

"Alison, Josh, and Marty have it now," Scottie told him, a little disappointed that they had to cancel their dinner with her.

"I might stop in and check on them," Dannan said, even as he studied Scottie's face, looking for some sign that she was aware of him.

Scottie looked into his eyes just then, and Dannan looked right back. He didn't want to draw attention from others in the room, so he turned and looked toward the front. Nevertheless, he spoke to Scottie.

"Tell me something, Scottie. Did you ever think about that first kiss?"

Dannan could feel her eyes on him but didn't turn his head.

"What first kiss?" she finally asked.

"Adam and Eve's."

"What made you think of that?"

That was a good question. "I don't know," Dannan admitted. "I was just thinking. I mean, God created lips, so He must have created kissing."

Scottie smiled a little at his casual tone.

"What are you thinking?" Dannan asked, eyes still front.

"I'm still wondering what got *you* to thinking about Adam and Eve kissing."

"I guess I might have kissing on my mind lately."

This time Dannan turned his head. He looked straight into Scottie's eyes and smiled. It took a moment for Scottie to catch his meaning. Her eyes grew a bit and her mouth opened, but no words came out.

"What do you think their first kiss might have been like?" Dannan asked.

"I don't know," Scottie admitted, her face growing pink.

"I think it must have been sweet and wonderful."

Scottie would have been forced to agree, but Corina chose that moment to call her name.

"Hi, Sottie." The little girl was standing next to her legs. Scottie looked down at her but didn't really focus.

Thankfully Corina didn't notice. That little person gabbed away about something, and although Scottie looked at her, she was really seeing Dannan.

Dannan, on the other hand, had eyes only for Scottie. He watched her expression, knowing that he'd thrown her into a whole new world and feeling inordinately glad about it.

"We'd better get going, Corina," Dannan finally announced.

"Bye, Sottie."

"Bye, Corina. Bye, Dannan. Enjoy your day," she managed in an afterthought.

Dannan waited until she looked up at him and said, "After talking to you? Always."

Scottie couldn't say another word. She didn't leave the meetinghouse immediately, but she also didn't comprehend another word that was spoken to her.

"You can't do that!" Scottie was on the attack first thing

Monday morning. Iris had just taken Corina to the kitchen, and she and Dannan were alone in the parlor.

"Do what?" Dannan asked.

"Talk to me about kissing in the meetinghouse. After you left I didn't hear a thing anyone said to me!"

Dannan smiled.

"Don't you smile about this, Dannan MacKay. I'm serious!"

"I'm sorry." He worked to school his features, but his gleaming eyes betrayed him.

Scottie's own eyes narrowed a bit. Dannan worked harder not to look pleased, but he was failing.

"Whatever possessed you?"

"I don't know."

"You must know," Scottie argued. "Do you think about kissing me?"

"Of course I think about kissing you."

This blunt, honest answer completely threw her. Scottie stared at him for a moment before finding her voice.

"Since when?"

"Since you became a widow."

"You never told me this."

"How was I to do that?" he asked, and then his voice changed. *"Oh, here's my daughter, Iris, and by the way, Scottie, I'm thinking about kissing you."*

Scottie thought about this, and Dannan watched her. The wheels in her mind were turning, and he wondered what would come next.

"Well," Scottie began, "I guess I'm glad you told me, but I don't want you to bring it up at the meetinghouse."

"Fair enough. Where can I bring it up?"

The question stopped Scottie again. She cast around for something to say but came up with nothing.

"I think I know what you want to say," Dannan put in.

"What?"

"Why talk about it, let's just go ahead and kiss."

Scottie's hand came to her mouth to keep from laughing. Dannan's brows had risen to an impossible height, and his eyes were huge with teasing. Scottie had to look away to gather her thoughts.

"Are we settled on this?" she asked.

"Yes. I will not discuss kissing you in the meetinghouse, but I can bring it up other places."

"I'm not sure that's what I meant."

"You could be the one to bring it up," Dannan suggested, and Scottie eyed him. He was having too much fun with this, and she didn't know what to do with that.

"I've got work to do."

Dannan smiled and lightheartedly warned her, "As do I, Mrs. Peterson, but mark my words, this topic will come up again."

Their eyes held for a moment, and then Dannan turned for the door. Once there, he paused and looked back at her. Scottie was still watching him, but Dannan made himself exit.

Once outside and the door shut behind him, Dannan stood and took a deep breath. He hadn't seen this coming. He never dreamed she'd actually mention the conversation from the day before. Dannan had thought about it plenty but not given Scottie enough credit.

Dannan didn't know what this courtship was going to look like in the days to come, but it certainly felt as though it was going to be fun.

It never occurred to Scottie that her conversation might

have been overheard. She went to the kitchen, determined to work and not think about Dannan or kissing, but the looks Iris and Finn were sending her way were all too clear.

"Did you hear my conversation with the doctor?" she asked, keeping her voice low, mindful of Corina's ears.

"What conversation?" Finn tried, but Scottie saw through it.

She looked back and forth between the pair of them and saw that they were much too pleased with themselves.

"I was going to work in here today, but now I'm not. I'll be cleaning upstairs."

Finn and Iris did not say a word, not to Scottie or to each other. But as soon as the young widow left the room, their eyes met and they shared a long, satisfied smile.

"What's that?" Old Mrs. Brasic frowned at the bottle in Dannan's hand, her look telling of her suspicion.

"It's the same mixture of herbs that's helped your toothache in the past. My uncle left notes for me about your needs and said this was the best treatment."

"He had no business going off like that," she sulked, tugging her robe about her, clearly taking Doc MacKay's departure very personally.

"He misses Tucker Mills," Dannan told her honestly and waited for the old woman to make the final decision.

"Can't you just leave the bottle with me?" She scowled at him.

"This is my only one, and I might need it. If you'll get some strips of cloth, I'll soak some for you. You can apply them as needed."

Mrs. Brasic was clearly not happy with this answer but still went for the cloths. Her front teeth were healthy, but her back ones gave her regular trouble.

"There you go, Mrs. Brasic," Dannan said when the cloths were ready. "Do you want me to apply one for you?"

"No," she told him shortly, heading to the door to open it.

Dannan didn't need it spelled out. He exited, not expecting a word of thanks and not getting one. On the way to his buggy, he passed Mr. Brasic, whose mood matched that of his wife's. Dannan prayed for both of them as he headed back toward the village green.

"Here, Corina," Scottie said, handing her a small feather duster. "You can dust that bookshelf right there by the door."

"I duss," Corina said.

"I'm sure you do. Do you help Dannan at home?"

Corina's little head bobbed in affirmation, and Scottie was suddenly struck with a thought: She could be Corina's mother in the foreseeable future. She had dreamt during her nap about Dannan asking her to marry him only to mother his child, and she had even wondered if Dannan might be looking only for a marriage of convenience, but actually becoming Corina's mother had slipped past her mind until just this moment.

That morning she had verbally sparred with Dannan over kissing. She knew he was not a man to play with a woman's heart. His talk about kissing had been playful, but in truth, they were contemplating something very serious.

"Sottie," Corina spoke, and Scottie realized she'd called her name a few times already.

"Yes, Corina?"

"I'n done."

"Thank you, Corina. I think you did a fine job."

Scottie hadn't even looked at the shelf before she said this because it didn't matter. At the moment all that mattered was this little girl's heart and the way she had so effectively walked into Scottie's.

∞∞

"The food was all wonderful," Alison told Scottie; both women were in the Peterson parlor. "Thank you so much."

"You're welcome. Were you able to enjoy any of it?"

"As a matter of fact, yes. Marty had the worst of it, but Josh and I pulled through pretty fast."

"Did anyone else get ill?"

"No, I'm thankful to say. Hillary stepped in and took care of us. It wouldn't have been very fun for her if anyone else had come down."

"Corina was sick last week. Dannan kept her home as much as he could."

Alison suddenly smiled. "Have I ever told you that Hillary is something of a matchmaker?"

"No!" Scottie said, having to laugh.

"She is. She was sure that Reese should have married Conner long before Reese even thought of it."

Scottie laughed again. "That's marvelous. Is she getting ready to find a match for herself?"

"No, but you're in her sites right now."

Scottie's mouth opened.

"I know it's soon, Scottie, and she's not being insensitive to your loss, but she wants Dannan to notice you."

Scottie only stared at her pastor's wife, unable to believe she'd just said that. Alison looked right back until she understood what Scottie was not saying.

"Scottie, has he said something?"

"Yes."

"And how do you feel?"

"My feelings are very confused right now."

"May I tell Hillary? She's very discreet."

Scottie shrugged. "I don't mind, but that doesn't mean anything will come of it."

Alison reached over and put her hand on Scottie's arm.

"He's a wonderful man, Scottie. Douglas is so impressed with his heart."

"It means a lot to hear that. I've talked to Reese, and she and Conner feel the same way. From what I know of him, he's very special."

Alison suddenly shook her head and observed, "This has been quite a time for you, hasn't it?"

"It's so true, Alison. If someone had told me six months ago that Eli would suddenly die, and Dannan and I would start to talk about a relationship, I would never have believed them, but here I am in the midst of it."

"Since Dannan brings Corina here each day, do the two of you usually talk?"

"Not every day, but it does give us more opportunities than just meeting on Sundays."

"Oh, Scottie, I don't know if God has this for the two of you or not, but please know that I'll be praying."

Scottie hugged her friend.

"Thank you, Alison. Please pray that I'll talk to Dannan about things that need to be shared and that I won't be anxious."

"I will pray, Scottie, and if you have time, I'll start right now."

It was not an offer that Scottie would refuse. Alison did not linger long in prayer when she was done, but when she left, Scottie knew that this wiser older woman would be remembering her.

"Have you noticed the change in Scottie toward Corina?" Iris asked of Finn at the end of the workday on Thursday. The widow and the little girl had just left for a walk.

"I don't think I have."

"When I went to visit Mercy and her new baby on Monday, they stayed here together. All week Scottie has invited Corina to do everything with her."

"Has she not done that all along?"

"No." Iris frowned at him, wondering how some men could be so obtuse.

Finn missed her frustration with the male population as well. He pushed to his feet and reached for the basket on the table.

"I'm for home. Thanks for the cookies."

"You're welcome. I'll see you in the morning."

Finn was barely out the door when Iris heard the first drops of rain. Her first thought was of Finn, wondering if he was going to make it home in time. Her next thoughts were of Scottie and Corina, and she puzzled where those two might have gone.

Already soaked to the skin, Scottie kept Corina close to her where they were huddled under a large tree. Scottie eyed the growing rivers of mud as well as the continued downpour. She knew that they could not wait it out—they were both shivering too hard—but she was equally uncertain of venturing forth.

"Sottie…" Corina's voice wavered a bit, and Scottie knew they had no choice.

"All right, Corina," Scottie spoke with more assurance than she felt. "I'm going to pick you up, and we're going to walk fast in the rain. It might be cold, but it's only water."

The little girl only shivered against her, and Scottie decided not to waste any more time. She lifted Corina into her arms, left the protection of the tree, and headed back onto the road. They were making good progress when Scottie's foot slipped. On her own she would have caught herself, but with Corina in her arms, they both went down hard. Corina began to cry, and all Scottie could do was wish they hadn't walked so far from home.

"Scottie?" Iris called when she heard the front door and rushed from the kitchen, only to stop short. Dannan was dripping on the rug right inside the front door.

"Scottie's not here?" he asked.

"No, Dannan. She's on a walk, and Corina is with her."

Nineteen

"Where did they go?" Dannan asked Iris, planning to head out and find them.

"I don't know," Iris admitted, her mouth looking strained. "Scottie said only that they were going for a walk and they would be back soon."

"So you didn't notice if they went toward town?"

"They didn't," Iris realized. "They went out the back of the yard past the chickens and then toward the road and trees."

"I'll head that way," Dannan said, moving toward the kitchen. Iris was on his heels, planning to heat water and gather blankets, when the kitchen door opened.

Gasping and shivering, Scottie stumbled in, Corina still in her arms. The little girl was crying, and Scottie was talking.

"Look, Corina, we made it. We'll be warm now. Oh, Dannan," Scottie exclaimed, suddenly spotting him. "We took a fall."

Dannan took Corina from Scottie's arms and began to give orders.

"I'm going into the buttery to undress Corina. Get out of those things, Scottie, and over to the stove. Iris, stoke that fire and put extra kettles on to heat. Where's the tub?"

"In the buttery," Iris answered, bustling between Scottie and the stove, grabbing blankets and towels as she went.

Dannan had disappeared with Corina, and Scottie was trying to work the pins on her dress, but her fingers were too cold. Iris stepped in, and just a minute later, her dress lay in a sodden heap at her feet. Mud was soaked through to her underclothing, but Iris didn't help Scottie out of those until she'd closed the buttery door. By the time Dannan returned to the kitchen, planning to put Corina in a warm tub of water, Scottie was wrapped in a large blanket next to the stove. Her face and hair were still muddy, and she was shivering, but at least she was home.

Iris had put a towel over Scottie's head and now stood behind her to dry her hair. Scottie closed her eyes, willing herself to stop shivering. Plopping Corina into the tub, Dannan told her she would be warm very soon.

"Tea for Scottie," Dannan said next. "Make it hot and strong, Iris."

"Coming right up," that lady agreed as she left the towel with Scottie and began the preparations. At the same time, she began to talk to Corina in a way that was familiar to that little girl.

"How are you doing, Miss Corina? You haven't had a bath in Iris' kitchen in a few weeks. Do you need a cloth in there to wash yourself?"

Through her shivers she managed to nod, and Dannan took the one Iris handed to him and began to sponge Corina's small shoulders and head. She was warming fast, but he could still see the upset and confusion on her face.

"Were you hurt when you fell, Scottie?"

Scottie opened her eyes and peeked out at Dannan, the towel still draped over her head.

"I'm not sure right now. Is Corina all right?"

"She's got a bruise on her back, but I don't see anything else."

"We fell in the road. There might have been a rock."

Dannan touched Corina's skin, satisfied to feel the warmth returning, and looked over to see the fresh clothing Iris had laid out. Dannan dried her briskly, rubbing more warmth back into her skin, and then helped her into her clothing. Iris had a blanket to go around her after that, and then Dannan's attentions shifted to Scottie.

"I'm going to take Corina into the parlor so you can check for cuts and bruises. Send Iris if you need me."

"All right."

When the women were alone, Scottie moved gingerly. She still felt a little cold, and she was beginning to ache.

"Why don't we get the rest of that mud from your hair," Iris suggested. "You lean over the tub, and I'll pour the water."

Scottie agreed, and in the process, Iris saw the bruises. Her arms were already beginning to turn black and blue, but there were no cuts.

"Dannan should look at those."

"It's just bruising," Scottie returned, trying to dismiss her, but Iris wanted her to be checked.

"I'll go and get some clothing for you, and then Dannan can look. How about the rest of you?"

"The rest of me is fine," Scottie stuttered through chattering teeth, but in truth she could tell she was going to ache all over. However, she wasn't going to mention this to Dannan or Iris. Still working to get warm, she dressed in the short-sleeved dress Iris had found her and then put on a sweater. Hair brushed but wet and hanging down her back, Scottie went to the parlor.

"How are you?" Dannan asked as he stood from his place on the sofa.

"Fine, thank you," Scottie answered but then turned her attention to Corina. "How are you?" she asked, taking the other side of the little girl and sitting close on the sofa. "Are you warm now?"

Corina climbed into Scottie's lap. Scottie winced but didn't object, putting her arms around the three-year-old and holding her close.

"There you are," Iris came from the kitchen saying.

"Yes, and leave those muddy things, Iris," Scottie spoke. "I'll get them later."

"Have you let Dannan check your arms?" Iris had come with her own agenda.

"They're just bruises," Scottie argued, but Iris was having none of it. Dannan, it seemed, wasn't willing to let it rest either.

"Here, Corina," he directed her. "Sit here on the other side of me a minute so I can see Scottie's arms."

After Corina had been lifted out of the way, Scottie pushed her sweater sleeve up and extended her right arm. Dannan held her arm to inspect the skin. Dannan took his time as the room was growing dim. It would be dark soon, but more than that, the rain was still falling so the cloud cover was heavy.

"Corina," Iris called. "Do you want to help me with the tea?"

The little girl didn't hesitate to accompany the cook, and just moments later, Dannan and Scottie were alone. Dannan was still checking Scottie's arms, but even when he finished, he did not let go of her hand. Scottie looked into his eyes.

"I was frightened today," Dannan admitted.

"About Corina being hurt?"

"Both of you," Dannan said, not able to put his thoughts into words.

"I wasn't scared, but I regret taking Corina out. The storm came on so fast, and the temperature dropped with it. I could have kicked myself."

"Thank you for bringing her home safely."

Scottie realized now his hands still enveloped her hand, and her eyes dropped to study them. Dannan's hands were larger and darker, his fingers long and lean, making hers look short by comparison.

"What are you thinking?" Dannan asked.

"That it's nice to have you hold my hand."

"Yes, it is," Dannan agreed, wanting to hold her as well but mostly wishing he could explain what had happened in his heart in the last hour. He was trying to find the words when Iris called them for tea.

Dannan knew it was best to let it go, but as soon as he had some time alone with Scottie, he planned to tell her what was on his mind.

Scottie did not want to get out of bed on Wednesday morning. She was no longer chilled, but she ached all through her shoulders and back. Her knees were also bruised, and it hurt to bend them. However, it was morning, and the need to relieve herself forced her to move. Dressing, on the other hand, was a different story. Still wearing her nightgown and bathrobe, Scottie made her way down the stairs. Ready for a cup of tea, she thought this would be a fine day to let Iris handle everything.

"How are you?" Dannan asked of Corina when she woke, sitting on her bed to lean close and kiss her.

"Danna?"

"Yeah?"

"Sottie wet."

"Yes, she was." Dannan laughed a little. "So were you."

"I'n hungry."

"Well that's a good sign. Let's head to the kitchen."

Corina climbed from the bed, just remembering to grab her doll, and preceded Dannan down the stairs.

Dannan watched her move with ease, and he knew beyond a shadow of a doubt that Scottie would not have fared nearly so well.

"Are you going to get dressed today?" Iris asked of Scottie. She had been at the kitchen table with a pot of tea since the older woman arrived.

"I should have before I came downstairs. Climbing back up to my room doesn't appeal to me at all."

"Have more tea," Iris offered, refilling the pot with boiling water and adding more leaves. She was in the midst of this when she heard the front door. "I'll get it," she offered, and Scottie was more than happy to sit still. She sipped her tea until Iris and Corina came in. Corina marched directly over to Scottie, who bent to hug her.

"Dannan asked after you," Iris mentioned. "I think he wanted to see you. I told him to come for dinner."

Scottie only nodded, watching Corina head to her little table to play. Scottie was learning what Dannan had already figured out: She had taken the worst of the fall.

"That was delicious, Iris, thank you," Finn complimented after dinner, a sentiment echoed by Scottie and Dannan.

"Scottie made that crumble," Iris added, more than willing to give praise where deserved.

Scottie rose to get the coffeepot and fill everyone's cup. The men had more dessert, Dannan's latest book selection was discussed, and Corina wanted more potatoes. The meal had come to a quiet close when Dannan said he had to leave. He asked Scottie to walk him to the door.

Scottie stood and waited until Dannan said goodbye to Corina.

"Have a good time this afternoon," he said gently, kneeling down to speak directly into her face. "And help Iris."

"I help."

"Yes, you do," Dannan smiled at her, loving her sincere little expression. "Give me a kiss."

As soon as the two had said their goodbyes, Scottie walked to the front door with Dannan. She didn't open it, sure that he had something to say.

"I don't have a lot of time," Dannan began, "but I needed to check one thing with you."

"Okay."

"Are you feeling as though we should continue as we are, or is there some reason you would wish us to not pursue a relationship?"

Scottie had not been expecting this. She studied Dannan's intense gaze and asked, "Did something happen, Dannan?"

"Yesterday," Dannan answered, "I thought you and Corina might be hurt, and that did things to my heart. I thought it only fair to tell you how serious I am about us. I also thought it only fair to my own heart to find out whether you're still in this with me."

"Yes, I am. I wish I could figure out what I'm feeling, but just because I can't define it doesn't mean I want us to stop."

Dannan nodded. That was all he needed to know.

"Can you explain a little more of what happened yesterday?" Scottie asked.

Dannan pulled out his pocket watch, touched the latch that opened the case, and consulted the time.

"Not at the moment," he said with regret, "but we'll plan on that."

Scottie had no choice but to nod. It seemed that they never got to finish their discussions, and she still felt a little off balance most of the time.

It was at that moment that Scottie realized Dannan hadn't left. Scottie met his gaze, her brows rising in question.

"Do you know how much I want to stay and talk to you?" Dannan asked.

"I guess I didn't." Scottie admitted. "I wish you could stay too."

Dannan sighed a little and stared at her face. He breathed, almost inaudibly, "You're so beautiful," before slipping out the door.

Scottie did not know what made her turn. The sermon had just started, but something caught her eye. She hadn't heard the door open, but it must have, since Finn was quietly slipping into the meetinghouse. He didn't look around or draw attention to himself but sat in a rear pew and looked to the front.

Scottie's heart clenched with so much emotion that all she could do was pray. She knew the song they stood to sing but didn't join in. In fact, Douglas was starting his sermon before Scottie stopped thanking God for sending Finn and began to listen.

Before Scottie could invite the Muldoon family for Sunday

dinner, Reese stopped by the house and invited her to join them, also telling her that Dannan and Corina would be there. Scottie was happy to be included and even took dessert.

The meal was a delightful time of conversation and good food until the topic of horseshoes came up. Troy had challenged both Conner and Dannan to a game. The men begged to put off dessert and trooped outside, looking for all to see like children at play.

"Well, Corina," Reese said as she turned to that little person when the women were alone in the dining room. "I think we need to have our own fun."

"Hair, Reese!" Corina said with delight.

"What does she want to play?" Scottie asked, rising to follow the two, who were now headed to the small parlor at the back of the house. She noticed that Reese was in the process of taking her hair down.

"She likes to brush and play with my hair," Reese answered, fingers still at work. "Doesn't she do that with you?"

"No."

"Sottie…" Corina had come to take her hand and was pulling her to the sofa to join Reese.

"Take your hair down," Reese directed as hers fell in thick waves around her shoulders and back.

Corina had gone to a small side table, opened the drawer, and taken out a hairbrush. From there she climbed onto the sofa to stand behind Reese, hairbrush ready. By the time Scottie had the pins out of her own hair, she had made a fine mess of Reese's dark red locks and was ready for Scottie.

Scottie's hair, also red, but with more blonde to it, had curls aplenty, and the three-year-old was swiftly fascinated. She discarded the brush in order to wrap the fat curls around her fist, her face rapt.

"What is she doing back there?" Scottie wished to know.

"She's quite taken with your curls," Reese laughed, picking up the hairbrush to fix her own hair and then brushing Scottie's where Corina had made snarls.

"Sottie has spurles," the women heard Corina say, and they laughed together. Corina's vocabulary was always a surprise.

The opening of the back door sounded during the midst of this, and the women waited for the men to find them.

"Well, now," Conner smiled at the sight. "Two victims today, Corina?"

"Sottie has spurles," Corina told the big man.

"She has what?" Conner looked to his wife, who was laughing once again.

"It's her word for curls," Scottie explained. Some hair had fallen into her face, but she could still see.

"What's the word for dessert?" Troy asked.

Reese laughed again before asking, "Who won?"

"I did," Troy announced, his smile only slightly proud.

"In that case, I'll get the coffee boiling."

Troy and Conner trailed after Reese, but Dannan had taken a seat across from Scottie and his daughter.

"This looks fun," Dannan observed, hoping he was masking his true feelings. Scottie looked even more appealing with her hair down.

"Corina certainly thinks so," Scottie said, pushing hair from her face.

"Corina," Reese called from the other room. "Can you come here?"

"You'd better go," her dad encouraged her, but he sat still. The moment Corina was gone, Scottie began to gather her hair. Dannan spotted the hair pins in her lap, quickly sat on the sofa with her, and plucked them into his hand.

"I need those," Scottie stated matter-of-factly, still gathering and twisting.

"Leave it down."

The look she shot him was withering, but Dannan only smiled.

"Is Scottie a nickname?"

"No. Give me the pins."

"Where did you get it?"

Scottie had her hair in place now and needed only to secure it, but Dannan had not relinquished the pins.

With one hand holding her hair in place and the other held out for the pins, Scottie negotiated, "I'll tell you as soon I get the pins."

Dannan gave her one.

"I need the rest," she said, stabbing the one into place.

Dannan gave her one more and then sat back. "Story first."

"And I'll get the pins?"

"Yes."

"All of them?"

"Yes."

"All right. I was born in a home for girls and was named by the matron. She'd been told I was a boy, so she named me Scott after her brother. By the time she learned I was a girl, she'd already documented my name in her book. She simply decided to add an *ie* to make it feminine."

The story told, Scottie's hand went out and Dannan gave up the pins. Scottie made short work of the task and then looked at the man on the other end of the sofa.

"You're a tease, Dannan MacKay."

"I think I'm just a man who knows what he likes."

"And what's that exactly?"

Reese called to say dessert was ready before Dannan could answer. They both stood and started toward the door, but Dannan took Scottie's hand and stopped her.

"This next week, I want the two of us to find some time to talk."

"Uninterrupted time?" Scottie asked.

"Yes!"

Nothing more was said on their plans to talk or Dannan's reaction to Scottie's hair, but Scottie was more aware of him that afternoon than she'd ever been.

"What did you think of the sermon, Finn?" Scottie asked Monday morning by the garden fence. After the service he had slipped away before she could catch him.

"I don't have an opinion yet," he spoke honestly, "but I'm thinking about it."

"Well, I'm glad you were there" was all Scottie said. She didn't press him. Finn expected no less from her, but when she only smiled at him and kept working, he felt himself relax. She hadn't even asked if he would be returning. He planned on it, but not having pressure on the issue was just what he needed to bring him back.

Dannan went to the Peterson house for dinner on Monday. Iris served a pork roast with all the trimmings, and the five of them feasted. Not until the end of the meal did Dannan take up his business with Iris.

"Do you cut hair?" Dannan asked of her.

"Certainly."

"I need some of Corina's to come off. She wants long hair,

but I've told her that has to wait. If she gives you a hard time, I need to know about it."

Iris agreed and went to work on the job right after Corina's nap. What she was not prepared for were Corina's sad tears. There was no fit, no fighting, and no disrespect, but the fact that this haircut broke the girl's small heart was more than obvious.

Corina sat quietly outside on a tall stool under the sheet Iris had draped around her, silent little tears trickling down her face. Iris got through it, but just barely. Indeed, she waited only until Dannan was back in her kitchen at the end of the day to tell him what she thought.

"I can't do it again, Dannan," she whispered. "It like to broke my heart."

Dannan looked over to see what Iris meant. Corina, sober as a judge, sat at her little table, not playing or even holding her doll. Dannan wanted to tell her how nice she looked, but he could see she was ready to cry again.

"You need a wife." Iris shared her view without warning, her voice still low.

"Is that right?"

"Yes! A wife would be willing to have it a bit longer."

Dannan smiled into the cook's eyes but didn't comment. Iris tried not to smile back, but it didn't work. Scottie chose that moment to arrive in the kitchen and go straight to Corina.

"Here, Corina." She lifted the little girl and stood her on the play table. She proceeded to tie a thin pink ribbon to a tiny lock of Corina's hair and stepped back to admire it. "You look so pretty. You can wear this every day. If Dannan can't put it in for you, bring it with you, and I'll fix it for you."

Corina reached for the ribbon, touching it carefully, and smiled at Scottie. Dannan and Iris watched, smiles appearing for them as well. Iris then turned with raised brows to Dannan, who whispered to her that he was working on the suggestion, but some things could not be rushed.

Iris did not look convinced, and once again it was time for Dannan to take his daughter home. He did so, telling himself it was time to get Scottie to himself. He didn't know when or how, but this was the week, and he was determined to do it.

Twenty

"I have an unusual request to make of you," Dannan said to Conner on Tuesday, having thought on the issue for hours the night before.

"Shoot."

"Scottie and I need a place we can talk. I'd like it to be somewhat private, but not so private that it would damage her reputation."

"Why don't you use our small parlor?" Conner suggested.

"I must admit I was hoping you would suggest that."

"That's fine. When are you thinking?"

"I haven't talked to Scottie about this yet, but I was hoping for tomorrow evening."

"Come for tea," Conner said in his usual welcoming way. "The two of you can talk afterward, and we'll keep Corina occupied."

"I'm going to ask Iris to keep her. Scottie and I very much need some uninterrupted time, and if Corina knows I'm in the house, that might not happen."

"Good enough. I'll tell Reese you'll be joining us."

Dannan thanked Conner sincerely, unbelievably excited to visit with Scottie in this way. Their lives were busy, and time to talk without interruption simply never presented itself.

Dannan left the bank building to go on with his rounds, his

step light. If tomorrow evening worked for both Scottie and Iris, it would be a date.

"Well, Scottie," Doyle greeted when she entered his store. "How are you this warm day?"

Scottie laughed. "I think hot describes it better, Doyle. Warm is what it was in the night."

"Yes, and after that cold rain last week."

"Corina and I got caught out in it. I didn't think I would ever get warm again."

"How is she doing, Scottie?" Doyle leaned across the counter with interest. "Cathy and I pray for her every day. How do you think Corina is managing?"

"I think she's doing well. Dannan has told me she'll ask for her mother when they're home, but she never mentions her when she is with us."

"Maybe Dannan will marry, and that will fill the need in her heart."

"Maybe." Scottie smiled, but Doyle didn't catch it.

"What can I get for you?" he asked as the conversation moved on.

Not until Scottie left did she realize how comfortable she was with the idea of marrying Dannan. She wasn't sure when her heart had settled in that place. It couldn't have been too long ago, considering how recently Eli had still been with them, but at the moment, marrying Dannan seemed like the most normal thing in the world.

"It's important to me that you know something," Scottie began early in their conversation in the small parlor at the big house. "I kept Corina at arm's length for a while. Her parents' death was too reminiscent of the girls' home."

"I couldn't tell you were doing that," Dannan admitted.

"Iris noticed and tried to push me, but I had to do it in my time."

"What was it like?"

"I didn't expect to feel that way, but I saw our faces in Corina. She adjusted to Iris in a way that only God could have planned, but at times she looked vulnerable, and when that happened it was like I was an orphan all over again."

"Did you ever know your mother?" Dannan asked.

"No, she had me and left. When I was about eleven, Matron did tell me that my mother was very young but from a good home. Years later I thought back on it and realized that was not how things normally worked at the home. If the mother lived through childbirth, she was expected to take the child with her. I get the impression that my mother's family must have paid handsomely to walk away like they did."

"Were you never tempted to look for them?"

"I wasn't tempted to find my mother, but even if I had, my last name of Davis was not my family's name. It was given to me by Matron. Without a name to work with, it would have been close to impossible."

Dannan nodded, taking it all in and then asked, "And you were there until when?"

"I was 12 when Mrs. Peterson came looking for a girl."

Dannan smiled. "Did she ever tell you what she saw?"

Scottie nodded, a little embarrassed to repeat it but willing to try.

"I was just starting to look like a woman. Mrs. Peterson told me that she took one look at my beautiful face and feared what would happen to me. We were worked hard at the orphanage. The threat of deserved punishment was very real, but we were never assaulted. Mrs. Peterson couldn't have known that. She just knew that she had to rescue me right then."

Something clenched in Dannan's gut to think of her in the girls' home, cared for but not loved.

"What was it like at first, coming to the Petersons?"

"Strange and a bit scary, even though they were all so kind. I went on a trial basis. Technically I wasn't adopted, but very soon it felt like I had been. I learned later that they knew right away that they wanted me to stay, but I didn't understand that for a while, even though I was treated so well with time off and my own room."

"And Eli? Did you get to know him right away?"

"Oh, yes. Mrs. Peterson took me everywhere. I read to Eli from the first week." Scottie's voice suddenly caught as a memory came flooding back. "The first time we met he pretended to get my name wrong. He called me Snotty just to tease me. We became friends because of that."

"And you married when?"

"When his mother died. I had found a place to live and was looking for work when Eli suggested that I marry him. At first I was appalled, but it didn't take long for me to see that nothing else made sense. With his mother gone, Eli needed me more than ever."

"What about your needs?"

"God was just taking care of me, Dannan. There is no other explanation. I was only 18, and although Tucker Mills is full of fine people, it's not perfect. I would have been rather unprotected had I left Eli's household."

"Were you connected to the church family at that time?"

"Yes, and I could have gone to them, but I didn't know as much as I know now, and I'm not sure that would have occurred to me."

Dannan was still taking it in when Scottie asked a question.

"What did you want to tell me last week after the rainstorm?"

"Only that my heart is certain about you."

"And that happened because of the storm?"

"Not just that, but if I'd had any doubts, they disappeared when I thought you might be hurt."

Scottie was thinking on this when Dannan asked, "What about you and your feelings about us right now?"

"You're going to think this odd. It makes perfect sense to me that we'll be married someday, but as to how I'm feeling, I'm still confused about that."

"I'm glad you told me. I think joining the lives of two people is very hard, and it would be harder still if we didn't love each other. We need to keep talking, but we can't get married until we're sure we're in love."

"Why is it so hard?" Scottie asked. Her own experience with marriage was nothing like Dannan described.

"I think because we each have our own set of needs, and sometimes those needs don't get met in the way we think they're going to. And look at how hard it's been for us to even find time to talk. If we were married, we'd see each other off and on during the day, but not necessarily be alone or able to talk."

"Which reminds me," Scottie put in. "At times I'm afraid to become Corina's mother. Her mother sounds like she was a wonderful person, and I don't know if I can fill her shoes."

"Corina adores you," Dannan assured her, not aware she felt this way. "And everything I've witnessed in you only reassures me that you're perfect for the job."

"Is that really how you feel?"

"Yes, but tell me why you fear this."

"It's ongoing. On days when I feel tired or even unthankful and complaining in my heart, I can take time for myself. A child's needs must be met every day. Corina can't wait for me to get myself settled. She'll need me no matter what."

"Your point is a good one, but I'm not seeing this selfish person, Scottie. You might have days when you're tired, but your care of Eli could not be faulted. I realize you had Finn to aid in that, but I haven't seen this unthankful, moody person who needs time alone."

Scottie stared at him. Where had all this come from? She realized she was not a moody person and did work hard to be thankful and keep on, no matter what.

"I guess I'm just being tempted to fear," she said.

"I can ask you about it in the days to come, but I'm not concerned about that."

Scottie was glad to hear that and then realized this was nothing like she'd imagined. How could they sit so calmly across the room from each other and discuss this life-changing event with such clear minds? Scottie said as much, and Dannan smiled.

"I'm glad to think I've fooled you into thinking my head is clear."

Scottie laughed. "What does that mean?"

"Only that my emotions concerning you are so strong, at times they gallop around the room."

"What kind of emotions?"

"Love, among other things."

"You already feel like you love me?"

"Yes."

Scottie stared at him as a thousand thoughts ran through her mind. Why hadn't she seen this? It was so obvious—the things he said, the way he watched her.

"I think Eli must have been right," Scottie whispered, her voice holding all the wonder she felt. "I don't know how to do this; I don't even know what it looks like."

"Courtship?"

"Yes. You've had feelings for me all along—you've even told me that—but I just didn't see it."

Dannan smiled a little. "I'll keep that in mind in the future."

"What exactly?"

"That I might need to explain things to you and not just expect you to know."

"It's true, Dannan." Scottie jumped to her feet. "I don't get this! It's all so new." She stopped and suddenly faced him. "Do you know what? You talked about Adam and Eve kissing, and I had no idea you were really talking about us. Not until right at the end did I catch on."

Dannan had to laugh.

"Don't laugh at this, Dannan. I'm pathetic."

"I think the word you're looking for is innocent, and it's very endearing."

His voice had changed. Scottie sat back down and looked at him.

"It's scary to be so far out of my depth."

"I'm sure it is, and I'm also sure it seems to you that I know exactly what I'm doing, but that couldn't be less true. I flounder around on a regular basis. I'm just not sure you know me well enough at this point to see it."

Scottie realized how much she wanted to know him. They had talked for several hours, but more was needed. Scottie told Dannan how she felt, and he agreed with her. His own feelings wanted to rush ahead, but just as he said, that would lead to disaster if she didn't love him.

It had become very dark outside by the time Scottie admitted she was tired. Dannan walked her home. At her door, he asked, "I'm sure Reese would welcome us on Sunday. Shall I check with her?"

"Actually, the Muldoons are coming here. Why don't you and Corina join us?"

"I'll plan on it," Dannan said, wishing her goodnight and knowing it was time to leave. If he stayed any longer, he would kiss her. Much as he would have enjoyed it, he didn't know how Scottie was feeling on that issue. Not to mention the fact that his daughter needed to be picked up and put in her own bed.

The last Sunday in August was just the beginning. Scottie started by inviting the Muldoons and then Conner, Reese, and Troy. After that, Jace, Maddie, Valerie, Doyle, and Cathy all ate at Scottie's house—Dannan and Corina always in attendance.

The hospitality that Scottie had yearned to extend when Eli was still alive became a normal part of her life. All of her renters were invited in turn, and one Sunday she even asked Finn and Iris to join her, not allowing them to lift a finger. The time between them was especially sweet.

September gave way to October, the days and nights cooling fast and colors changing all around them. Reese had asked Scottie and Dannan to join them at the big house for dinner, but the meal no more began when Reese's pains hit her.

All could see that, for Conner, having Dannan on hand was his idea of a miracle. The anxious father hovered in the background while Troy and Scottie played downstairs with Corina.

Conner came and went, as did Dannan, but hours passed. At one point, Reese asked to see Scottie, who ventured upstairs, her heart begging God to keep her friend safe.

"You're still here," Reese said with tired pleasure. "I wasn't sure."

"It's too exciting to leave." Scottie took Reese's hand as she spoke. "I wish it wasn't so long for you."

"Dannan says it will be a while yet."

"But it is going to happen," Scottie said with a smile. "And October is such a nice month to be born."

"When is your birthday, Scottie?"

"October."

Reese was still laughing when the next contraction hit. And unfortunately for Reese, Dannan was right. Troy ended up walking Scottie and Corina home so that the little girl could sleep through the night. At the big house, midnight came and went, and still no baby. Not until the wee hours did Reese need to push, and then things happened very quickly.

Howling for all he was worth, the youngest Kingsley entered the world at nearly two o'clock. Troy had still not gone to bed. He sat in the upstairs hallway and waited for Conner to emerge. The older man shed his own tears when he saw Conner's.

"A boy." Conner's soft voice was hoarser than usual.

"Reese?"

"Worn out, but that's all."

Conner didn't linger. After hugging his friend and business partner, he went back to his wife, and Troy sought his own bed. Daylight would arrive before anyone was ready. Troy did not fall immediately to sleep, but that was all right. They had a baby boy, and Reese was doing fine.

"Danna!" Corina squealed when he arrived at the Peterson house just after breakfast.

"Hey, you," he said, scooping her up to share a hug and kiss.

All the adults had come when they heard her voice and were waiting for the news.

"A boy," Dannan wasted no time in sharing. "Big and healthy. Reese is doing great."

"If I know Reese," Iris said, "she's already out of that bed and about her business."

"You're probably right," Finn agreed.

"How late was it?" Scottie asked.

"About two o'clock."

"Did they name him?" Iris thought to ask.

"Not before I left."

"Will you be stopping back today?"

"I'm headed there now."

"Tell her we'll have dinner ready for them today," Scottie offered. "Finn can bring it at about noon."

"I'll do it."

Dannan took a few more minutes with Corina and then left. Scottie joined Iris in the kitchen, working alongside her because two meals were needed. Iris added ingredients where she could, but Scottie made a separate dessert. And just as they'd said, Finn made a noon delivery to a grateful Troy and Conner.

Finn, still smiling over what he'd learned, delighted in telling the ladies he knew the baby's name. He didn't give it up that easily, however. Iris was serving their own dessert when Finn announced that the newest person in Tucker Mills was named Levi Conner Kingsley.

Scottie waited until later in the week to visit Reese, and when she arrived, it was to find Maddie in attendance as well. Valerie was with Cathy. The three women, Maddie holding Levi, settled in the parlor, and neither Maddie nor Scottie could believe how good Reese looked. In fact, when the women offered to come and help, Reese had to be honest.

"It's kind of you, but I don't need it. I've been up and around since early yesterday morning."

"What did Dannan say about that?" Maddie asked, concern in her voice. "Every time I stood up, I bled heavily. Are you sure you're all right?"

"I'm fine, and Dannan doesn't seem to have issues with my being active this soon."

Maddie was glad to hear it. It had taken her a while to feel good again. She bent her head over the baby again, a round bundle in her arms. He was so pretty and looked to be pounds heavier than Valerie at this age.

"How is he doing?" Scottie asked.

"He likes to be awake in the night. Eventually I'll let him cry, but not now." Reese's smile was very content. "It's too fun to hold him."

"Speaking of which—" Scottie prompted, her eyes on Maddie.

"Must I?" Maddie teased.

"Yes, it's my turn."

Maddie surrendered Levi into Scottie's waiting arms, but the move was not successful. Levi woke and wanted to eat, and Reese ended up having to take him. Still working on her breast-feeding skills, Reese was thankful Maddie was on hand. Levi settled down after a bit of work, allowing the women a comfortable visit for the next hour.

"Danna, I sleep here," Corina told him when he arrived to get her on Friday.

"Yes, you did," he agreed. "The night Levi was born."

"No, Danna. I sleep here."

Dannan looked at her in confusion and then to Iris.

"She's been saying it all day. I believe she wants to spend the night."

"Is Scottie here?"

"Not right now."

"Not tonight, Corina," Dannan had no choice but to say.

"We'll have to ask Scottie about that some time, but not tonight."

The little girl was not convinced. She turned toward the kitchen, calling Scottie's name. Dannan went after her.

"No, Corina. It's not going to work. You cannot stay here tonight."

The expression of disappointment gave way to stubbornness and anger. Dannan didn't wait for tears or an outburst but knelt down swiftly to speak into Corina's face.

"You will not pout or cry about this. Do you understand me?"

Corina did understand. She was sober as she said goodbye to Iris and thanked her. There was no scene. Dannan had brought the buggy, so they arrived home swiftly, and as Dannan expected, Corina put the whole thing behind her.

Not until they'd had tea and cleaned the kitchen did Dannan realize he'd been so concentrated on Corina's behavior he hadn't even asked Iris where Scottie might be. Wanting to see her and wondering how she was spending her evening stayed on his mind the rest of the night.

"Have I made any sense, Finn?" Scottie asked that man as the two walked along the road.

"You love Dannan," Finn stated plainly, and Scottie stopped.

"I guess that is what I'm saying to you, isn't it?"

"Yes, but something is still bothering you. I can hear it in your voice."

Scottie's brow furrowed with concern, but she didn't speak.

"I think I know what it is," Finn offered.

"What?"

"Eli. You feel disloyal to him."

"Yes." Her voice wobbled slightly. "I never had this feeling with him. We were friends, and we cared for each other, but it wasn't like this."

"And he didn't expect it to be like this, Scottie." Finn began to walk again, not moving fast but wanting Scottie home before it grew much cooler. "He struggled with his inabilities at times, but for the most part, he knew what he was capable of and rested in that. Do you know what peace it gave him to have you take over the accounts and learn them so well?"

"Why was that?"

"He knew you would know what to do in the future and how to manage it all. He was constantly correcting his mother's mistakes. She was terrible with ciphering, but he rarely had to correct you. In fact, you caught his mistakes more often than you made any."

Scottie felt a little better, but there was still a weight.

"Have you told Dannan?" Finn asked.

"No, but I want to soon."

"Good. After the wedding he can move into the house, and from then on his house can be used for his office."

Scottie stopped and stared up at him.

"You've thought this all out."

"Of course. Iris and I have been working on it for weeks. You and Dannan will take Mrs. Peterson's room, and Corina will go into Eli's. Your room and my room will be free for any new little ones who arrive."

Scottie couldn't keep her mouth closed. When Finn saw her stunned expression, he only laughed without apology. He also told her to be done worrying about the issue. He left her at her front door with a final word about telling Dannan and took himself home.

Twenty-One

"Mrs. Greenlowe was here again?" Conner questioned on Saturday night.

"Yes, it's the third time," Reese said with a pleased laugh. "She's utterly taken with your son."

Conner's smile matched her own as he looked down at the baby in his arms. Reese watched them for a moment, amazed over the miracle of Levi's birth.

"I think he looks like my nephew, Blaine," Conner mentioned. "Did you meet him?"

"I think so." Reese took a moment to remember. "Actually, I'm glad you mentioned your family. I hope you know that as soon as Dalton gets your letter about Levi's birth, he's going to be here."

Reese was talking about Conner's oldest sibling, a huge man like Conner with a heart and personality to match.

"I'm sure you're right. And he might bring the family. Will you be able to manage?"

"I think so. I'll have to tell you if I can't."

"I hope you do. Oh, my," Conner exclaimed. "Someone is wet."

"I can take him," Reese offered.

"No, thank you," Conner replied, refusing the help. "We'll get along just fine." The new father, looking very pleased with the task, headed out the door and upstairs to take care of his tiny son's needs.

Reese smiled at the sight of her very small son securely tucked in the arms of his large father. She could see Conner's face in her son, and that gave her no end of pleasure.

Settling back on the sofa, knitting needles in hand, Reese had a chance to wonder how Scottie was doing in the other room.

"Thank you for coming." Scottie spoke to Dannan in a formal manner as she paced the small parlor floor, sounding as though she were addressing a meeting.

"Certainly." Dannan watching her carefully, nervous about what might be coming.

"I've been thinking about things. I even talked to Finn, and he said I should tell you right away."

Dannan waited, watching her walk back and forth, wishing she would just say what was on her mind.

"I'm in love with you," Scottie said, not stopping or even looking at him. "I think the realization came on me slowly. At first I felt so disloyal to Eli that I tried to ignore the reality of it, but Finn told me this was just what Eli wanted. He said it was right and good."

Without warning, Dannan was in front of her. Scottie had no choice but to stop, her eyes looking up into his. Dannan touched her cheek with his hand, loving the soft silkiness of her skin. He looked into her eyes, saw how tense she was, and forced himself not to kiss her. Instead, he took Scottie's hand

and led her to the sofa. He sat down on the arm, leaving Scottie to stand in front of him, putting his head slightly below hers.

"Why did we come over here?"

"Because I think you're a little afraid of our first kiss. I'm so much taller. This way, you can start or stop at any point."

Loving his thoughtfulness, Scottie brushed the lock of hair from his forehead and saw the tiny scar she'd put there.

"Do you remember when I gave you this?" she asked, touching the spot with a gentle finger.

"Yes, I do." Dannan smiled. "I was already taken with you, and then there you were, looking all concerned and adorable in that bonnet."

"I can't believe you didn't find me dangerous."

"Only to my heart."

Scottie smiled. She was slowly seeing what a romantic he was. Unable to help herself, she put her hands on either side of his face. Bending just enough, she kissed him so briefly he thought he might have imagined it.

"I've never done this," she whispered.

"Technically, I haven't either."

"What did that mean?"

"Just that I've *imagined* kissing you many times."

Scottie smiled. "I have too. Yesterday for the first time."

"And does this match what you imagined?" Dannan asked.

Scottie bit her lip and stepped back.

"Stand up," she told Dannan. "Now, let's try."

The kiss they shared was slow and sweet, Dannan's arms holding her close, and Scottie's arms squeezing him tight. After a moment, Dannan pulled back enough to look into her face.

"Like you dreamed?"

Scottie just kept the teasing smile from her face. "Not quite. We'd better try again."

"Scottie and I want to be married," Dannan told Douglas on Sunday evening, Scottie's hand in his. Both Douglas and Alison were in the parlor with their guests, Corina playing in the other room with the children.

Douglas smiled before requesting, "Tell me how this came about."

"As a matter of fact," Scottie began, "Eli instigated it."

Douglas' surprised face was comical to Scottie. She laughed a little and then waited to hear what he had to say.

"I've got to know more." Douglas' voice was very dry, and again Scottie laughed.

"He spoke to me," Dannan filled in this time. "It was during one of his spells. He could barely talk, but he wanted me to know that when he was gone, I was to love and marry Scottie."

"I must be honest, Dannan—I've never heard of such a thing."

"So he didn't discussed it with you?" Scottie asked. "I've wondered about that."

"No, he didn't. I can't think of too many topics we didn't discuss, but—" Douglas suddenly stopped. "That's not true. I do recall his telling me that he prayed almost daily that a man would come along to take care of you should he die. I'd almost forgotten about that."

Dannan and Scottie watched emotions chase across Douglas' face. They could tell his mind was casting back in time to his many visits with Eli.

"He spoke to Finn about this, didn't he?"

"Yes, and that's been very helpful."

Douglas nodded and had more questions about Eli's involvement, but eventually he began to question Dannan and Scottie about their relationship and the future. He spent a long time asking Scottie how she felt about marrying again so soon. It was good to hear the way they'd both been talking to Conner and Reese about the subject.

Douglas ended up so impressed with their answers that he could not object to the marriage for any reason. Nevertheless, he asked if he could meet with them one more time before they chose a day. Their willingness to do as he asked further confirmed for their pastor that Dannan and Scottie were making the right move.

"How did she do?" Dannan asked when he arrived a few weeks later at the Peterson house. Corina had spent the night.

"Very well," Scottie replied from the parlor sofa where they were alone. Corina was eating her breakfast.

"What's this?" Dannan tapped the paper in Scottie's hand and sat next to her.

"Just a list of things I want to get done for the wedding."

Dannan's hand came up, and Scottie felt him touch her hair. Not until a lock of hair fell over her ear did she understand what he was up to. She was turning to tell him no and found his face very close.

"Wear it down," he entreated softly.

"No," she whispered right back. "If Corina sees it like this, she'll want to play, and I have a full day of work ahead."

Dannan's only answer was to reach to the other side and steal another pin. When Scottie had hair over both ears, Dannan smiled at her.

"You'll just have to tell her no."

"And what do I tell you?"

Dannan smiled. "Always yes."

Scottie could not resist his smile or voice. When he leaned to kiss her, she melted inside. They were still sitting close, talking and occasionally kissing, when Corina found them.

"Hair, Sottie!" She didn't miss a thing. "Sottie has spurles," she told her father, looking for the brush.

"Come here a minute," Dannan called to her. "Scottie can't play hair with you right now, but as soon as she can, she'll tell you. All right?"

Dannan was very proud of his daughter when she agreed right away. They had been talking about obeying the first time she was asked, and she was making an effort.

"Sottie has spurles," she announced once again, this time from Dannan's lap.

"I think you might have curls too, Corina," Scottie told her, reaching up to adjust the ribbon. Scottie had found a new one, this time in green.

"I've got a dress for you to try on today," Scottie remembered and told her future daughter. "Remind me after dinner."

"You do know," Dannan said, keeping his voice quiet, "that she's going to ask you about that a dozen times between now and then."

"Do you mean she might nag me," Scottie teased, "like a certain man concerning my hair?"

Dannan could not hold his smile, but he still teased right back. "It won't be long before I'll be living here, Scottie Peterson, and you might find that you can't locate a single hairpin in all the house."

Scottie was ready with a comeback of her own, but Corina was watching them, her young eyes not appearing to miss a thing.

"We'll finish this later," Scottie warned, and well-pleased with himself, Dannan only smiled, kissed his daughter, and sent her to the kitchen.

He was at the door, saying he had to get to work, when he remembered to ask, "Is Finn here?"

"I haven't seen him today," Scottie answered. "In fact, I didn't see him yesterday at the meetinghouse either. Why do you ask?"

"Oh, I just have a question. I'll find him later."

"All right."

Dannan came back long enough to kiss Scottie goodbye, both remembering that it wouldn't be long now.

"I'm glad you told me, Finn," Scottie said sincerely, even as her heart ached. "Have I done something to make you doubt?"

"No, it's nothing like that. I think Douglas Muldoon is a fine man, and I respect him, but I can't swallow what I'm hearing about the Bible. There is some good in man. I've seen it all my life."

Scottie thought fast, wanting to give Finn something to think about without pushing him in this matter.

"Do you believe any part of the Bible, Finn?"

"I don't know. No one is perfect, not even God. He has power to a degree, but it's not limitless, or this world would be a better place."

"Have you had a chance to discuss any of this with Douglas?" Scottie tried.

"No, but I told him on Sunday that I wouldn't be back. He said I could stop in and see him anytime."

Scottie nodded and prayed. She could do nothing outside of that. The decision had to be Finn's, and true to his word when Eli died, he had attended services at the meetinghouse.

"You know what I believe, Finn," Scottie said, her voice as

kind as ever. "Just as you knew what Eli believed. I do believe God is perfect and limitless, but if you don't see the Bible as God's Word to man about who He is, then you are at an impasse. I know I can believe anything written in His Word and be sure of it.

"I want you in my life—I need you in my life, Finn—so never think I would shun you over this decision, but know that I'll pray for you because I still believe you need a Savior."

Finn's face actually looked open. Scottie was expecting some sort of anger, but his face looked as it always did.

"I would never want you to deny your beliefs, Scottie."

"Thank you, Finn."

The conversation ended there. Confident that it was not her place, Scottie had never pushed this man and knew God didn't need her to do so. However, she did pray in belief. Just as she had said: Finn needed a Savior, and Jesus Christ was perfect for the job.

Scottie turned 24 at the end of that week. She knew Iris was baking a cake and that Dannan was coming for tea, but she did not expect the others who showed up to wish her well.

A simple evening tea turned into a party when Jace, Maddie, Conner, Reese, Douglas, and Alison all arrived within a few minutes of each other, wishing her well and laughing at the surprised look on her face.

"Where is the baby?" Scottie asked as she hugged Reese.

"Home with Troy," Reese answered with a huge smile.

"That Troy is a keeper."

"Yes, he is," Reese was happy to agree.

"And what about you, Maddie?" Scottie asked. "Where is Val?"

"I left her with Doyle and Cathy, much to their delight."

Iris, Finn, and Dannan had been planning it all week. Food that Scottie had not seen Iris preparing was brought out, and they feasted. The cake was delicious, and with only Corina in their midst, it turned into a lovely "grown-up" birthday party that Scottie knew she would remember for a very long time.

"Do you want to know something completely odd?" Scottie confided in Douglas after services that Sunday. They had talked about Finn for a time, but then Douglas had asked her how she was feeling about the wedding.

"Tell me," Douglas encouraged.

"I wish Eli could see Dannan and me be married." Scottie shook her head a little. "Eli and Mrs. Peterson taught me everything I know about taking care of a home and a husband, and it seems only right that Eli know how it's turned out."

"I can certainly see why you feel that way. In many ways, Eli was more like a father to you, or an older brother."

"I'm starting to see that, but it's taken some time," Scottie agreed. "At first, I was so hurt he'd spoken to Dannan that I didn't know if I could move past it, but now I realize how pleased he'd be to know that Dannan will be in my life, taking care of me the way he always did."

"I think he would be pleased. I even think he would be pleased that you didn't grieve for years."

"I still miss him," Scottie admitted. "I suspect that having Dannan and Corina in the house will change some of that, but it's always been Eli's house, and I still miss walking to his room and talking to him."

"He was a wonderful friend."

"He certainly was," Scottie agreed.

The two shared a smile, and then Douglas noticed Dannan moving in their direction.

"I believe someone might be looking for you."

Scottie glanced long enough to see Dannan, but she still turned back to Douglas.

"He's a wonderful friend too."

"Yes," Douglas agreed wholeheartedly, "the very best type to marry."

The wedding was on a Friday afternoon, November 20, and was held at the big house. Reese had asked to do this for the new couple and was very excited when they agreed. Corina would spend the next few nights with Iris, giving the doctor and his new wife a few days alone.

The church family and a few folks Scottie knew from town were invited to this celebration, but for the most part, it was a quiet affair. Feeling just a bit scared and very excited, Dannan and Scottie stood before Douglas to repeat their vows.

Cake and small sandwiches were served afterward, and Dannan and Scottie were able to visit and hear the well-wishes of everyone who came. When it was time to say their goodbyes, they loaded into Dannan's buggy, Iris and Corina in tow, with plans to drop off the two of them.

Corina, who loved to sleep at Iris' house, barely noticed when they left her, and for himself, Dannan was in no mood to linger. Urging the horse along, he landed Scottie at the front door and made quick work of stabling the animal. By the time he got to the house, Scottie had lit a lantern and put her coat away.

"Do you want help lighting the fire?" Scottie asked when he stepped into the near-dark room. The moon was full, and the lantern seemed dim after the large parlor and dining room at the big house.

"First things first," Dannan said, joining her in the middle of the room.

Scottie stood still while his hands went toward her hair, his eyes lighting with pleasure as her hair fell in soft, light red curls around her shoulders.

"That's better," he whispered as he bent to kiss her and take her in his arms. "I think marriage agrees with you," he continued, holding her close.

"What makes you say that?"

"Only that you look more beautiful than ever."

Scottie laughed with pure contentment and put her arms around his neck. Dr. Dannan MacKay was finally hers to have and to hold, and there was no better time to start than now.

Once darkness had settled all around them, the slow rocking of the train put Corina to sleep. Dannan had settled her on the seat across from them and returned to put an arm around his wife. It had taken some months of planning and waiting for winter to pass, but at last they were making the trip to see Dannan's family.

Scottie was on her first train ride. A little nervous and very excited, she had exchanged letters with Dannan's family but had also been asking about them for weeks.

"Do they know I have red hair?" she asked.

"I'm not sure. Does that matter?"

"It might. Not everyone likes red hair."

Because they sat close, Scottie could feel Dannan laugh, but he controlled his voice before answering. "My family will like red hair."

"You're laughing at me."

"Some of your questions are funny."

His voice was much too logical, and Scottie hadn't been very serious. She suddenly felt him lean toward her.

"We could be kissing, you know," he whispered in her ear.

"On the train?" she whispered right back with just enough scandal in her voice.

"It's very fun," Dannan coaxed.

"You speak from experience?" Scottie teased.

"I will as soon as you kiss me."

Scottie put a hand over her mouth to keep from laughing, and Dannan felt her body shake against him.

"Let me cover that for you," was his last whisper before he moved her hand and covered her lips with his own.

Epilogue

A little bit more to their stories...

"Maddie," Jace stood at the bottom of the stairway and called to his wife.

"We're coming," she called down, and Jace waited for his family. They were headed to the train station to pick up Jace's sister, Eden, who was coming to visit for the weekend. As soon as they had Eden, they were all going to Doyle and Cathy's for dinner.

Valerie was first down the stairs. Fifteen years old now, she had her mother's hair and her father's eyes, including his long lashes.

"What's taking so long?" Jace asked.

"Walt has outgrown his good pants again," Valerie said simply. "Mama's trying to button them around him."

Slipping past their father, 12-year-old Jenny and 11-year-old Eden made their way downstairs. They followed their sister, even as 8-year-old Walt came into view. Jace had to smile when he noticed how short his pants were.

Taking the stairs in last place was Maddie. Their 2-year-old daughter, Paige, was in her arms and reached for her father the moment she was close.

"All set?" Jace asked, Paige settled on his arm.

"I think so," Maddie answered. "I've taken those pants out so many times the seams are weak. If he bends, folks in town will be scandalized."

While Jace was laughing, Maddie had another idea.

"Jace, next time I'll hitch the team and you can stuff Walt into his pants."

Jace laughed again and put an arm around her, moving them to join their children in the yard.

Conner and Reese listened to footsteps on the stairs, knowing Levi was headed their way. No one else had feet so big or so loud as that boy, and it always made his parents laugh.

"Levi," Reese called to him from the dining room. "We're in here."

Levi went that way and found his parents already seated. He joined them at the table and prayed for their tea when he was asked, his voice almost as soft as his father's.

Reese watched him when they started to eat, never tiring of thanking God for this child. He was their only one. Not in all of Levi's 14 years had Reese conceived again. Still a marvelous caregiver, and having assumed their large home would be filled with children, Reese did at times wonder that it had not been God's plan.

It was true that Troy's health had not been the best. More than two years had passed since he moved back to Linden Heights to be near his daughters, but prior to his going, Reese had taken care of him like the beloved father he'd become.

And it wasn't as if Reese ever lacked for something to do or company to look after. She was as busy as ever with many opportunities to do good works for the church family and in the community. Conner could not have been prouder of her work and was good at telling her how he felt.

"What are you thinking about?" Conner asked, and Reese realized she hadn't touched her food.

"Just wool gathering," Reese told him, her look saying more.

Conner didn't press her, but just as soon as Levi wandered off, Conner cornered his wife in the kitchen.

"Are you upset about something?"

"Not upset. Just wondering and wrestling a bit about God's plans. Levi would have made a wonderful big brother."

"Yes, he would have," Conner agreed, "and you mustn't forget, it might still happen."

Reese looked up into Conner's face, thinking that she would have never seen things as she did without his solid confidence in their saving God. He never failed to remind her of God's goodness and that in Him there was always faith and Someone to trust.

"Thank you, Conner," Reese said, slipping her arms around him.

"For what?"

"For being you."

Reese went up on tiptoes to kiss him. Conner, who loved her even more now than the day they were married, kissed her right back.

"Scottie?" Eli, four years old and the youngest MacKay, found his mother in the kitchen.

Scottie was used to it by now but still liked to laugh a little over the fact that all six of her children called her by her first name. They had grown up listening to Corina and simply followed suit.

"What do you need, Eli?"

"Where's Rina?" he asked, using his nickname for his oldest sister.

"Corina is helping Mrs. Muldoon today."

"Where's Annie?"

"Also helping Mrs. Muldoon."

"Where's Matthew?" came next, and Scottie knew Eli was going to ask about all of his siblings. Distracted as she was by more than one subject, she stopped what she was working on and sat down to hear him.

"Matthew is sweeping at Doyle's store today."

"Where's Grant?"

"He's at Uncle Finn's."

"Where is Jonas?"

"He's with Grant and Uncle Finn."

Eli sighed when he realized there was no one to play with. Scottie was about to suggest he look at books when Dannan came in the kitchen door.

"Someone's missing you," she wasted no time telling her husband.

Dannan didn't need much time to catch on but still teased, "Eli or you?"

"Both, but if you can spare a little time to play with Eli, we would both be very grateful."

Dannan came over to kiss her. She could see by his eyes that he wanted to tease her some more, either that or keep kissing, but he took pity on all of them and invited Eli to accompany him back to his office.

Scottie saw them on their way and went back to work on the casserole she was making for the next day. Iris had been gone for almost four years, dying unexpectedly in her sleep. Scottie still missed her but enjoyed working in the kitchen, preparing meals and gathering her family around her. And indeed, the family would gather tomorrow. Scottie had to force herself to calm down when she thought of what it was going to be like. It was going to be a wonderful day.

Sunday brought a very special service. Douglas and Alison were celebrating 35 years of marriage and 25 years with the Tucker Mills church family. Joshua Muldoon, who worked with his father, took the service, and memories were shared at every turn.

Tears, some of grief and some of joy, filled eyes in all corners of the room as folks stood and shared what this church family had meant to them. By the time Douglas went to the platform in front, taking Alison with him, his eyes were red and a bit swollen.

"Thank you," he said softly. "There isn't much I can add to all the wonderful praise you've given today. We do have a God of salvation, mercy, and forgiveness. I have needed those so greatly over the years, and He has never failed me.

"I won't start a sermon, but you must allow me to tell you that I could not have accomplished a thing without this woman standing next to me."

Alison's fingers came to her lips, but she could not stem the tears.

"I praise God for her and for my children, my in-law children, and my grandchildren. And before I step down so we can eat and fellowship more, will you please allow me to share some news with you?

"It's no secret that our son Martin has been seen in the

company of a certain young woman. It is official." Douglas'
smile nearly stretched off his face. "Martin has asked, and Miss
Corina MacKay has accepted."

Cheers and clapping threatened to raise the roof, even as the
young couple seated in the front row holding hands laughed in
delight. When it grew quiet, Douglas simply thanked everyone
yet again before Joshua came forward, thanked God for the food,
and dismissed everyone to eat.

With their meetinghouse filled just seating each family, they
had no choice but to use the green for their celebration. The
next few hours were spent in good eating and fine fellowship.
All who attended said it was a day of remembrance, not a day
to remember only the past, but a day to serve as a memory
stone to God's goodness to them and His work on their behalf
in the future.

The weary MacKay family, short of Corina, who had gone
with the Muldoons for the evening, finally found their way home.
There were dishes to wash and food to put away, and even some
children who were told to ready for an early bedtime.

Dannan and Scottie had not been relaxing in the parlor for
an hour when someone came looking for the doctor's services.
Scottie walked him through the kitchen to see him off.

"I hope I won't be long," he said, shrugging into his coat.

"It's not as late as it feels, but it's sure getting dark early."

"Leave a candle burning?" Dannan asked, an arm going
around her waist to pull her close.

Scottie went on tiptoe to kiss him just before saying,
"Always."

Glossary

∽ **bells:** New England towns had their own system for announcing when someone died. Nine bells for a man, six for a woman, and three for a child. Then a bell was rung for each year the person had lived.

∽ **bonnet:** this word needs no explanation in form, but I found it interesting as to why women wore them. It was simply for practical purposes, not out of propriety or coming of age. After marriage, most women didn't have time to do much with their hair and found it simpler to wear a bonnet.

∽ **broomcorn:** a tall, cultivated sorghum with stiff branches used to make brooms or brushes.

∽ **buttery:** pronounced but'ry, it's a room where dairy goods were worked, cheese and butter, for example.

∽ **dinner:** the noon meal, always a full-blown affair.

∽ **green:** also called the center or common, it's the middle of town, a grass area where homes and shops sit in a rectangle or on a square. I know of one in Connecticut that's a mile long.

∽ **kitchen garden fence:** marauding animals were not the main problem with a kitchen garden—people were. A kitchen garden was a lifeline for many families. The fence was usually high enough to keep thieves out.

∽ **laying out:** preparing a body for burial, usually done by family or neighbors.

⁓ **meetinghouse:** the building for public assembly, including the church on Sunday.

⁓ **millpond:** the pond of water that feeds the mill and is fed by spring thaw, or in the case of Tucker Mills, by a huge river that doesn't run dry in summer.

⁓ **parlor or sitting room:** where you sat in the evening, entertained visitors, and unless your house was very large, ate your meals. The table in the kitchen was mostly for work rather than eating.

⁓ **pins:** straight pins were often used to hold dresses on. Buttonholes were a lot of work, and women didn't try to use them on their clothing.

⁓ **purging, puking, and bleeding:** not a pretty idea, but folks of this time wanted some proof that their doctor was doing something for them when they were ailing. Often doctors gave things to people to flush their systems one way or the other. Purging and puking were not fun, but typically folks survived. Bleeding was not so kind. Many did not live to tell about it.

⁓ **set bones:** some towns had bonesetters, people who could set broken bones. They were usually not doctors.

⁓ **short hair:** if you've ever seen an old painting or a daguerreotype of a young girl who looks like a little boy in a dress, you're seeing history as it truly was. It wasn't practical for hardworking mothers to take extra time with their young daughter's hair, so it was kept short.

⁓ **tea:** also called "snack"—this was the evening meal, which used leftovers from dinner.

⁓ **townball:** townball descends from the British game of rounders. Played in the United States as far back as the early 1800s, some considered it to be the steppingstone between rounders and modern baseball.

About the Author

LORI WICK is a multifaceted author of Christian fiction. As comfortable writing period stories as she is penning contemporary works, Lori's books (over 5 million in print) vary widely in location and time period. Lori's faithful fans consistently put her series and standalone works on the bestseller lists. Lori and her husband, Bob, live with their swiftly growing family in the Midwest.

The *English Garden* *Series*

By Lori Wick

Set in the early 1800s in Victorian England,
the English Garden series takes you back
to another time and place.

THE PROPOSAL

William Jennings is a man who has never known the love and companionship that marriage brings—and doesn't want to. But when a relative dies, leaving Jennings three young children, his whole world is turned upside down. In seeking counsel from his sister, Jennings meets her neighbor, Marianne Walker. Will Jennings find himself drawn to this woman—and to the God she so obviously loves?

THE RESCUE

When Robert Weston visits her cottage, Anne Gardiner accidentally topples from a ladder into his arms. Coming upon the end of the scene, Anne's unstable father demands honor for Anne. Can a real marriage cure the heartache caused by a false one?

THE VISITOR

After a throw from a horse, Alexander Tate retreats to the country to see if time and quiet can restore his sight. But when his aunt asks a young woman to read to him daily, the intriguing voice of the visitor sparks new light in the heart of the young man. Soon he understands that he is not the only one struggling with blindness, though hers is of a different kind entirely. Will these two young hearts trust God's healing touch, however it comes?

THE PURSUIT

Edward Steele has enjoyed a great adventure in Africa with his brother, Henry. But now Henry has returned to England, and Edward, hoping to be home for Christmas, is ready to follow. However, when aboard ship Edward tells two strangers he will help them, he never dreams that meeting them will cost him so much or put a woman into his life who captivates and confounds him in equal measure. A story of betrayal and learning to trust. A story of God's sovereignty in every moment of life.

Current Books by Lori Wick

A Place Called Home Series
A Place Called Home
A Song for Silas
The Long Road Home
A Gathering of Memories

The Californians
Whatever Tomorrow Brings
As Time Goes By
Sean Donovan
Donovan's Daughter

Kensington Chronicles
The Hawk and the Jewel
Wings of the Morning
Who Brings Forth the Wind
The Knight and the Dove

Rocky Mountain Memories
Where the Wild Rose Blooms
Whispers of Moonlight
To Know Her by Name
Promise Me Tomorrow

The Yellow Rose Trilogy
Every Little Thing About You
A Texas Sky
City Girl

English Garden Series
The Proposal
The Rescue
The Visitor
The Pursuit

The Tucker Mills Trilogy
Moonlight on the Millpond
Just Above a Whisper
Leave a Candle Burning

Other Fiction
Sophie's Heart
Pretense
The Princess
Bamboo & Lace
Every Storm